The NonCon

Storming out of the elport, I raced into the apartment. Gran was on the couch, her arm around Dee, the two of them wet-faced and sniffling. Harriet was next to Gran, murmuring sympathy. The apartment had been torn apart, things everywhere, but one thing was obviously missing.

My voice trembled. "Pops?"

"B.O.S.S. took him." Dee's voice cracked, fresh tears streaming down her face.

"The scrambler ran out of time. That silly old fool kept on talking. It's my fault. I should have stayed in here with him. Kept an eye on him." Gran twisted her hanky, her voice shaking. "He's so sick. He won't survive reassimilation."

OTHER BOOKS YOU MAY ENJOY

Fat Kid Rules the World	K. L. Going
Looking for Alaska	John Green
Matched	Ally Condie
Nightshade	Andrea Cremer
The Rules of Survival	Nancy Werlin
Sunshine	Robin McKinley
Willow	Julia Hoban
Wintergirls	Laurie Halse Anderson
XVI	Julia Karr

TRUTH

Julia Karr

speak
An Imprint of Penguin Group (USA) Inc.

SPEAK

Published by the Penguin Group

Penguin Group (USA) Inc., 345 Hudson Street, New York, New York 10014, U.S.A.

Penguin Group (Canada), 90 Eglinton Avenue East, Suite 700, Toronto, Ontario, Canada M4P 2Y3
(a division of Pearson Penguin Canada Inc.)

Penguin Books Ltd, 80 Strand, London WC2R 0RL, England

Penguin Ireland, 25 St Stephen's Green, Dublin 2, Ireland (a division of Penguin Books Ltd)

Penguin Group (Australia), 250 Camberwell Road, Camberwell, Victoria 3124, Australia
(a division of Pearson Australia Group Pty Ltd)

Penguin Books India Pvt Ltd, 11 Community Centre, Panchsheel Park, New Delhi - 110 017, India

Penguin Group (NZ), 67 Apollo Drive, Rosedale, Auckland 0632, New Zealand
(a division of Pearson New Zealand Ltd.)

Penguin Books (South Africa) (Pty) Ltd, 24 Sturdee Avenue, Rosebank, Johannesburg 2196, South Africa

Registered Offices: Penguin Books Ltd, 80 Strand, London WC2R 0RL, England

First published in the United States of America by Speak, an imprint of Penguin Group (USA) Inc., 2012

1 3 5 7 9 10 8 6 4 2

CIP Data Is Available

Speak ISBN 978-0-14-241772-0

Text set in Bulmer MT

This book is dedicated to Amy, because . . .

ACKNOWLEDGMENTS

There are a lot of people who helped to make this book happen, but two in particular who should be named. My awesome editor, Jen Bonnell, who made sure that there was no sophomore slump for me. And Justin Vollmar, without whom I would've starved. Thank you both!

TRUTH

I was contemplating what would happen to me if anyone discovered that I'd killed Ed when Mr. Haldewick's voice broke through my brooding. "Miss Oberon, if you please!"

"Yes, sir?" Hopefully my expression and manner were sufficiently contrite to reach Mr. H's soft side, which he did have—no matter what most of the other students thought.

His forehead wrinkled in a frown, but he repeated the question. "What is the importance of the XVI tattoo? And you should know this, since I see you now have yours."

I twisted my right hand around my inked wrist, glancing across the aisle at my best friend, Wei. Thistles encircled her XVI, snaking around her hand and up her fingers, completely overshadowing the obligatory government brand. She was a Creative, and her ultra tat was legal. I reminded myself that I'd recently gotten my Creative designation and I could get something similar, if I ever got enough credits to afford—

"This century, Miss Oberon?"

Snapping back to reality, I opened my mouth to give the rote text-chip answer, but what came out was, "The XVI tattoo is a government-mandated brand designed for easy identification of females who are sixteen and legally old enough to be sexually active. Even though it fades away in about six years, when girls get it they become immediately vulnerable to unwanted sexual advances and easy targets for rape. A crime that is rarely, if ever, prosecuted because—"

Mr. H's mouth dropped open; his glasses flew off his pointy nose and dangled from their silver chain. Slamming his pointer on the desk, he roared, "That is NOT an acceptable answer, Miss Oberon!" Even from my seat in the back, I could see little beads of sweat forming on his forehead.

Skivs! I clapped my hand over my mouth. What was I thinking? Actually, I wasn't thinking. Because of everything that had happened to me in the past few months, my real feelings were finding their voice—which wasn't necessarily a good thing. Out of the corner of my eye I saw Wei grinning. Various titters erupted around the room.

No sooner had I started to breathe again, figuring my outburst had gone unnoticed outside the classroom, than Hal, the robotic hall access limiter, marched into the room with a request for my presence in Mrs. Marchant's office. Caught! Mr. H waved me out with one hand, mopping his brow with the hanky in his other. Wei squeezed my arm as I headed for my self-made disaster.

***

Hal ushered me into the principal's office and withdrew into the corner, silent as death, which might have been preferable to the unknown that awaited me. I'd never been in trouble at school, ever. A sick feeling burbled in my stomach, and I swallowed, attempting to keep my fears down.

Mrs. Marchant sat behind a gleaming acrylamite desk. Its transparency allowed a full view of her—transchair and all. Like everyone else at Daley High, I knew her story. She and her husband had been low-tier college students. There had been a horrible multitrans accident: her husband had been killed outright, and she had been partially paralyzed. Expensive restoration surgery had not been an option. Rumor was that she preferred the aluminoid shell encasing her from the waist down, even though she could now easily afford a reconstructed spine and bionic legs. I averted my eyes, focusing on her face instead.

"You are aware that classes are observed, Miss Oberon?" Mrs. Marchant pointed to a bank of AV screens mounted on the wall like pictures, one for each classroom.

"Yes, ma'am." Hands clasped in front of me, I shifted my weight from one leg to the other, until I became ultra-aware of the fact that I was standing and she couldn't. I froze.

"Those feeds are periodically reviewed by the government." She raised one eyebrow, giving me a sharp look. "Understand?"

"Yes." Prickles of fear raised goose bumps on my arms.

"Based on your outburst, it would appear you have an inclination toward the ideas of your father." Her fingers wrapped around the edge of the desk, and she pushed, the transchair gliding backward. "I know all about Alan Oberon."

There was a subtle but distinct whirr as she skimmed across the floor, then stopped in front of me. Even though the chair placed her a good foot shorter than me, the intensity of her gaze made me feel as if we were eye to eye. "Should you plan on spouting any more antigovernment rhetoric," she said, "join the debate club. That's what he did."

"Yes, ma'am." She was right. My father had won several citywide debates. Media had even wanted to make him a star broadcaster, that is, until he began actively speaking out against the Governing Council beyond the safety of sanctioned debating. Eventually, he had faked his own death. A fact I'd discovered only when my mother lay dying in an Infinity machine after a brutal attack. Now I knew for sure he was alive. We'd even talked once. We just hadn't met, yet.

Mrs. Marchant grasped my arm, her slender fingers warm and surprisingly strong. She turned my wrist over to reveal the XVI tattoo. Our eyes met. Something in her expression made me pretty sure she didn't approve of the government's branding either.

"Your permanent records indicate you're no longer a candidate for FeLS." She let go of my wrist.

An odd statement. "My contract was bought out." My mom had saved for ages to be able to buy my contract back from the government so I wouldn't have to be a part of the Female Liaison Specialist program. They said FeLS was diplomatic service: a good way, practically the only way, for low-tier girls to work themselves up a few tiers. But only a few knew the truth. Was one of them Mrs. Marchant? I studied her face.

No, she couldn't know. Really, no one who wasn't in the Governing Council knew the truth—the horrible things they really did. No one except for a few of my friends and me. But now the proof of its nefarious dealings—which had cost my mother her life—was safely in the hands of my father, and the Resistance. I'd risked my own life to get it from Ed, and Wei's father had delivered it, along with my little sister Dee's baby book, to my dad just a few weeks ago. He'd know when and how to reveal it to the world.

"You were recently awarded your Creative designation, and you've taken a part-time job at the Art Institute. Correct?"

"Yes, ma'am."

She maneuvered her chair in a circle around me, before skimming back behind her desk. "I suppose you'll get a fancy tattoo like Miss Jenkins did. Perfectly understandable. I've heard you are quite the artist." She waved her fingers toward Hal. "Escort Miss Oberon back to class. Miss Oberon, keep that contract safe. I'd prefer you remained a student here. I'm sure your grandparents would, too."

I followed Hal, puzzling over Mrs. Marchant's veiled warning to watch my back. I wasn't planning on causing any trouble, at least not me personally. If my father's revelations about FeLS caused an uproar . . . well, that would be a good thing. It couldn't be traced back to me. Could it?

Maybe she was concerned that I'd quit school to work full-time at the Institute. A lot of kids in my tier didn't make it to graduation. And even with the survivor benefits from my mother's death, Gran and Pops were struggling to support Dee and me on their meager retirement credits. That must be it. Or maybe she was worried that I'd mouth off about the Governing Council again and that B.O.S.S., the Bureau of Safety and Security, would come and take me away from the only family I had left.

Bile crept up my throat. B.O.S.S. The GC's security force scared me—galactically. People who were arrested by B.O.S.S. were either never heard of again, or were reassimilated—turned into shells of their former selves. B.O.S.S. did whatever it wanted, and no one could stop it. No one.

My worrisome contemplations were diverted by a slight catch in Hal's step every time his left foot made contact with the ground. Step, hitch, step, hitch, step, hitch . . . It was hypnotic. A little Lube-All in the hip socket would fix that, I thought. My ruminations on robot maintenance came to a halt when Hal stopped, abruptly, in front of my classroom. Several students cast furtive glances at me as I took my seat, probably wondering what tortures I'd been subjected to.

For the remainder of the period, Mr. H divided us into small discussion groups on gender-specific roles in society and, more specifically, in tiers. I kept quiet, surreptitiously doodling tattoo ideas for my wrist.

II

erek, Mike, and I headed to Mickey's for lunch. The nanosec they were out the door, kids whipped out their Personal Audio/Video receivers to check messages and watch broadcasts. A barrage of verts about everything from the latest tunes to the best acne meds filled the half block between school and café. The noise was overwhelming, so I switched on my PAV to block them out. Once inside Mickey's, we managed to muscle our way into a window booth.

"Heard you got to visit Marchant's," Derek said.

"Yeah, I got carried away with my views on tattooing and the government. I suppose I should watch my mouth." I glanced around. You never knew when or where the Bureau of Safety and Security had surveillance turned on. There were some dead zones in the city, but Mickey's wasn't one.

"You and Sal coming to Soma on Saturday?" Derek asked. "Riley and I are playing again. It's going to be a steady gig, if we're lucky. Wei's coming." He beamed.

I was thrilled that two of my best friends liked each other—a lot. As a matter of fact, Derek and Wei had been dating since my sixteenth birthday, and from what I'd noticed, I thought they were getting serious. "As far as I know we'll be there." I fingered the half-of-a-heart charm dangling from my necklace. Sal had given it to me for my birthday. My half said "I LO"; his half said "VE YOU." Absentmindedly glancing out the window, I saw Sal and Wei walking by with a girl I didn't know. My shoulders tensed. I'd seen her before, hanging on Sal in the hallway at school. She was definitely upper tier, like Wei, but unlike Wei, she had all the attitude of privilege. "Who's that?"

"I dunno." Mike shrugged and went back to eating.

"Oh, I know that girl. She moved here earlier this year from New York," Derek said. "Her father's some big-shot Media consultant. Wonder what she's doing with Sal and Wei?"

I was wondering the same thing when I saw her grab Sal's arm. A twinge of jealousy pricked me. I shook it off. Maybe I'd ask him about her later. Maybe not. I loved Sal, and he said he loved me. And he'd shown it by being there for me these past few weeks. Hard weeks. But the one thing I'd been able to do after my mom Ginnie's murder was count on Sal to be my bright spot.

***

After school, Sal was waiting for me on the front steps. "You working this afternoon?" he asked.

"Nuh-uh. You?" He worked with his brother on personal transits, retrofitting them with Resistance-friendly security devices, like antisurveillance covers and such for NonCons, a covert arm of the Resistance. I'd gotten to ride in one. It was ultra.

"Nope. John's got an appointment with the big trannie dealership in Evanston, so I have the afternoon free."

Tucking my arm in his, I smiled. At least he wasn't off on any NonCon business for the rest of the day. Sal usually disguised himself as a homeless person and helped with vert interruptions, when the NonCons would silence all of the verts and broadcast short messages of the Resistance. The NonCons were like foot soldiers for the Resistance, and it was public and dangerous work. I had to admit, sometimes, when I didn't know what he was off doing, I worried about his getting caught. I guessed that was the price one paid for attempting to uncover all that was wrong with the government.

We headed out to meet Dee at the trans stop closest to Dickens Elementary. Snow was falling, and I stuffed my hands in my pockets, having left my gloves at home, again.

"You need those clips like little kids have," Sal said. "The ones that fasten their gloves to their coats."

I stifled a giggle. I'd been trying to keep a good upset on about the girl I'd seen him with earlier, but it wasn't working.

"And," he added, "a hood on your coat, because you never ever remember your hat." He put his stocking hat on my head, pulling it all the way down over my eyes.

"Hey!" I tossed it back at him.

One thing led to another, and we'd thoroughly pelted each other with snowballs before he pulled me close and kissed me. Nothing was cold after that. I swear, when his lips are on mine, summer runs through my veins.

"We'd better hurry. Dee will be waiting, and it's getting colder." As if to punctuate my statement, a frigid gust shrieked down the street, stabbing right through me. Sal put his arm around me.

"Who was that girl you and Wei were with at lunch?" I asked.

"Paulette Gold. Why?"

"Oh. I saw you with her a few weeks ago, in the hallway. Remember? When we were fighting? She stuck something in your pocket." I refrained from mentioning how she'd looked like she was trying to crawl inside his skin. I hated thinking about that time, when we'd just started kind of dating. Right after my mom died, everything was such a mess. I was a mess. And then I met Sal, a NonCon. He'd told me things I didn't want to hear, like about the Media controlling our society. About the GC and their oppressing the people. About my family—my mom and my dad. And he had been right about everything. We'd made up, but it still hurt to relive that.

After a long moment, he said, "Oh, yeah, *that*. It was the security code for her dad's Janji. John had it in the shop for some repairs." He took hold of my shoulders, bringing us face-to-face. "Hey, Nina. She's just some girl. You, however, are *my* girl." And he kissed me again.

I believed him. It still didn't quite quiet my nerves about this girl, but the kiss certainly helped. I could've stayed there until the spring thaw. After indulging myself in a much-too-short dose of Sal, I said, "We'd better go. Dee's probably turned into an icicle by now." When it came to my little sister, I was hyper-responsible. With good reason, I thought to myself.

Sure enough, when we reached the transit stop, Dee was huddled in the doorway of a nearby store. "Geez, Nina. I could've frozen to death. What took you so long?"

"Why didn't you go into one of the shops?" I asked.

"'Cause they're ultra boutiques, and the salespeople watch me like I'm going to steal something." She wrinkled her nose. "Just because people are low tier doesn't mean they're thieves."

"Don't let it bother you, Deeds." I sighed, knowing exactly how she felt. "Some people are jerks. Plain old jerks."

"Hey, how about some hot cocoa from Rosie's?" Sal asked. "My treat."

***

In fifteen minutes, we were cozied up in a booth, sipping steaming hot cocoa and munching on cookies. There were only three other people inside, an older couple and a man at a table by himself.

Rosie joined us. She'd offered to teach me Cliste Galad martial arts after Holiday break. But right now, after all I'd been through, what with killing Ed, I wasn't sure I wanted to learn to be a finely tuned murder machine. But then Wei was practically a Cliste Galad master, and she wouldn't hurt a fly—unless there was no other way. I was still processing my feelings about what I'd done to Ed. I cringed at the thought of learning other ways I could've dispatched him.

"Rosie, about your offer . . ." Rosie's was DZ, even PAV reception was spotty. But that didn't stop someone inside from overhearing conversations, so I chose my words carefully. "I want to wait. I'm not ready."

"When the time is right, you will know." She patted my cheek. "You are a wise one."

I didn't feel wise. I did feel relieved.

"I've got more cookies in the oven," Rosie said. "I'd best get back to them."

"Can I help?" Dee was in a love-to-cook phase. My similar phase had been very short. I could find my way around the cook center, but wasn't a whiz like Gran.

"Of course. But I might put you to work."

"Cool." Dee followed Rosie into the kitchen.

Sal and I sipped our cocoa, held hands, and acted exactly like I never imagined I ever would. Even just a few months ago, I'd been so determined not to be a typical sex-teen, falling all over boys, dressing to attract them—and every creepy pervert in the galaxy—that I'd decided never to have a boyfriend. Yet here I was, enjoying the major bright spot in my life—Sal.

The only thing we ever argued about was his inclination to be overly protective. I understood why he felt that way. After all, it can't be easy to see your girlfriend threatened by a former B.O.S.S. agent. I shuddered, thinking about Ed. About how he took my mother from me. The power he had wielded over Dee and me. Dee, who still thought Ed was her father . . . But Ed was gone. And I didn't need protecting.

If anything, I wanted to be more active in the Resistance. If guys as young as sixteen could be NonCons, why they made girls wait until eighteen made no sense to me. Guys didn't get tattooed at sixteen; girls did. Every day for a sixteen brought unwanted sexual advances, or worse. And yet the leaders of the Resistance thought Resistance activity was too dangerous. Ridiculous.

It seemed like guys everywhere—even the NonCons and Resistance fighters, who should know better—bought into at least some of the Media propaganda about women not being as strong or capable as men. I sipped my cocoa, swallowing down the negativity.

While we were talking, a woman came in and joined the lone man. Her chestnut hair, caught in clips above her temples, cascaded over her shoulders like in a shampoo vert. Her clothes were definitely not Sale-o-rama. They were ultrachic, showing off her perfect figure. She was tall, too, almost Amazonian. At first, I thought she was beautiful. Looking closer, I noticed a hardness to the set of her mouth that didn't seem so attractive.

Sal was looking at her, too. I squeezed his hand. "What's wrong?"

"Nothing." He frowned slightly before turning his attention back to me. "I should have been thinking about you." He brushed his lips over my fingertips. I forgot everything except how he made me feel.

***

After Dee returned from helping Rosie, we bundled up to go. We were nearly to the door when a voice called, "Miss Oberon." Dee and I turned simultaneously. "You might need this." The chestnut-haired woman was holding up one of Dee's mittens. "It's awfully cold outside."

"Miss Maldovar!" Dee hurried over to the table. "Thank you! Mom gave these to me last Holiday. I'd hate myself if I lost one." She snugged her hand into the errant mitten.

"I can imagine. So sad about your mother." She laid a hand on Dee's shoulder. "Be careful with them." She glanced up, scrutinizing me. "You'd better run back to your sister now."

Sal held open the door and asked Dee exactly what I was wondering. "Who's that?"

"My new teacher, Miss Maldovar. She's so ultra."

I glanced in the window at the same moment the woman's eyes met mine. The hairs on my neck involuntarily prickled. I buttoned my coat. It was icy cold out.

When Dee and I got home, Pops was sitting in his favorite chair, his prosthetic leg propped up against the side table, his crutch lying on the floor next to it.

Dee flung herself into his arms, planting a big kiss on his cheek. "Tons of homework right before Holiday. Can you believe it?" She straightened up. "Will you help me with my math later?"

"Sure enough, Deedles." He chucked her under the chin. "Try 'em yourself first, though. I'll check your answers."

Dee bounded off to her room.

"How about you, Little Bit? School okay today?" he asked.

"Uh-huh." I wasn't going to tell him about my visit to Mrs. Marchant. He'd only get worked up and frustrated because he couldn't help me. In the few months since Dee and I had moved in with Gran and Pops, Pops's health had gotten worse, and he was growing more forgetful. Not wanting to dwell on depressing subjects, I asked, "Anything exciting happen here?"

"Checkerheads came by again."

So much for changing the subject. A stranglehold of anxiety knotted my gut. The same anxiety that had been my constant companion since my mom's murder, but which had subsided somewhat since Ed's death. I wrapped my arms about me, not even bothering to chide him about the derogatory slang for the police. "What did they want?" As if I didn't know.

"Had a couple of Bureau agents with 'em this time." He rubbed the day's worth of stubble on his chin. "Still looking for that no-good, worthless, piece-of-crap Ed. I told 'em he'd never been to see Dee, didn't care a whit that she was his daughter, and I didn't give a damn about him or where he was. Probably out cheating on his wife with some other woman now that Ginnie's dead."

"Pops!" There was no reasoning with my grandfather about the government. I understood his contempt perfectly, but—old and disabled or not—I was terrified he'd get himself into some kind of trouble he couldn't get out of. "You probably should have been a little . . . nicer."

"Nicer?" He snorted. "Like anything the government's ever done to me was nice?" He patted his stump, a reminder of the shoddy treatment he'd received when he'd lost his leg in an accident while working on a government project years earlier.

I tried logic. "They're B.O.S.S. They can, you know . . . reassimilate you."

"I ain't scared of reassimilation, Little Bit. It'll take more than some warped technology to turn this old geezer into a pile of mush."

I doubted Pops knew how zombified reassimilated people were. Like the teacher I'd had who'd strayed from GC-mandated texts. He was never the same after he came back. But it took more than vague threats to scare Pops. "Did they say anything?" I asked. "What leads do they have?"

"Same as before. His last PAV signal was from around Lincoln and Wells. Said it might have come from the old Robin's Roost hotel." His eyes flashed, and he straightened up. "That's where your father and his friends hung out. Been deserted for years. What business would Ed have had to be there?"

I shrugged, as if I hadn't a clue that Ed had been there, looking for me, while I'd been there looking for evidence my mom had hidden. I had found the evidence. And Ed had found me.

Pops sighed, and slumped back into his chair. "Alan and Ginnie's wedding reception was there. Place all done up in silver and Neptune green. Fairyland. That's what it was like. A magical fairyland."

His eyes lost focus, clouded by what was becoming a much too frequent faraway look. I needed Pops to stay present. I perched on the arm of his chair. "Did they say anything else?"

"Huh?" He cocked his head to the right, his eyes a muddled mix of long-past memories and current events.

"The Bureau of Safety and Security agents, Pops. What else did they say?" I held his gaze. His vision cleared, and he sat upright.

"Oh, yeah, those S.O.B.'s. You ever notice that, Little Bit? B.O.S.S., kind of like S.O.B. backward." He patted my leg, chuckling.

"Yes, Pops." I hid the impatience from my voice as best I could.

"Well, the city demolished Robin's Roost on your birthday. Fine old building once upon a time. Flat as one of Edith's flapjacks now." He shook his head. "Tell me, Nina, if Ed were in the city to see Dee, what would he have been doing in an abandoned hotel? Doesn't make any sense, does it?" He didn't wait for a response from me. "I told 'em they were crazy." He waved like he was pushing the whole lot of them out of our lives. "They won't be back."

"I hope you're right, Pops." I threw my arms around him, squeezing hard, but not hard enough to dispel my fears. "I'd better go do my homework, too."

As soon as I got to my room, I messaged Wei on my PAV. I couldn't risk a conversation being overheard by the audio surveillance I was sure was trained on our apartment. Especially with B.O.S.S. looking for Ed, and with the entire world thinking Dee was his daughter, we had to be somehow suspect. The fact that I had actually killed him, and Dee *wasn't* Ed's daughter, and Alan Oberon was alive—skivs! It was a good thing they didn't have thought surveillance yet, or I'd be dead already.

"Meet you in Lincoln Park. You know the place," Wei messaged back.

There was a tech tower in the park that caused a lot of satellite and radio frequency interference. It wasn't as good as a full-on dead zone, but almost.

"Twenty minutes," I replied.

Bundling back into my coat, I stopped by the kitchen and told Gran I'd be late for dinner.

***

"Wei, what am I going to do? B.O.S.S. was at our apartment today." I paced back and forth. "They're going to find out, aren't they? And when they do, I'll be reassimilated. Or they'll send me to Mars."

"Stop. You're making me dizzy." Wei held up her hand. "They

aren't going to find out anything. And they only send guys to the prison on Mars."

I came to a halt. "What am I going to do?"

"Seriously, Nina. They are not going to arrest you, because there is no evidence of anything. Trust me. I know what happened afterward, the cleanup. You have nothing to worry about. Nothing. Besides, I've got some friends. I'll ask them to check and see if anything about you is making the rounds."

"What do you mean?"

"This." Wei pointed to the thistle tattoo on the back of her hand. "There are a few of us . . ."

"Creatives? What can they do?"

"Not just Creatives." Wei pulled me close. "We're the Sisterhood. Kind of like . . ." She glanced around. "Like NonCons, but girls," she whispered.

My eyes widened. "Are you serious?"

"Uh-huh." She kept scanning the area around us as she softly said, "The NonCons, well, you know the guys won't let us do much. But we do Rogue Radio and the tech for vert and vid interruptions. We see things, hear things, and then supply the NonCons with intelligence that they pass along to the Resistance. The only problem is, we don't get to do any of the more dangerous things they do. Like guarding high-level Resistance members when they come through town, saving FeLS girls—even before your mother found out the whole truth about FeLS—or stopping a convoy of political prisoners heading to Mars."

"Really?" My heart quickened, and I latched onto her arm. "I want to join. How? I'll do anything."

"Whoa. Slow down. I need to talk to the others before I say anything else. Although, you saved my life and you're Alan Oberon's daughter . . . How could they not—"

"You can't tell them that. At least not *what* I did—no one can know what happened with Ed. No one except you, Sal, Derek, and Mike—and whoever did the cleanup—can ever know. Promise!"

"I won't say a word. But, Nina, you can't tell Sal anything about the Sisterhood. I know he doesn't want you doing anything that might put you in danger again. When Ed was . . . well, I shouldn't—" She shook her head.

"Shouldn't what? Spill."

"It's not a huge thing. But when Ed was harassing you and Dee, Sal would borrow John's trannie and go sit outside your apartment building, watching for Ed. Keeping an eye on you and Dee. He loves you so much, Nina. He'd do anything to protect you."

"He did what?" I barely heard anything past "keeping an eye on you." Sal had been guarding me without telling me? Part of me was touched, and part of me was mad. While I appreciated his concern, so far, I'd been able to take care of myself—and Dee.

"I shouldn't have said anything." Wei bit her lip. "Don't tell him. Okay?"

I tamped down my rising anger. It was already done. No sense fighting after the fact. I sighed. "I love him, too, but . . . this issue of what girls can and can't do is something we completely disagree on."

"Oh, yeah, I argue about it with Sal *and* with my dad. They think we have enough to deal with, just running the gauntlet of being sixteen every day. They don't get that we need to be able to do things that prove to us how powerful we really are."

"What about your brother, Chris? Does he give you a hard time, too?"

"Not really. We haven't talked about it much. He's always been my sparring partner in Cliste Galad, and he knows what I'm capable of. I don't think he has the same hangups my dad has."

"I bet Derek doesn't worry about you either." I knew all about Derek's admiration for strong girls.

Wei actually blushed. "He doesn't." She looked up at me from under her lashes. "Actually . . . I decked him one night."

"You're kidding!"

"Nope. We were goofing around. He grabbed me, I reacted without thinking. Bam! Flat on his back."

"Derek? Really?" I unsuccessfully tried to stifle a laugh. Wei was tiny, and Derek was, well, he wasn't huge, but he was definitely bigger than Wei.

"At least some guys have a little faith in girls. Even if they have to find out the hard way. So to speak." She chuckled. "Of course, we did kiss and make up."

"So do the other girls in the Sisterhood want to do more, too?"

"Uh-huh. We're waiting for the right time to do something, or to help someone, outside of our regular activities. Something that will prove our capabilities."

My mind flashed on Joan, Mike's sister, who was an escapee from the FeLS program. She'd been rescued and brought back to Earth from the training station. Based on what Wei'd just said, it must've been NonCons who'd saved her. She was living with a group of homeless women. I wondered . . . would the Sisterhood . . . No. I didn't know enough about it. And I wasn't even a part of the Sisterhood yet. I'd talk to Wei some other time about Joan.

"Has your dad said anything about what's taking so long to expose FeLS?"

"Nuh-uh," Wei said. "I know he gave that information to your father weeks ago. I'm sure they are waiting for just the right moment."

"They need to get it out there, and the sooner the better." When FeLS was exposed, people like Joan would be helped. Even though I couldn't do anything for her right then, maybe joining Wei's group would give me some ideas. "Listen, is there some sort of initiation for the Sisterhood? I'll do whatever it takes."

"You are the last person in the universe who needs to prove anything," Wei said. "I'll talk to them tonight and let you know the outcome tomorrow." She smiled at me. "They're going to want you. I know it."

"I hope so. I really hope so."

IV

I t was the last day of school before Holiday break. No one wanted to be there, not even the teachers. Mr. Haldewick had propped his pointer in the corner and stopped lecturing for once. The entire class was having an actual discussion of Holiday traditions through the centuries. I was anxiously awaiting the last bell so Wei and I could talk, but during my second to last period, Hal showed up for me. I was going to the principal's office, again. I scuffled along behind him, going as slowly as I could, all the while imagining numerous things that could be wrong. Along the way I saw Sal and Paulette sneaking out a side door together. Fortunately, Hal didn't notice them. No matter what Mrs. Marchant wanted with me, it couldn't possibly be worse than seeing the two of them together.

"Sit down, Miss Oberon." Mrs. Marchant pointed opposite her. "Your grandmother has called . . ."

Oh, no. "Pops . . ." It had to be. I clutched the arm of the chair "Is he okay?"

"It's not your grandfather." She inclined her head slightly to the right.

That was when I noticed the two women, both in black,

perched like giant crows on the bench that sat under the AV screens.

"These ladies are from Child Protective Services." Mrs. Marchant wheeled around her desk, stopping next to me. "They want to ask you some questions."

I glanced at her. Somehow it felt like sides had been drawn, and I could tell Mrs. Marchant was on mine.

"Yes, ma'am," I said.

"We will be recording this," one of the women said.

Her voice startled me. It was soothing and melodious, more like a songbird than the rasping caw I'd expected.

"Give me a moment, please." She tugged the pouch off her shoulder, fumbled with the clasps, and eventually produced an AV recorder. Glancing apologetically at the other woman, who was frowning over her beakish nose, she said, "It's a new model, I'm not quite used to—"

"Then stop explaining and figure it out," her partner snapped. "We haven't got all day." That one's voice fit her appearance perfectly.

I wished Songbird would be asking the questions, but I knew it would be Crow Face. If only I knew more of Wei's emotion-regulation tricks. Wei had shown me some simple breath-control exercises to check emotions, but still the familiar heat radiated up my neck. My hands were sweating, too.

Mrs. Marchant whirred herself between me and the pair of women. She produced a tissue from inside her all-encompassing chair. "Know the truth, but tell only what needs to be told," she whispered, handing it to me. Spinning around, she faced them, kind of like a mother protecting her child. "This won't take long,

I hope? We are running a school here. You could have done this at the home." Her last remark was almost an outright accusation.

Crow Face's jaw tightened, but she didn't reply.

"It's ready." Songbird had the recorder affixed to a tripod, and it was pointing right at me.

I pressed the tissue between my hands and tried to remember to breathe. I made it through the routine questions without any major problems. Name, age, relationship to Dee, Gran, and Pops were all confirmed when Songbird scanned my hand. A sympathetic flicker crossed her face.

"How old are your grandparents?" Crow Face towered over me.

"Pops is eighty-seven, and Gran is, uh . . ." Did I even know how old she was? Besides, I was pretty sure they already knew the answers. "I think she's eighty-five."

"Tell me about your grandfather's drug use." Her beady eyes locked onto mine.

The hackles on my neck rose. "He takes prescription drugs for pain, for his leg." How dare she accuse Pops of being a drugger! "The leg that he lost in service to the Governing Council's space program," I added.

Crow Face tapped something into her PAV receiver. "It would serve you better if you watched your attitude, Miss Oberon."

I tugged at the tissue in my hands, shredding one corner of it. Mrs. Marchant caught my eye. Her expression was enough to remind me that this was neither the time nor the place for outbursts.

"I'm sorry." Which, of course, I wasn't. But even though my nerves were eating me up inside, I could lie with the best when I had to. Contritely, I said, "The GC and Media did more than they had to for Pops." The exact opposite being the truth. The bare minimum, that's what they did. And that was only after the story leaked out about how the government wasn't covering any of the medical bills or rehab for Pops and the other guy, who'd lost both legs and an eye. The Media couldn't hide that particular truth.

"Your grandmother has a friend, Harriet Pace?"

"Yes, ma'am."

"She's at your apartment often?" Her black eyes bored into me.

"I suppose so."

"Suppose so?" Her eyes narrowed to slits. "Is she or isn't she? Daily? Hourly? How often?"

"She usually comes over every day, or Gran goes to see her." What could possibly be the problem with Harriet? "Mrs. Pace is nice," I added.

"Are you acquainted with John Pace?"

Johnny, Harriet's son, had been arrested weeks ago for being a NonCon.

Miss Crow Face leaned close to me; her breath smelled of rotting, dead things. Vegetarianism was the law, but everyone knew there was a black market in animal flesh. A mental image of her gnashing into a cow crossed my brain. Clenching my teeth, I swallowed hard, struggling to keep my lunch down.

"Answer the question, Miss Oberon," she said. "Do you know John Pace?"

"Yes."

She straightened up, smirking. "Does your sister know John Pace?"

"Yes." What did Dee have to do with this? I plucked at the tissue in my hands.

"Has she ever been left in his care?"

"I don't think so. He might've been around when Mrs. Pace was watching her." Where this was going I didn't know, but it couldn't be good. I looked at the shredded tissue in my hands, then at Crow Face. "Why?" I asked.

"I ask the questions." She drew close again. "How long has your grandfather been a subversive?"

"What?" My eyes flew wide open.

"You heard me. Answer the question."

"Pops isn't a subversive." I felt the sweat beading on my forehead. "He's just, well . . . outspoken. I don't understand what's going on here."

"There have been complaints, Miss Oberon. A Writ of Unsuitability has been filed against your grandparents." She grabbed my wrist and twisted my arm over with more force than was necessary, exposing the XVI tattoo. "We know you are of age—you can take care of yourself." She dropped my arm, turning her back to me.

"I'm old enough to take care of Dee, too." I protested.

Crow Face pivoted around and raked her eyes up and down me. Her lip curled. "You may be sixteen, but you are not emancipated. You're just a tier-two orphan." She punctuated each of the following words with a jab of her finger. "You. Are. Nothing."

Nothing. Tier two. Orphan. Sixteen. Nothing. The words wrenched some vital plug deep inside me, and I felt myself draining out. Had I stopped breathing? I couldn't even feel my heart beating. Staring at the recorder, I wondered how it would document me as nothing. A black hole where I was sitting? An empty silhouette in the middle of the room?

I was vaguely aware of Mrs. Marchant rolling her transchair in front of me. As if through a barrel of water, I heard her say, "Are you quite done?"

From that same far-off place, Crow Face said, "We most certainly are. Put that away," she ordered Songbird. "As for this case . . . you . . . Oberon!" I snapped my eyes to her face. "Your grandparents will have received notice to appear in Upper Court on December twenty-third. You are permitted to be there if you want." She spun around and strode off. Songbird, still stuffing AV equipment into her bag, scurried after in her wake.

December twenty-third. Two days before Holiday. I was staring at Mrs. Marchant's back when the room began to spin. Next thing I knew, Hal was hovering over me with a glass of water, and I was lying on the bench previously occupied by the Child Protective Services women.

As quickly as I rose, I fell back down.

"Drink this," Hal intoned. "You will feel better."

Hesitantly, I propped myself up on my elbow. When I was sure I wouldn't collapse again, I took a sip.

Mrs. Marchant glided over to me. "You'll be as well as one could expect." She dismissed Hal. As the door closed behind him, she said, "Your tutor will be a great help with this."

"Who?" I raised myself to sitting.

"You are beginning tutoring in ancient sciences soon, are you not?"

Rosie. My Cliste Galad lessons. How did she know? "Not for a while. I couldn't . . ."

"I understand. No matter, you will learn other things. You are far from alone."

"I need to go home. Gran and Pops must be worried sick."

"Yes, you should go straight home." Mrs. Marchant handed me another tissue. "Now that CPS has the case, they will do whatever they will do." She checked the wall clock. "You have friends. Ask for their help." She whirred back to her desk.

"Thank you," I said.

"The truth will out, Miss Oberon." She didn't even look up from her papers. "Carry on."

V

When I got outside, Wei was waiting for me. "You look terrible. What happened?"

I glanced around, this wasn't something I wanted overheard. "There's been a Writ of Unsuitability filed against Gran and Pops. CPS came and questioned me in Marchant's office. Someone's trying to take Dee away." I checked out each student who filed out of the building, hoping against hope to see Sal. "Where's Sal? I saw him with Paulette when I was going to Marchant's."

"He . . . yeah, business." She gave me a knowing look.

"Yeah, right." It took a minute for me to stop peering at the faces trickling past. I bit my tongue. Sal had been straight with me. I had no reason to doubt him. But Paulette . . . Gah! I didn't want to waste more than that one sarcastic moment on Paulette. I'd talk to Sal later.

The last bell rang. "Skivs! Dee's been waiting." I called her on my PAV. She'd taken refuge from the cold inside a designer shop and was wondering where I was.

"We'll be right there." I clicked off and motioned to Wei. "Come on. I'll tell you the details while we're walking."

I filled her in: "You know, I could ask Mr. Long if he'll let me work full-time. If Gran and Pops can't . . . Well, I can. I'll quit school and look after Dee. I will not let her go." A thought grabbed me. "Wei, what if it's not the CPS system they send her to? What if they send her to Ed's family? I can't let that happen! I—"

"Dad will know what to do," Wei said.

Dad. What about my dad? And my sister's dad—her real one, that is. Wei's mother was the only person besides my father and me who knew that he was Dee's father, too. Surely he'd do something if they took her away. He had to, right? But then I realized what would happen. It wasn't safe for anyone to know that Dee was really Alan Oberon's daughter—things were dangerous enough after the incident with Ed. And the only way anyone could be absolutely sure that Dee would be safe was if she went into hiding with him. Underground. Disappeared, presumed dead—just like him. Chills ran through me. I'd lost my mom; I never had my dad. I couldn't lose my sister, too—there had to be a different way.

"Hey, Wei, did you talk to your friends?" I asked. Maybe, just maybe the Sisterhood could help. How, I didn't know.

"Yep. Whenever you can come over to my house, you can meet them. We'll set up a face-to-face."

"I don't work again until tomorrow. So, maybe tonight?"

We were still trying to figure out timing when Dee came running out of the shop. "They were about ready to throw me out." She gave a dismissive wave of her hand. "Oh, never mind that. Guess what? Miss Maldovar chose me to be her assistant for the rest of the school— Zats! Nina, you look awful." Like a little nurse, she swiped her wrist across my forehead. "Are you sick or something?"

Wei gave my arm a quick squeeze. "See you later. Bye, Dee."

Taking a deep breath, I explained the situation to Dee, stopping only long enough for us to board the trans.

When I was finished, instead of breaking down or crying, although her chin did quiver once, she said, "That's ridiculous. Pops is not a drugger." Fire lit her eyes. "I'm going to tell that . . . that crow-faced woman who bullied you . . ." She smacked her fist into her hand.

"Deeds, calm down." I quickly surveyed the other passengers, to be sure no one was watching us. I don't think I'd ever seen my little sister so visibly angry. "Wei is going to talk to her dad. He'll help. Right now we need to get home and find out exactly what happened."

She bounced back in the seat, a determined set to her mouth. "Nobody is going to take me away from Pops. Nobody."

I hoped she was right.

***

When we got home, Gran and Pops were in the middle of a heated debate, which stopped as soon as Dee and I entered the room.

She ran to Pops's side. "I'm not going anywhere," she said, curling her arm around his shoulders. "I don't care what anyone tries to do."

"So you've heard," Gran said to me.

"Uh-huh. CPS came to my school and questioned me," I said. "I told Dee on the way home."

"I'm calling my friends," Pops growled. "We'll take care of this. Get me that dang—"

"Hush up!" Gran wagged a finger at him, but left the room,

then returned with the scrambler, taken from its hiding place above the chiller.

Dee watched her plug it in and turn it on. "What is *that*?"

"Keeps prying ears from hearing everything we say," Gran said.

"It scrambles sound waves so that audio surveillance can't understand what we're saying," I said. Gran had showed it to me a few weeks ago and explained how to use it. I'd gotten some good use out of it when Ed was still alive. But Dee had never even known it existed before now. I didn't think she'd even known something like that could exist.

"Surveillance? Why would they listen to us?" Dee glanced from Gran to me. "Because of your father? He's dead. Don't they know we're not a problem?"

"The GC doesn't let the past lie," Gran said. "They'll hound us till we're in our graves." She turned to Pops. "Now, don't forget, old man, when it starts beeping, turn it off."

Brushing her away, he said, "I know. I know. It's my machine, remember?" He fumbled with his PAV receiver until he got one of his cronies on the other end.

Gran motioned Dee and me to follow her into the kitchen. "We will fight this thing." She sat at the table, rubbing her chest. "You know, arguing with your grandfather takes it out of me. I'm not as young as I used to be."

"Are you okay?" I asked. She was breathing hard, her face ashen.

"I'm . . ." She paused, taking a ragged breath. "I'm not used to getting all het up about things."

Dee glanced at me, a concerned frown creasing her forehead. I mustered as much reassurance as I could into a weak smile.

Gran slid a paper across the table. "Here's the writ. I can't imagine who could've done such a thing. Why would anyone think that we're unsuitable to take care of our own grandchildren?" She drew in another uneven breath. "I wonder if it's because of Dee's father? Maybe he isn't missing. Maybe he's—" She took in Dee's expression and quickly changed course. "I have the papers from Ginnie, signed and notarized, appointing us as guardians to both of you. There should be no question . . ."

"Are you sure you're okay?" I'd never seen Gran so pale. "Maybe you should lie down? Or I could call the clinic doc downstairs." That was one thing about living in a building full of retirees: there was an on-site medical clinic, open twenty-four hours, every day.

She shook her head. "It's the shock of getting that." She jabbed a finger at the paper. "Give me a moment, I'll be right as rain."

I poured a glass of water and gave it to Gran. Her hand trembled as she took a sip.

"Gran, I should show this to Mr. Jenkins." I picked up the document. "Wei said he would help. I'm going to digi it with my PAV and send it over now. She can give it to her dad right away."

Gran sighed. "They've done so much for us already. But, yes. I suppose we'll have to ask for their help again. If only your grandfather . . ." Her voice trailed off.

"What about me?" Dee piped up. "What can I do? This is all about me, but I feel so"—she threw up her hands—"helpless."

I wondered if Gran was as surprised as I was at how grown up Dee sounded, not at all like a little kid. Of course, she was nearly twelve. She'd be a preteen in less than a month. That hardly seemed possible, my little sister, a Pre. As that, surely the authorities would let her have some kind of say in all this. A faint voice in my head, sounding a lot like my mom, informed me, *They'll do what they want—there's something more behind this, Nina. Seek the truth.*

"I can use help cleaning up this kitchen," Gran said. "No sense in me moping around. Nothing to be done right now anyway. Let's get cracking." Belying her words, Gran stayed seated.

Dee, however, began to bustle around. "I'll start dinner. What shall we have?"

While the two of them formulated the menu, I slipped out of the room with the writ. I'd just sent it to Wei when my PAV beeped.

"Can you come to our place?" Sal asked. "I'll be there, waiting."

I raced down the hall, pulling on my coat, when I noticed Pops, still ranting to his friends. The scrambler's light shone green. Kneeling beside him, I caught his attention. "Pops. Don't forget what Gran said. Stop talking when the light blinks and the beeping starts. Okay?"

He stuck his hand over his PAV receiver. "I've been using this thing since before you were born, Little Bit. I'd never forget something that important. See? I've got it right in front of my eyes." He made a face at the scrambler.

"Gran and Dee are in the kitchen. I'll be back soon. I love you!" I brushed a kiss across his forehead, then swung past the kitchen, calling out, "I'm going out, I won't be long."

"Come back by dinnertime," Dee replied. "I'm cooking."

When I got to the street, the number 33 had just pulled away. I raced alongside, banging on the door. Thankfully, the driver had a heart and let me board. My stomach was flip-flopping like a fish out of water. I couldn't wait to see Sal. I had to tell him about the writ, and I wanted to find out what he'd been doing with Paulette again. Except I had to remind myself to not be jealous. Curious, is all.

I leaped off at the stop in the middle of Lincoln Park, taking all four steps at once. Before my feet hit the ground, I was sprinting in the direction of my mountain, the place where my mom and dad would meet after he'd faked his death. The place where I first met Sal. It was a dead zone. The perfect place for two people in love to meet.

My breath caught when I spied him. He was dressed homeless, like when we'd first met. Over the past couple of weeks I'd come to know what that meant: NonCon business. No one looked at the homeless, and so it was the perfect disguise for NonCons doing saboteur work, like Sal. My heart sank. This meant he'd be gone again. Sometimes it was just a day; sometimes he'd be gone nearly a week. Before I had the chance to wallow, he drew me down the far side of the mound, out of view of the street and prying eyes.

"Nina, I'm so sorry. I know this isn't a good time to leave. Wei told me CPS is trying to take Dee." His fingers laced between mine. "She said her dad is going to help, so you'll be in good hands."

His eyes searched mine, waiting for a response. Maybe he expected me to be mad that he was going again, but I wasn't. I was sad. I felt like I hardly saw him anymore. I knew his work was important, but so was I.

And as much as I wanted to talk to him, I wanted to kiss him, too. Lots of kisses. Enough kisses to make me forget that my life was, once again, falling apart. I reached for him and pulled him to me.

After several minutes of pure bliss, I backed off. "I'm going to miss you. I know Wei's dad will do what he can for us with Dee, but what if it isn't enough? I feel like I should do something myself to stop the writ. I'm Dee's closest relative. If I quit school and become emancipated, they won't be able to take her from me."

"Nina, Mr. Jenkins will figure out something. You can't quit school. You're a good enough artist to get a scholarship and go on to design school. That will boost you up at least three tiers. You'll be—" He stopped abruptly and reached over to push my hair out of my eyes.

"Be what?" I blocked his hand midswipe. "Up to your tier?" I shot him a questioning look. "Are you ashamed of me because I'm low tier?"

"Of course not." He leaned in to kiss me, but I dodged left to avoid it.

"You've thought about it. About me being lower than you." My temper was rising. "Is that how come you've been hanging out with Paulette? She's closer to your tier, more acceptable than I am?"

"Stop being ridiculous. This has nothing to do with what tier you are. Nina. Has that ever made a difference to me?"

"I don't know. Has it?" I waited, watched, as he collected his words, measuring what to say next.

"Tiers may mean something to you, but they don't mean crap to me. Do you think I do this"—he raked his hand up and down his homeless garb—"because I give a shit about what tier someone is? The amount of credits someone has doesn't make her somebody worthwhile. It's what's in the person, not what's in her account."

I wanted to believe him. He and Wei and their friends had never treated me differently because of tiers. It may not have meant anything to them, but that didn't mean it didn't mean anything to me. They could ignore tiers because they were upper. I wasn't. If I managed to get a scholarship, on top of having my Creative designation, I could work my way out of my lower-tier status. Then I'd be closer to equal . . . ugh. I shook my head, trying to clear away my negative train of thought. Hadn't anything Ginnie taught me sunk in? She had always tried to impart to Dee and me that everyone was equal. That the tiers were imposed.

Maybe Sal was right. This was my problem, not his. And whoever's problem it was, it was taking precious time away from the two of us.

"I know you're—" My PAV beeped. "Hang on, it's Dee." I clicked it on. "What? No! I'll be right there. Dee, I'll be right there."

VI

Halfway home I was lucky enough to snag a trans and got there faster than I'd thought possible. I'd left Sal in his homeless clothes standing by our mountain. He couldn't follow me, not dressed like that.

Storming out of the elport, I raced into the apartment. Gran was on the couch, her arm around Dee, the two of them wet-faced and sniffling. Harriet was next to Gran, murmuring sympathy. The apartment had been torn apart, things everywhere, but one thing was obviously missing.

My voice trembled. "Pops?"

"B.O.S.S. took him." Dee's voice cracked, fresh tears streaming down her face.

"The scrambler ran out of time. That silly old fool kept on talking. It's my fault. I should have stayed in here with him. Kept an eye on him." Gran twisted her hanky, her voice shaking. "He's so sick. He won't survive reassimilation."

"There, there, Edith." Harriet stroked Gran's shoulder. "You don't know that's what they're going to do. They just took him for questioning."

"Surely they won't . . . He can't have said anything important.

He was spouting off with his cronies." I arched my head back, staring at the ceiling, gathering together my swirling thoughts. This could not be happening. "Pops isn't a threat to anyone."

"It's not what he said. It's the machine, Nina . . ." Gran said. "The machine is the problem. They found him with contraband. There was no way to explain it away. If he hadn't insisted that Dee and I didn't know what it was, they'd have taken us, too." She thrust a paper in my hand. "We're supposed to be *there* on Monday."

"He doesn't have his leg," Dee cried. "Nina, they wouldn't let him take his leg. We have to *do* something."

I started pacing back and forth. There was nothing for us *to* do, not until Monday. I looked at Gran sitting on the couch. Her skin was ashen, and her breathing was worse than before I'd left.

"Gran, are you all right?" I bent down and touched her arm. She laid her hand on mine and let out a breath.

"Nina . . . I can't breathe." She grabbed her left arm and collapsed back on the sofa, eyes closed.

"Gran!" Dee cried.

"Dee, call the clinic! Now! Nina, do you know CPR?" Harriet's voice wavered.

Dee sprang to the door, pressing the emergency button on the entry pad to alert the medics. Harriet helped me slide Gran off the couch and onto the floor. Her eyes fluttered but didn't open. She was still breathing, but just barely. I loosened her collar and felt for a pulse on her neck. Her skin, the near-translucence of old age, slid across her bones, fragile, breakable, like an antique china cup. Rhythmically, I pressed on her chest. With each movement, I said, "Gran." Push. "Don't leave." Push. "Please." Push. "Gran . . ."

The medics rushed in, swept Harriet and Dee aside, and took over for me on the chest compressions. Dee's arms circled my waist, mine hers, and Harriet's wrapped around us both. She was whispering prayers.

I knew Gran believed in a god. I'd never been sure what I believed about God and prayers, but where else could I turn? I silently echoed Harriet's words, begging Gran's god to hear me. To not let her die.

"She's stabilized," one of the medics said. "Let's get her to Metro."

Moments later they had Gran on a stretcher and were wheeling her out of the apartment.

"Who's coming with us?" the tech asked. "Only got room for one."

"You go," Harriet said to me. "Dee and I will meet you there."

I squeezed my sister to me. My words tangling in her hair. "Be brave." I hoped I could do the same.

***

The E-Med trans screamed through the city. I kept twisting around from the front seat to keep an eye on Gran. Although I couldn't see her, I could see the lines on the machine to which they had her hooked up. Those lines were still moving. That was a good thing.

When we arrived at Metro, the hospital for all low-tiers and welfare people, the medics transferred Gran to a hospital gurney and left without a word. I was lost. The only other time I'd been in the hospital was when my mom, Ginnie, died, and that had been with a police escort in and with a B.O.S.S. escort out. I wrapped my arms around myself, holding in those awful memories.

A woman in slacks scanned Gran's info while several nurses and hospital techs crowded around her. The blur of their colorful scrubs reminded me of an Impressionist painting come to life. Life. Hang on, Gran. I peered at her through the sea of colors. *Please, Gran. I can't lose you, too.* B.O.S.S., hoping for information no doubt, had arranged to keep my mom alive long enough for us to talk, to say good-bye. But I knew there'd be no Infinity machine keeping Gran alive if . . . I blinked back the tears crowding to get out. I was an adult now. I had to handle this like an adult.

A girl, not a whole lot older than me, guided me away from the cluster. Her badge said INTAKE. She pointed down the hall. "You need to wait in there. The sign that says WAITING ROOM." When I didn't move, she said, "You can read, can't you?"

I glared at her. "Of course I can read."

"You welfs are all the same." She smirked. "You still have to wait—"

"I am not on welfare," I said through clenched teeth. "This is where government retirees have to come."

"Yeah." She glanced over my clothes. "The low-tier ones." Before I had a chance to retort, she said, "The doctor will be in to see you when they're done with her." She gave me a final once-over before going back to whatever rock she'd crawled out from under.

It wasn't like she was making a ton of credits working intake at Metro. She was no better than me. Sal's words rang in my head, *It's what's in the person.* Well, what was in that person was a whole lot of nasty. I trudged to the waiting room.

It was filled with anxiety, fear, and sadness. I perched on the edge of a vacant chair near the door, ashamed of the thoughts running through my head about my fellow occupants. Judging thoughts, mean thoughts, the same thoughts that awful girl had insinuated when she'd ordered me out of the emergency area. My PAV beeped me out of my self-loathing. It was Sal.

"Nina. Are you okay?"

"They took Pops. Gran had— She had an attack. Gran's at Metro. Can you come? I need you."

His response was cut off by another voice—a girl's voice. Paulette.

"Sal. We've got to go. Now."

"I can't come, Nina. I have to—"

"Sal," Paulette urged.

"I'll call when I can." His PAV clicked off.

Sal was with Paulette. NonCon business? It had to be. I knew that I shouldn't mind, but I did. Sal was my boyfriend. I really needed him now. Was this what it was like for Ginnie when my dad took off? How did she deal? I knew the answer. She got tough. She took Ed's abuse. She gave her life. Was I going to do the same? I stared at the floor, even though it could give me no answers.

"Nina!" Dee burst into the room, with Harriet right behind. I hugged Dee tight and explained what I could. There was little I could update them on, other than the fact that Gran was being attended to. A commotion across the room put a stop to our conversation.

"My baby!" a woman shrieked. "No! You're lying! She just turned sixteen. She's my life!" She made a grab for the med tech who had apparently just given her the news that her daughter was dead. "They killed her! You've got to do something!"

Her companion restrained her. "Mona. Sis." Holding and stroking her sister, she said to the tech, "What do we do now?"

"If you insist, we can call the authorities," he said. "But, there's no medical indication that the sex wasn't consensual." He shrugged.

"Consensual? Those animals!" The mother broke free, lunging at the man.

I hustled Dee behind me. Harriet grabbed my arm, and we became a barrier between the frantic woman and my little sister.

"Five of them! Do you hear me?" the woman screamed. "Five! It's murder! All because of that damned tattoo! How can you say—"

Her anguished tirade was immediately silenced when two policemen in their checkered hats burst into the waiting room. One stun-stick to the neck subdued her, and they dragged her off. The sister scrambled after them, tears streaming down her face.

The room was silent. No one made eye contact with anyone else. I pulled Dee close. "You shouldn't have seen that," I said. "Harriet, you should take her back to—"

"Nina, I'm staying here with you." Dee was trembling, but there was a determination in the set of her chin. For a moment, she reminded me of Ginnie. "I want to be here when Gran wakes up."

"I'll get us something to drink," Harriet said.

Dee and I took seats near the door. I kept my arm around her shoulder, and she didn't protest. Harriet returned with Sparkles for all of us. I excused myself and went to the ladies' room to throw water on my face.

Staring into the mirror, I couldn't blink away the haunting picture of that woman's daughter fighting off a gang of boys. I could hear my mother telling me how important it was to be on guard, not to act sex-teen—to push against the system, but not too openly. It wasn't safe. Words. At the time, that's all they had been. But since her death, and Sandy's—my best friend who'd been raped and killed by Ed—and knowing what I now knew, what Ginnie'd uncovered about FeLS being a front for a sex-slavery network for high-ranking government officials, I wondered how long I could keep quiet. Someone had to speak up. I fingered the T on my charm necklace. Pops had given me the T, he'd said it stood for Truth. Pops spouted truth, my dad debated truth, my mother exposed truth . . . was I the Oberon who simply had to tell the truth? But how?

***

When I got back to the waiting room, Harriet was dozing and Dee had fallen asleep in her arms. I retrieved a rapido and sketch pad from my bag. The tormented face of the mother as the cop jabbed her flowed out of my fingers. I was still drawing when a nurse stuck her head in the door. "Is there someone here for Edith Oberon?"

I leaped up, stuffing my artwork away. "Me!"

VII

The nurse would allow only one of us at a time in the cube, so Harriet and Dee stayed in the waiting room. Gran was surrounded by a tangle of tubes and wires, hooked to a monitor that beeped and hummed softly. I scooted a chair close to her; wrapping my hand around hers, I sat, transfixed by the lines on the monitor indicating her heartbeat. Mine beat twice before the faint blip of hers registered. Even then, it barely made a bump on the horizontal green bar pulsing across the screen.

A tall man in a white coat, carrying some kind of digi-pad, entered. "I'm Dr. Silverman."

Jumping up, I extended my hand. When he didn't take it, I withdrew mine.

"You're sixteen?" he asked.

"Yes."

"We'd like your permission to try a new procedure on the patient. She is your grandmother, correct?"

"Yes." I gulped. Who was I to give permission? Then I realized: Pops was in custody. Dee was underage. I was the only relative who could.

"The procedure repairs damaged heart tissue and . . ." He

glanced at the pad in his hand—Gran's chart—then back to me. "Given her age, it will add three, maybe five more years of life. There are, of course, risks, as with any new medical technique."

I felt the blood drain from my face. "Risks? What if she doesn't have the operation?"

"Without it she'll be dead in a few hours." He tapped his rapido against the chart's edge. "I don't have all night, Miss . . ." He consulted the chart again. "Oberon. Your decision."

"Decision?" I stared at him. "There really isn't any except 'do it,' is there?"

He raised an eyebrow, as if he hadn't expected anything but a simple yes or no. "You could decide that the burden of caring for an elderly woman whose use in life—"

"She is not useless." I glared at him. "And how dare you—"

"There are other patients who won't hesitate." He headed toward the exit.

"Wait. Please."

He turned back.

"Yes. Do it. Please." I was groveling. Gran was worth that, and so much more. "I'm sorry if I got out of line. I'm not used to making—"

The doctor snapped his fingers, and two orderlies hustled in. "Get this patient down to three. Stat." Within seconds, they had trundled Gran out of the cube. Silverman was busy on his PAV. "Have Heart Team Fifty-ought assembled in three. We've got a live one."

Live one? My eyes widened, and I swallowed another huge lump. What if I'd just sentenced Gran to die at the hands of some government quack practicing an experimental procedure?

"Are you sure this is—"

Dr. Silverman cut me off again. "This is science."

I stuffed all my premature guilt down deep. He had to be right. Had. To. Be.

Cutting out of the cube as sharply as he'd entered, I hurried along behind. Terror crawling up my spine.

***

Dee ran up to me. "How's Gran? Can I go see her now?"

"Not now," I said. "They took her to the operating room."

Dee clutched my hand. "She's going to be all right, isn't she?"

"Let's sit." I led her back to where Harriet was waiting. "It was definitely her heart," I said. "This really great doctor is operating on her right now. She's going to be better than ever when this is done."

Dee threw her arms around me, squeezing tight. "She has to be all right."

I couldn't shake the memory of that awful night when Ginnie died. "It's going to be fine," I said, with much more conviction than I felt. Although there had been something about Dr. Silverman . . . I doubted he would allow Gran to die, simply because he couldn't stand to lose a patient. Looking closely at Harriet, I realized how exhausted she was. As much as I didn't want to be alone, I didn't want to be a burden on her. And Dee, too, was obviously worn out. "You should both go home. It's going to be a while. I promise I'll call you as soon as there is news."

"I don't want—"

"Dee, don't argue with me," I snapped, and immediately felt awful. "I'm sorry. One of us needs to get some real sleep. I have to be here to sign papers or give permissions. Please go. I'll call as soon as I know something."

"We'll go to my apartment," Harriet said. "It will be fine, I'm sure. Your grandmother's a strong woman."

"Call right away. Promise?" Dee hugged me.

"I promise."

When they were gone, I called Sal. No answer. I didn't want to think about him with Paulette, or anything that had to do with his not being there with me. I finally called Wei.

"I'll come right down to the hospital," she said.

"It's too late. I just wanted to talk for a minute."

"Nonsense. I'll have Chris drive me over. See you in a few."

I called Sal again. Even if he couldn't be with me, at least talking with him would be reassuring. No answer. I didn't leave a message. Alone in the waiting room, I poured my fears and frustrations into the drawing I'd started earlier.

***

"Took me forever to find you," Wei said. "The people working here are not helpful at all. Actually, the girl in intake was outright evil."

I snorted. "Yeah, I met her. That's how everyone treats low-tier and welfare people. And this is Metro"—I shrugged—"so those are the only people you'll find here."

"Really?" She tilted her head, casting me a quizzical look. "That's no reason to be rude. People are people."

It was my turn to be surprised at Wei's naïveté. The thought had never occurred to me that Wei wouldn't have any experience with life at the lower end of society. "Some people don't consider anyone below tier three to be real people. Not worth much of anything, unless they're doing them a common service, or, like Mike's dad, testing out experimental meds for research."

"Huh." She sat back, a pensive expression on her face. "I hadn't thought about that." She glanced at my lap. "What's that?"

"Nothing." I flipped the cover over my drawing.

"Can I see? It looked cool."

I didn't show my work around, except for art class. But I trusted Wei.

I pulled back the cover. "It was this woman who was here earlier. Her daughter was gang-raped and died." I'd divided the page and done the drawing as a triptych. One panel was of a girl, unconscious and hurt, with boys walking away in the distance. The middle panel was the mother weeping over her daughter's body. And the third was the mother being stunned by the cop.

Wei looked at it for the longest time. "That's amazing, Nina. As eloquent as one of your father's speeches, and just as powerful."

Wei was maybe thinking about the picture, and I was wishing that more people could see, really see, that this is what the XVI tattoo meant, when a family came in. The woman, puffy-eyed from crying, held a sleeping baby in her arms. An older woman, possibly her mother, was with her, a boy of about five in tow. They sat on the other side of the room and turned on the Family Audio/ Video. The baby fussed itself awake. Between its cries and the FAV, there was enough noise that Wei and I could talk, carefully, without fear of being overheard or monitored.

"Nina. After we talked this afternoon, I called and set up a meeting with my friends for tomorrow. But now that Gran's here, maybe we should—"

"No! I'll make it work." The Sisterhood. I had to make it—this was my chance, and I needed to do something other than sit in this room, waiting for bad news.

Just then, the waiting room door swung open. All eyes turned toward the entrance. My heart leaped into my throat as Dr. Silverman entered, expressionless, like a sphinx. It felt like an eternity as he walked across the room to me.

When he finally reached me, he said, "Your grandmother came through the procedure as well as can be expected. She'll be moved to a private room where we can keep her under observation."

I seized his hand. "Thank you! May I see her? Please?"

He extricated his hand, waving over one of the nurses standing near the door. "Sani-cloth. Stat. Then take this girl to the eighth floor." Without so much as a glance in my direction, he said, "Five minutes tonight, that's all."

Snatching the wipe from the nurse, he walked out, vigorously scrubbing the hand I'd touched.

"Nice guy," I muttered to Wei.

"Oh, he's so much more than that!" the nurse gushed. "He's a miracle worker." Her adoring gaze followed him.

I bit my tongue. If the operation saved Gran, I guess it didn't matter how much low-tiers, like me, disgusted the man.

***

On the way to the eighth floor, I called Dee. "Gran's out of the operating room. I get to see her for five minutes. The doctor said she did well." I didn't add his caveat. No need to upset Dee, and no need to dampen my own little spark of positivity. "I'll pick you up from Harriet's in about half an hour."

While I was talking with my sister, Wei called Chris to come and pick us up.

"Nina, maybe you guys should stay with us tonight?" Wei said.

"We'll be fine at the apartment." My thoughts ran to the mess the B.O.S.S. agents had made and how empty everything would feel without Gran and Pops. "It's closer to Metro," I reasoned. "And I know Dee will want to come down here first thing."

We opened the door to Gran's room quietly. I couldn't tell just by looking whether she was better or not. There was more color in her face, for sure. She was asleep and had a tube in her throat, and was hooked up to a machine that appeared to be controlling her breathing. I stood beside her bed for my allotted five minutes, remembering back to the allotted ten I spent with Ginnie when she was in the Infinity machine, after which the doctor had switched it off and my mother was dead. This time, however, things were different. The hypnotic blips on the monitor were stronger and more frequent than they'd been earlier—tiny pulses of hope.

VIII

It was freezing outside, and dark. The glare of the canopy of overhead lights temporarily blinded me.

"Hey, I'm over here." Chris was half out of his multi, waving to us. "Ladies, your chariot awaits."

"You sit in front." Wei crawled into the back and stretched out. "I'm pooped." She let out a big yawn, and then silence.

I sank into the seat, too wired to relax.

Chris slipped into the driver's side. "So how's your grandmother?"

"Better, I think. She was still under the anesthesia when I left, but they said her heart rate was good and she wasn't gray anymore."

"That's great. I'm sure she'll be fine. She's an Oberon. I've heard they're pretty tough cookies."

That did it. I burst into tears.

"Whoa! I didn't mean to start a river. Although it's completely understandable." He pulled a napkin out of the console and handed it to me. "Here."

Wei leaned over the seat, groggy. "You okay?"

"Fine." I sniffed, wiping my cheeks. "A momentary lapse of control."

Chris reached over and squeezed my arm. "Your family's been through so much. But you guys always bounce back." He put the trannie in gear and eased out into traffic. "Dad and Wei told me about the writ, and then your grandfather . . . Now this." He shook his head. "Lots of stuff going on in your life. You know, I'm sure it's because you're Alan's daughter. I wonder if B.O.S.S. suspects he's alive."

"Ed thought so, but—" Catching myself just in time, I pointed skyward. Surveillance.

"Oh, not to worry. Trannie's been modified by John and Sal. You can say whatever you want. No one can hear us."

Sal. What I wanted was not to be reminded of Sal. Sal who wasn't there when I needed him most, who was off somewhere with Paulette. Like my dad had not been there for my mom.

This whole night had brought back so many memories. How Ginnie'd had to face life alone after my father went underground. Sure, it had been for our safety as much as his—but, still . . . Ed, her boyfriend and Dee's presumed father, murdered her all because she wouldn't tell the truth about Alan's being alive. I knew some of how Ginnie had felt, from reading one of her hidden notes in Dee's baby book. She'd loved my dad, all the way to end. But what about him? How had he felt all those years? There were so many unanswered questions.

For those last few weeks, I'd managed to keep myself pretty upbeat about an eventual meeting with my father. But there were times I was angry, really angry at him for choosing the Resistance over my mom and me. To stave off any more thoughts, I dove into the conversation with Chris. "Ed wasn't sure my father was alive until right before my mother died. The nurse who was taking care of the Infinity machine that kept my mom alive those last few minutes was working with Ed. She overheard Mom tell me to find my father."

"Yeah, I know," Chris said. "She was dealt with."

I sat up with a jerk. "Dealt with?" What did that mean? "You don't mean . . . killed . . . ?" Was the Resistance no better than the GC, removing people who disagreed with them?

"Of course not." Chris glanced at me out of the corner of his eye. "We have a holding camp in the Himalayas. People there are as free as we can let them be. Most of them were coerced into working for B.O.S.S. anyway, but we have to keep them, uh . . . out of circulation, just in case. They'll all be released after the Governing Council is brought down. Anyway, back to Ed. We found out that he'd been in regular contact with someone we only know as 'A,'" Chris said. "But as near as we can tell, he didn't have any solid proof about your dad to pass along. So maybe I'm wrong. It's entirely possible that all of this is coincidence."

"Even the writ?" I wasn't convinced.

"Well, your grandfather wasn't . . ." Chris seemed to be choosing his words carefully. Which was a good thing. I was at the end of my last nerve and knew I wouldn't deal well with someone accusing Pops. "Let's say, he had a lapse in judgment."

He was right. Completely right. "That happened after the writ was filed. You're definitely not wrong about the Oberons. We do have a habit of speaking our minds at precisely the wrong time."

"Well, the right times, too. You should hear your father's speeches. He's an amazing orator."

The best I could muster was a lame smile. Pride swelled my heart, yet at the same time, pain pricked it. I'd only "heard" my father once, ever. That had been weeks ago on my birthday when he called me. I wanted to hear more—lots more. Like how everything got so messed up in my life. Surely, once he knew about Gran and Pops, he'd do something. He'd have to.

***

Chris parked his trannie in front of my building, "I'll walk you up."

"You don't need to," I said.

"Where are we?" Wei mumbled from the backseat, where she had been sleeping.

"Go back to sleep," Chris said. "And you, Nina—humor me." He bounded out of the multi, raced around, and opened my door before I could say okay. Bowing low, his eyes twinkling, he stretched out his hand. "Madam."

When I placed my hand in his, I felt some of his strength flow into me. A smile tugged the corners of my lips, and I gladly went along with his silliness. It was the perfect touch of humor to lighten my mood. "Thank you, sir."

"My pleasure."

Placing my hand on the recognition pad, I said, "Nina Oberon and guest." Chris put his face next to mine for the ID.

"Proceed to your apartment at once," an automated voice intoned. "Important notification posted at eleven-thirty p.m."

"What's that about?" Chris cocked his head.

"I have no idea. We'd better go up there before I pick up Dee from Harriet's."

I paced around the elport while Chris tried to calm me down. "I'm sure it's nothing. Probably a change in procedure of some sort."

The message screen by the apartment door was flashing. I pressed it and a paper slid out. Bolded across the top, it said: NOTICE OF EVICTION.

"What?" I slumped against the wall for support. "How could this happen?"

Chris cupped my elbow. "Let's get inside."

My hands were shaking as I pressed in the code. "Why would they evict us? We haven't done anything wrong. The rent goes straight from Pops's pension to the building fund."

Once we were inside, Chris let out a low whistle. "Wei said B.O.S.S. paid you a visit. This is their version of home decorating?"

"Yeah." I saw Pops's ginger tin on the floor, open, dented, and bits of candied ginger were scattered everywhere. I knelt down and started picking up the pieces. It was the only thing I could think to do.

Chris squatted beside me. "We should look at this notice," he said gently.

He helped me up and sat next to me on the sofa. Our legs were touching. Oddly, that was comforting.

"'Dear Mrs. Oberon,'" he read. "'Due to the subversive activity of Mr. Oberon—'"

"My dad? They don't know he's—" Chris clapped his hand over my mouth, shaking his head.

Surveillance. Pops's arrest was undeniable proof B.O.S.S. had us under surveillance.

"Dead. He's dead."

"Okay." Chris scanned the paper. "It says here that because of your grandfather's recent arrest, the building management is giving you, your grandmother, and Dee twenty-four hours to vacate the premises."

I stared at the marks on the paper, unable to focus on the fact that they made words. "Twenty-four hours? Where will we go?" A shiver ran down my spine. I pictured Dee and me, homeless, like Joan, eating out of garbage cans, wearing rags, always cold. And Gran. Where would she go when she got out of the hospital? I was so deep in my misery that I hardly noticed Chris making a call on his PAV.

He clicked off. "It's settled. Mom said all of you are going to live at our house. At least until this business with your grandfather is straightened out and your grandmother is healthy again. So where's your room? Let's get you enough things to see you through tonight. You want to get Dee's things, too? Then we'll stop by your neighbors' and get her."

I pulled myself together. It was no time for me to fall apart, even if I was exhausted, emotionally and physically. So much had happened in less than twenty-four hours. Pops, Gran, and now this. But—I wasn't helpless. I wasn't alone. I had friends, friends who were helping me.

And now I had a focus. "How about you go get Dee while I pack some things. Harriet Pace is in D14. I'll call and tell her you're coming." Chris took off and I called Harriet, telling her that we had been evicted, and explaining the plan, and trying not to get sucked into the rabbit hole of grief that threatened to envelop me. "Yes, Dee knows Chris. He's a good friend. We'll be fine. I'll be sure to call you tomorrow from the hospital and let you know how Gran is doing."

I started gathering a few things from the mess in the living room—a digi of Ginnie and my dad, and Pops's ginger tin.

The door opened, and Chris and Dee came in. "I told Dee what was going on," Chris said. "Hope you don't mind?"

"Not at all." I hugged Dee. "Deeds. You okay?"

"I'm tired." She pressed against me. "Gran's going to be okay, isn't she?"

"Uh-huh." As if I knew.

"And Pops. You'll get Pops out on Monday, won't you?" She gazed up at me.

I threw Chris a look of complete despair. Pops's hearing. "I'll do my best."

"You know," he said, "there isn't a lot we can do right now, except sleep. Let's get your stuff, and we can talk tomorrow about what to do. Want me to help you get some things together, Dee?"

After Ginnie's death, we'd had six days to vacate the modular we'd been living in. Because Dee and I didn't have much, it had been relatively easy. Gran and Pops had come and helped us move. This time wouldn't be much different. While Chris and Dee were in Dee's room, I stuffed a bag with the finds from the living room, my art supplies, and most of my clothes. We met back in the living room.

"What are we going to do about this?" I waved my arms at the mess of things. "We can't get all of it now. And the big things . . ."

"Nina, let me see the eviction notice again." Chris took the notice from me and scanned it quickly. "Damn. Everything has to be out by six p.m. Tomorrow." He rubbed his chin. "Okay. I'll come back early with a couple of friends. We'll pack everything up and get stuff moved. Mom's putting you guys in the downstairs apartment, the one my sister Angie and her husband didn't want. It's furnished, but we can move whatever you don't need into storage to make room for your stuff."

"That won't be much," I said. "All the furniture belongs to the building. Except for Pops's chair and my bed, we hardly have anything."

"Don't worry. I'll take care of everything. We'll move it all, and then when your grandmother is feeling up to it, she can make the decisions of what to keep." He took Dee's bag. "You ready?"

She nodded.

"Then let's go."

IX

To me, Wei's house was the most beautiful place I'd ever been. It was an ancient three-story brownstone walk-up. Even as exhausted as she was, Dee's eyes widened in amazement as we walked up to the front of the house. Lights glowing on the stone-pillared front porch welcomed us. "This is ultra," she whispered to me.

Chris activated the retinal scan hidden behind the brass numbers. "I'll program you guys in tomorrow."

Mrs. Jenkins must've heard us coming, because she was descending the marble stairs as we stepped into the foyer. Showering Dee and me with motherly hugs and murmurs of reassurance, she said, "Consider this your home, girls. I've put a few things in the chiller in your place, in case you get hungry. We'll figure out everything else tomorrow."

There were two apartments on the first floor. One was Mr. Jenkins's office. The other was now ours.

"I hope this will be comfortable." Mrs. Jenkins opened the door to our new home. Even as tired as we were, it would've been impossible not to be impressed.

The living room was furnished with an overstuffed sofa and

two chairs that were so big I was sure I'd sink down and get lost in one. A FAV hung on the wall across from the sofa. Flanking it were two bookshelves, filled with books—real books, not just chips like we used at school. I was awestruck at being surrounded by so many precious historic things. We'd had a few real books back when my mom was still alive, but they'd all been confiscated by B.O.S.S. after she died

"It's more than comfortable," I said. "I don't know how we can ever repay—"

"Nonsense." Mrs. Jenkins waved off my mention of indebtedness. "It is an honor to be able to help the family of my dear friends." I remembered her telling me how close she and my mom had been. "Let me show you the bedrooms. You must be exhausted."

"Nina, you shouldn't be alone tonight," Wei said. "I'll go grab my PJs and be right back."

When Wei returned, Mrs. Jenkins left, reminding us that there would be breakfast in the morning upstairs.

"We should get to sleep," I said. "I'm totaled."

"Me, too." Wei stifled a yawn.

"I guess so." Dee looked ready to drop, but hesitated at the door to her room. She obviously did not want to be alone.

"You know, the bed in my room is huge," I said. "There's plenty of room for three."

As it was, we could've fit in a fourth, it was so huge. Even with all that space, Dee fell asleep curled up in my arms.

***

A warm beam of sunlight across my face woke me. I bolted upright. "Where am I?"

"Huh?" was the muffled reply.

"Wei?"

She threw back the comforter, stretching her arms over her head. "You're awake."

"Yeah. It took me a minute to remember what all's happened." I patted the pile of covers next to me. "Where's Dee?"

"She woke up just after I did. I sent her upstairs for breakfast."

Just the mention of food made my stomach come to life, growling like an angry dog. But I had other things to take care of before my hunger. "Where's my bag? I have to call Metro and check in on Gran. Will my PAV work in your house?" With all the antisurveillance technology that Wei's house was wrapped up in, I didn't know what would and wouldn't work.

Wei produced my bag from beside the bed. "PAVs work fine here. If you want to know how, though, you'll have to ask Chris. All that techie stuff is space jargon to me." She rolled out of bed. "Come up when you're done."

***

I lightly tapped on the door. Wei's mother welcomed me, putting an arm around my shoulders, like Mom used to do. It made me sad, but it felt good, too. How I wished . . . no sense in that. There was too much for me to figure out. I didn't have time for what Gran called pie-in-the-sky thoughts.

"This is so kind of you." I felt myself tearing up. "I don't know—"

"It is the least we can do," she said. "We are fortunate to be in a position to help friends. Your father, although distressed about his parents, was glad to know that you and Dee are safe with us."

They talked to him—my father. I had spoken to him only that one time, weeks ago. But they'd already gotten word to him. How many emotions and questions just hearing "father" brought up. I settled them all back to sleep.

"Dee doesn't know about him—I mean, about him being alive, that is," I said.

"I thought not. She also doesn't know that he's her father, does she?"

I shook my head. "Just you and me, well, and my father—we're the only ones who know."

"And that is how it will stay until he decides to tell her. We will not talk openly of Alan around Dee. I'll be sure that Chris and Wei are aware."

"It's so hard to keep secrets. Like the FeLS information. Because of it, Ginnie's dead."

"Yes, that and so many other reasons." Mrs. Jenkins hugged me tight. "Someday the truth about everything will come out."

"Do you know when or how my father is going to let the world know what FeLS really is?" It was naive of me to think that one chink in the Governing Council's armor would bring them down. But at least exposing the FeLS sex-slavery side would stop low-tier girls, like Mike's sister, Joan, and me, from being exploited in that way.

"I have heard that there will be an announcement soon. Let's not focus on that today. When you go to see your grandmother, you want to be happy, positive. Take a few hours to enjoy life and not be worried about it." She cupped my chin in her hand. "I hope staying here will bring you some happiness, Nina. You so deserve it."

I craved happiness. As to whether I thought I deserved it, I wasn't so sure.

We walked into the kitchen. Chris was at the cook center, using it on manual, like Gran liked to do. Wei and Dee were already tucking into plates full of food.

Dee put her fork down. "How's Gran? Can we go see her now?"

"The doctor is going to call me when he gets in. The nurse said Gran was 'as well as could be expected,' but we can't see her again until the doctor approves visitors."

"Sit here." Wei pointed to a chair next to her. "I'll go with you if you want."

"You can go if it's after you've practiced your piano lessons." Mrs. Jenkins gave Wei a stern look.

Wei rolled her eyes. "Okay."

"Here you go." Chris came over with a plate of French toast, dusted with powdered sugar. A pat of spread in the middle was melting into a steaming pool. "Strawberries. Blueberries." He scooted a tray with two pots of toppings in front of me.

I spooned strawberries on one side of my toast and blueberries on the other. As I was eating, I realized Mr. Jenkins wasn't there. "Where's your dad?"

"He's taking care of a storage unit for your things," Wei said.

"After breakfast, if you haven't heard from the doctor yet," Mrs. Jenkins said, "you can go back to your apartment with Chris to deal with the rest of your things."

All at once, it hit me. "Oh, no! I almost forgot. I have to go to the Art Institute. I'm supposed to work today."

"Dee can get me into the apartment." Chris said. "My friends and I will do the packing, and she can make sure we don't miss anything. We might still be there when you're through with work."

The thought of my job, which entailed sitting in the middle of a cavernous storeroom filled with art, was inviting. It would be a little bit of sorely needed peace for me. But there was so much to do, and Gran . . .

"Why don't you go on and see what happens?" Wei said. "It's better to do something than to just sit around here worrying. If the doctor calls, you can get in touch with Chris and he'll bring Dee to the hospital. Don't stress."

***

But stress I did. I spent the entire ride to the Art Institute trying to clear my head about thoughts of FeLS. Thoughts like what my dad would do with the information I'd given him about a supposed diplomatic corps really being all about sex trafficking of low-tier sixteens. Thoughts of how Ed used to be the Chooser—the man who would go to schools and choose which low-tier sixteens would be enrolled into FeLS. Shipped off was more like it. Thank goodness we were able to buy out my contract so that I never had to go through that. But so many other girls did. Thoughts of Joan, who'd been broken by the FeLS induction "training." When I first saw her with a group of homeless women who hung out near the Chicago River, I'd wanted to help her. A thought flashed through my head, again: maybe the Sisterhood could do something.

The Sisterhood. Wei had said we'd meet later today. That was good—there was hope. I had something positive to hold on to.

X

I hopped off the trans and looked across Michigan Avenue at the front of the Art Institute. Two massive bronze lions had flanked the entrance since 1893. The south lion was "standing in defiance," and the north one was "on the prowl." Today I felt a kinship with both.

I got off the elport on the third floor and walked through the hallway. Floor-to-ceiling glass windows made up one entire wall. Light shimmered through them onto a huge hammered-silver disc that hung opposite. I loved this walk. In the three weeks since I'd started working for Martin, I had discovered that traversing this particular hallway had a calming effect on me. Actually, the entire Institute was a place of solace and comfort to me.

I tapped on Martin's door. He needed to know what was going on with Gran, and everything else. He was one of the head curators, so he was in charge of several special exhibits, as well as a lot of the rest of the collection. He knew more about art than anyone I'd ever met. It was amazing being in this place, working in this place. I'd often wondered if it was more than luck that Martin had spotted me sketching in the Postmodern exhibit one day. We'd talked briefly and he'd offered me the job after I got my Creative designation.

"Come in," he called.

I pushed open the tall, white door. Martin was at his floating desk. At least, that's what I called the shiny, black slab of stone that was supported by invisible power beams. An invention of Martin's partner, Percy.

"Oh, there's my lifesaver! Come, come." He motioned me over so I could see his PAV projection. "Say hi to Percy."

"Hi, Percy," I said to the projection.

"Nina, dear. Looking lovely, as usual."

I smiled. "Thank you. And you're looking lovely, too."

"You flatterer." Percy grinned. "I love it! Well, Marty, I guess this means you have to get back to work. Remember, the Winnackers' tonight. Better make the wine white, otherwise Iona will spend the entire time fretting over her white sofa and rug." He turned to me. "The woman has no sense at all, decorating or otherwise. None!" He threw up his hands and clicked off.

"Oh, my dear little Percy. He is much kinder than yours truly." Martin leaned forward conspiratorially. "I think I'll bring the red wine and sit in the middle of her ghastly whale of a sofa, waving my glass like a flag on End-of-Wars Day."

"Really?" I still was not sure when Martin was joking and when he was serious.

"No, not really. The Winnackers are one of the largest donors to the Institute's antiquities acquisition committee. They're having a Holiday party for the curators. I'll be on my best behavior, as usual. But I'll be wishing it was the red, all the same." He got up. "Is there something you needed?"

I told him about Pops, Gran, the writ, and the eviction notice.

"Oh, my dear sweet Lord." His smile faded into a concerned frown. "You need the day off? Don't spend a nanosec worrying if you do. I've been without an assistant for so long . . . and I want you to take care of what needs to be taken care of." His face was awash with concern.

"Oh, no," I said. "I'd go crazy sitting outside Gran's room. Besides, they told me no one's allowed to see her until Dr. Silverman says so. And as far as moving . . ." The tiniest smile hesitantly lifted the corners of my mouth. "I really don't mind if someone else does it for me."

"Really? Wonderful. Then come with me."

I followed Martin down the white hall, into the Twenty-first Century Postmodern exhibit. He uncovered the security box and keyed in the code; a hidden panel door slid open and we went in, the door slipping shut silently behind us. My workspace was a huge room filled floor to ceiling with crates, boxes, and tubes of all sizes and shapes. There were tall, skinny windows all around the room that gave the effect of stripes of light throughout. As my eyes adjusted, the vast art treasures stored there came into focus. My job was assisting Martin in cataloging everything from primitive cave-dweller tools to current pseudomodern vandal art. I actually loved being alone with centuries of art, the results of man's need to communicate nonverbally his deepest emotions. That kind of language I understood. Raw truth. You couldn't lie when it came from the soul.

It suddenly hit me. Martin had explained the curiosities of the

Art Institute my first day. Certain places in the Institute, especially back rooms and storage areas, were dead zones. And because of the fragility of many of the pieces, there was no surveillance at all in the storeroom. Damn.

"Martin. Since this room is protected, how will I know if the hospital calls?" I really wanted to stay at work, but I couldn't risk missing a call about Gran.

"M'dear, I've thought of almost everything it takes to protect the art. And Percy, bless his little self, has thought of everything it takes to protect me. Don't you know? He loves me. I know, we're talking about necessities. Although"—he leaned toward me, affecting a very serious look—"love is definitely a necessity."

I pursed my lips. "I'm not too sure about that."

"Uh-oh. You're too young to be cynical about love. But that is a conversation for another day. Let's attend to the conundrum at hand. Surveillance shields—taken care of, like so." He moved a lever on the side of the light on my desk. "Up, no surveillance." He pressed it again. "Down, surveillance."

"What does it do?"

"It turns the safety shield off and on. Percy's always been afraid that I would get trapped in here by Lord knows what. An earthquake? A flood? A marauding band of river rats? And I wouldn't be able to call for help. Anyway, since B.O.S.S. taps into everything . . ." He checked the light. "Up. We're safe. Because the entire downtown is bombarded with whatever electromagnetic folderol they use, all exhibit areas and storage rooms in the Institute are protected by shields. Only security can turn them on and off, except for this room." He lifted his eyebrows. "Percy's a peach, don't you know?"

"But won't B.O.S.S. or Security notice?"

"Not if you aren't in here making noise. If the hospital calls, go out to the hallway. You'll be fine. Just don't forget to turn the shield back on. And don't tell anyone about it. Our secret."

"Not a word." I would be able to stay and still get the hospital's call. Things were looking up.

"If you're absolutely sure you want to work today . . ." he said.

"Yes, I really need to be busy."

"As long as it doesn't involve packing up boxes, right?" He wiggled his eyebrows. "Well, no packing today, although you may be required to ready objets d'art for shipment to another museum."

"I think I can handle that."

"If that's the case, let us go to the Chinese artifacts room. I need to get a little something to take with me to the Winnackers. Have to keep the patrons happy. And, nothing makes Iona happier than, well . . . a clean sofa"—he chuckled—"and the loan of something ancient and unique. Rather like me—well aged and idiosyncratic." He made a silly face.

Martin was such an interesting mixture of down-to-earth, kind of pretentious, and really goofy, I couldn't help but like him.

"Come now. We'll traverse the secrets of the maze of the museum. There is surveillance in these corridors." Shifting his eyes back and forth like a comic detective, he led me to a door I'd never noticed before. Probably because it was covered by a thick tapestry. On the other side of the door, tunnels snaked out in several directions. "We're behind the walls now," Martin said.

"From here you can gain access to every exhibit hall, to the vaults in the basement, and even up to the helipad on the roof. In case you ever need to make a quick getaway."

"Just what I was looking for," I joked. "I'll let my helio pilot know to park there next time."

As we padded through the dimly lit corridors, I said, "It's a good thing you're here. I would be so lost if I were alone."

"Exactly why I needed a new assistant. Last one was sent off to Egyptian antiquities and hasn't been seen or heard from in months."

It was a struggle to keep my jaw from dropping open. "Are you—" Then I noticed the twinkle in his eyes.

"Gotcha! Didn't I?"

"Yes!" My insides had been tied up for so long, it was a huge relief to laugh aloud. "I can be a little gullible."

"We all are, sometimes. It's good to see you smile, Nina. You're much too serious for a teenager. Now is the time when you should be having fun, learning about life, trying out new things."

"I've been trying a lot of new things," I said ruefully. "Most of them haven't been much fun, though."

"That will change, love. That will change." He ushered me into a small room. Several wooden storage frames were leaning against the wall, and a huge glass-topped case was in the center of the room. This place was completely different from my usual workspace.

"As in main storage," Martin said, "there's no possibility of surveillance here." He glanced around the ceiling before continuing, "But no cutoff switches either."

72

"Guess I'd better not get caught here during an earthquake, then."

Martin threw back his head and laughed. "You know, Nina, you remind me so much of your father."

My father? I was a little taken aback. I knew that Martin was a friend of the Jenkinses, and so probably was, at the very least, sympathetic to the Resistance, but I had never expected this! Since I'd been working here, he'd never even hinted that he actually knew my father. So many secrets . . . it made my head spin. "You knew my dad?"

"Knew Alan? Indeed I do know him." His eyes twinkled. "And more than that. Certain friends of your father, like myself, are doing our best to make sure you are safe. After all, he can't be everywhere at once." As he talked, he perused the contents of the glass case.

"You're a NonCon?" My mouth fell open. Martin hardly seemed the type to be involved in Resistance work.

"Oh, I do so hate that word." He rolled his eyes. "I much prefer *dissident*. But I've learned to live with the majority rule. Not everyone has my taste for classical Latin derivatives. More's the pity, don't you know?" He flashed a quick smile. "Now, this will do." He removed a small flask from the case and held it to the light, inspecting it. "Iona will love showing this little beauty off, and there's little damage anyone can do to it." He slipped it into a velvet pouch. "We'll check it out when we get back to your desk. Come on."

No sooner had we stepped into the tunnel than my PAV beeped. "It's the hospital." After a short conversation with a nurse, I clicked off. "Gran's awake. They want me there. I have to go."

"Of course you do. Work will wait." He rushed me through the maze of corridors back to the main storeroom. "I won't expect to see you here until Monday," he said. "My best to your grandmother."

***

I called Chris to meet me at the hospital with Dee. When the trans pulled up to Metro, it seemed as if every passenger was getting off there. I shouldered my way through the crowd, looking around for them, torn between racing to Gran's room and waiting for my sister. I knew Chris wouldn't drop her off if I wasn't there. Fortunately, I didn't have to wait long.

Once inside, Dee and I grabbed the first elport going up. When the doors opened, there was Dr. Silverman, at the nurses' station.

Wary of his attitude and how it might affect Dee, I whispered, "That's Gran's doctor. He's kind of, uh . . . well, he's not real friendly."

Almost as if he knew I was talking about him, he looked up and motioned me over.

"Two of you." He frowned at Dee. "How old is this one?"

"I'm Delisa Oberon. I'll be twelve next month." She stuck out her hand. "Thank you for saving my grandmother's life."

He stared down at her. Begrudgingly, or so it seemed, he shook her outstretched hand. "It's what I do." He withdrew his hand. "Nurse, a sani—" He stopped short.

I'm not sure what kept him from asking for that wipe. Maybe it was Dee's open smile. Whatever the reason, I hid my astonishment by asking, "How is our grandmother?"

Fully recovered, and drawn back into his I'm-top-tier-and-you-are-disgusting-low-tier persona, he said, "Of course, the surgery was successful. Assuming Mrs. Oberon continues her present rate of recovery, I anticipate releasing her to the Edgewater Rehabilitation Center on Tuesday."

"Rehabilitation center?" Metro was one thing. Everyone had free medical care. But rehabilitation—that cost credits. Lots of credits that we didn't have. "Can't she come home? I can take care of her."

"Always about the cost, isn't it?" He flared his nostrils, as if something stank. "Because the surgery was experimental, all the care is covered. You won't be out anything."

"May we see her now?" Dee asked.

"Yes. Go. Ten minutes," was his snappish answer.

We stopped outside Gran's room. I took a deep breath, releasing my anger. Gran didn't need to feel my exasperation with some jerk like Dr. Silverman. I had to remind myself that he'd saved her life, and he'd been almost nice to Dee. Although, in my corner of the galaxy, that didn't give him a free ride.

"Gran?" I peeked around the door.

"Girls." Gran was reclining in the bed. Smiling, albeit weakly, she said, "I'm not in much of a position to hug you two." A tube dangled from her arm to a bag of clear fluid on a stand.

I took one hand, and Dee took the other. Gran felt warm, alive. Color was back in her face, replacing the deathly gray from the day before. "You look great." I kissed her cheek. "How do you feel?"

"Like a new woman," she said. "Tired, but alive."

Dee stroked her hand. "I was so worried."

"No need to worry any longer, dear."

"I know." A tear trickled down Dee's face. "It's just with Pops gone . . ."

"Your grandfather, yes. And the writ." Gran's face clouded. "Nina, dear, you will have to handle this alone. Can you do it? I'm sure Mr. and Mrs. Jenkins will help."

"Especially now that we're living with them," Dee said.

"What?" Gran's eyebrows knotted. "Why are you living with the Jenkinses?"

"We were evicted." I hadn't wanted to tell her, not just yet. "But it's all right. I've got it all under control."

"Oh, no, Nina. Our things? How will we—" She rubbed her forehead, her monitor beeps speeded up.

Dr. Silverman swept into the room, a nurse scurrying in behind him. "No disturbances. Out."

"We didn't mean to," Dee said. "It's just—"

"Out!"

As we slunk through the door, I saw him take a needle from the nurse, inject something into one of Gran's tubes, and then the monitor slowed down, back to its hypnotic *beep, beep, beep.*

Silverman strode into the hallway. "She cannot be subjected to anything that will agitate her. If you can't keep from upsetting her, you can't come back."

"I'm sorry." Tears swam in Dee's eyes. "I'd never do anything to hurt her."

"See that it doesn't happen again," Silverman said, a softness crossing his face. "I will not have my work ruined. No more visits today. Call tomorrow to find out when you are allowed back."

"Yes, sir." I took Dee's hand, and we walked silently to the elport. Neither of us said a word until we got outside the hospital.

"He's not so bad," Dee said. "He's just worried about Gran."

"Uh-huh." I let her think what she wanted. I, on the other hand, thought he was more worried about his precious reputation as a doctor.

XI

By the time we got back to our old apartment, Chris and his friends had already packed and moved most of our things to a storage unit.

"I sent the guys home," he said. "Everything's done except the kitchen and these from your grandparents' bathroom." He pointed to a collection of bottles on the dining room table.

"Pops's medicine!" Dee exclaimed. "He hasn't had his pills since yesterday. Nina!" She grabbed my sleeve. "He's got to be hurting, really bad. We have to do something."

Chris said. "You might be able to drop these off, although . . ." He glanced at Dee, like he wasn't sure how much more he should say.

"Although what?" She waited for him to finish.

"You might not get in. And if you do, they might not give them to him."

"They have to," I said. I'd had enough. Pops needed his medicine, and I was sick and tired of being told what to do. "In Government class we learned that it's against the law to withhold medical treatment from prisoners if it's doctor ordered. And all these prescriptions are doctor ordered." I whisked them off the table into a bag. Then scrolled through my PAV for the copy of the digi I'd sent to Wei of the order the cops had given Gran. It said Pops would be taken to the downtown detention center at the main B.O.S.S. building on LaSalle and Jackson. "I'm taking these to him. Chris, take Dee with you when you're done. I'll meet you back at your house." Grabbing my coat, I rushed out the door.

"Nina!" Dee ran after me to the elport. "You can't. What if they arrest you?"

"Dee. They will not arrest me. Go back there and finish packing."

Chris came up behind Dee. "I'll drive you. You could use some backup."

"I can take care of this myself. Dee needs your help more. Our twenty-four hours are up at six p.m., remember?" The elport doors opened. I stepped in and hit Close before either of them could stop me.

***

"Where's detention?" I asked the reception bot.

"Stand for weapons detection," it said. A bright light flooded over me. "No weapons found. Place hand in reader for ID scan."

I did as I was told.

"Nina Oberon, who do you wish to see?"

"Herbert Oberon, my grandfather. He needs his medicines." I placed the bag of bottles on the desk in front of the bot. Apparently, that was the wrong thing to do.

Sirens blared, and a booming voice intoned, "Code blue at reception. Contraband. Code blue at reception. Contraband."

By the third Alert, I was ready to run. But there was nowhere I could go that they wouldn't find me.

"May I ask what you are doing?" said a female voice behind me.

I spun around to find myself face-to-face with a woman in uniform, a look of curiosity on her face and a stun-stick aimed at my neck.

"I'm looking for my grandfather." My voice radiated a confidence internally negated by the quivering in my belly. "He's required to take these." I reached for the bag.

"Hands up," she commanded.

I threw my hands over my head, but I wasn't about to back down. "Those are his meds. It's not legal to keep them from him. It's illegal to withhold medical necessities."

"You seem well versed in Governing Council law."

"I'm in school. They teach us that in Government." My arms were getting tired, and I was more than a little scared.

The woman opened the bag with her free hand and perused the content. Gesturing with the stun-stick, she said, "Pick it up and come with me." Keeping her weapon at the ready, she marched me across the atrium, where we went into a small office. The door clicked behind us. "Put the medicine there." She indicated a spot on her desk. "You may sit, if you'd like."

"I'd rather not." Sitting felt like surrender. My eyes swept through the room. Besides the desk, there were two chairs, and a tech rack hung on the wall. That was it.

"Suit yourself." Sheathing the stun-stick in a pouch on her belt, she selected an ID reader from the rack and scanned my information. "Hmm, Nina Oberon." Scrolling through a digi-pad, she eventually stopped. "Ah, here we are. Herbert Oberon." After she studied the info for what seemed like an eternity, she pressed a button on her desk. "Send a detention runner to purple corridor security office."

Detention runner? Were they going to arrest me? My heart pounded in my chest. Gran was in the hospital, and if I got arrested, both Pops and I would be in jail, and Dee would all alone. Just as I was contemplating making a run for it, a nonhumanoid bot whirred through the door.

The woman removed Pops's medicine bottles, scanning each one into her desk unit. "You know, you didn't have to create a scene," she said. "All prisoners are allowed personal medications after they are approved by the detention facility physician. I'll have that confirmation in a moment."

Create a scene? How was I to know the reception bot would think I was trying to get contraband to Pops? Adrenaline abating, I felt the need to move around, or I was sure I would collapse on the floor, a mass of quivering body parts. However, the room was tiny, and any movement on my part could easily be read as hostile or combative. So I stood as still as possible, even though the bot's sensors were picking up on every twitch and sigh I made.

"All medications are approved," the woman said. "They will be administered at the appropriate times." She opened the bot's front compartment, put Pops's meds inside, shut the door, and pressed a code on the keypad. It spun around and skimmed out the door.

The woman scrutinized me. "Due to your youth, the recent loss of your mother, and your grandmother's sudden illness,

I've requested my superiors overlook your flagrant disregard of protocol. Should it happen again, however, you will be detained and charged with attempted breach of Bureau offices. Do you understand me?"

"Yes, ma'am." My age was on my ID, but it was beyond me how she knew so many personal details about me and my family.

"Good."

Pops's incarceration, it made sense that they'd know that. But Ginnie's death and Gran's heart attack. There was no doubt in my mind, B.O.S.S. was tracking me.

She escorted me to the entrance. "There is not to be a repeat performance. Correct?"

"Uh-huh."

The door shut behind me.

I was headed for the trans stop when Chris's trannie pulled up in front of me. Dee jumped out and flew into my arms. "Nina! Are you all right? Don't ever do that again," she said. "You scared me to death."

"I had to, Deeds. Pops needed his medicine."

Chris leaned out the window. "You guys mind getting in? I'd rather not get a ticket."

Dee took the front, and I slid into the back.

"We packed the things, and I made Chris come here first. We've been waiting forever," Dee said. "Chris was ready to go in and see if you were okay."

"Really?" I looked over at him. "I was fine." Liar.

Chris shrugged. "Wei'd kill me if I let anything happen to one of her best friends." Changing the subject, he said, "So they let you give him the meds?"

"You saw Pops? How is he?" Dee swiveled around.

"They didn't let me see him. They scanned in the meds, and then a robotic carrier took them to wherever he is."

"Were you scared?" she asked.

"Not really."

Chris glanced in the rearview, raising his eyebrows.

I looked away, not planning ever to admit how terrified I'd been.

XII

When we got back to our new home, I put Gran and Pops's things in the room they would eventually share. I was being as positive as I could be about Pops's eventual release. Dee was busy arranging her clothes in the huge dresser in her room. We could've fit everything—hers, mine, and our grandparents' clothes—in those drawers and still had room left over.

My room was beautiful. Like most everything in the apartment, the bed was antique. Solid, warm, and comforting. I loved it. I was putting away my clothes when there was a tap at the door.

"Hope you don't mind that I let myself in," Wei said. "I won't do it after your grandmother comes home."

"I'm sure she wouldn't care," I said. "Besides, it *is* your house."

"Don't be ridiculous! This"—she threw her arms wide—"is your house now."

My room was luxurious by any standards. "You know, it's going to take some getting used to. And in a way, I don't want to get used to all these beautiful things." I knew Wei wouldn't understand what I meant as soon as the words were out of my mouth, and her quizzical look confirmed that. "I don't mean that I don't want to feel like they are . . . well, not mine, but you know . . ." I could tell she didn't. "Look. This—everything here—can all be taken from me in a nanosec. Everything. I mean, even my family can be taken away from me. This stuff, it's not mine. It belongs to your family. I'm a tier-two girl who might get something better someday, but only if I work really hard and get lucky. I'll never be up in your stratosphere."

"You know..." Wei whisked one of my T-shirts from the bed and began folding it. "You have got to get over this tier crap. You think way too much about it. I've told you before, it means absolutely nothing to me. Period. Okay?" She laid the shirt on top of the others in the drawer.

I sighed. It meant nothing to her, but that didn't mean it meant nothing to everyone else in the world. I resigned myself to the fact that she, like Sal, might never understand where I was coming from. "Sure."

"Listen, I came down because Dad wondered if you'd mind talking with him now. He needs to know everything you know about all that's happened to your grandfather and about the writ. He said to bring the arrest papers."

I took the order for Pops's arrest out of a folder. As we went by Dee's room, I let her know I'd be across the hall. She was on her PAV, chatting away with her friends.

***

Across the hall, Wei and I stood in front of Mr. Jenkins's desk while he read both papers. "I heard you made a trip down to Bureau headquarters today. Did they let you see your grandfather?"

"No." I couldn't help turning red. The tone of his voice

registered his disapproval. Wei gave me an admiring glance, which made me feel a little less guilty of recklessness. "They did log in the meds, though. So I guess they took them to him."

Mr. Jenkins made notes on a digi-pad. His voice softened. "How is your grandmother doing?"

"She got upset about the eviction. The doctor had her sedated. Before that, she looked much better."

"Her doctor is Silverman, right?"

"Yeah. He doesn't seem to like low-tiers very much."

Mr. Jenkins tapped his rapido on the table. "I don't think he likes anyone very much. There's no denying he's a brilliant physician, but . . . I'm not sure what kind of person he is." He projected a page from his PAV onto the desk. It looked kind of like the genealogy charts we'd studied in Personal History and Health when I was in fifth grade.

"What's that?" Wei asked.

"Dr. Silverman's career path. He's been on the Resistance watch list for a while." Mr. Jenkins studied the graphic. "See here?" He pointed to a line on the projection. "He was head of research at Utar Seriosus Research and Development, before moving to Chicago as head surgeon for Metro."

It sounded as if I should understand the significance of that information, which I didn't at all. "What does that mean? What's Utar Seriosus?"

"He went from being top man at a prestigious research-and-development laboratory to taking a job at an inner-city hospital that specifically treats low-tier and welfare citizens. Utar Seriosus is where the Infinity machine was invented. They were rumored to be working on a cure for the Ocri virus."

"Wouldn't that mean the miners on Mars could come back to Earth when their time was up?" Wei asked. Being sent to the prison mines on Mars was nearly a death sentence, since few if any escaped being infected with the Ocri virus while there. Once infected, they could never return to Earth.

"Yes," her father agreed. "But there are people who would prefer that never happened."

"Why?" I asked.

"There's not enough money in the research end of it. The possible users of the drug are limited to ocribundan miners. Men who aren't even at the bottom tier, but way below that. Most of them are criminals who were given a sentence of labor on Mars or death."

"I thought some were just low-tiers who went off to work and send money home to their families." My stomach clenched as I thought of Joan. Part of the information Ginnie'd uncovered about FeLS was that girls, like Joan, who broke down during sex training were sent to Mars as "wives" for the miners. "Are they all . . . murderers?"

Mr. Jenkins pressed his fingertips together, pursing his lips. "Many are nonrehabilitatable criminals who, for a variety of reasons, would be better kept far from America's society. Some are people who fared poorly during reassimilation. And more than a few of them are NonCons or Resistance sympathizers." He dropped his gaze.

I got a sick feeling in my gut. "People you know?"

"Yes." He clicked off the projection, clearing his throat.

"I don't get it. Why don't they just send the criminals to a prison station?" Wei asked.

"Someone has to mine ocribundan, or we'd have no fuel. Without a cure, no regular people would do it. The symptoms of the Ocri virus are eventual debilitating pain and gradual loss of motor skills, followed by an excruciating death."

"But if they could find a cure for Ocri, then anyone could go work there," I said.

"I know it seems that simple and humane," he said. "But the current system is much more convenient and a permanent solution for the Governing Council."

"Do you think Dr. Silverman found a cure?" I asked.

"I doubt it," Mr. Jenkins said. "But the thought has crossed many Resistance minds that he must have been very close to have been removed from Utar and sent to Metro. Something of a sentence for him, no doubt."

I couldn't help being grateful that someone as skilled as Dr. Silverman was at Metro to, hopefully, have saved Gran. Although now, the seed of the tragedy of those miners—many who didn't deserve their exile, and none who deserved being infected with Ocri—was sown. I wouldn't forget it.

Mr. Jenkins picked up the papers I'd given him. "Nina, unfortunately, neither Mrs. Jenkins nor I will be able to go with you to the meeting at the Bureau on Monday. Since it's not a hearing, I'm sure you'll be okay. In all likelihood they will merely give you further instructions as to charges against your grandfather and an anticipated trial date. But as far as the unsuitability hearing," he said, "Mrs. Jenkins will be able to accompany you to that."

"Can I go with her to the Bureau, Dad?" Wei asked.

Mr. Jenkins shook his head. "They'll be making records of whoever shows up with any interest in Mr. Oberon's case. The fewer people who are concerned with him, the safer it is for everyone."

"I'll be fine." *Yeah*, I thought, *I've already been there once—and nearly got arrested*. Why should going back be any scarier? Right. I'd be terrified. But that was two whole days away. The way things were going in my life, anything could happen in two days.

"Dad," Wei said. "Have you heard anything about the FeLS information that you gave to Nina's dad?"

"As a matter of fact, there should be an announcement soon. I believe it's important enough that it will come as an Alert."

"*Très* cool! You're the best."

Mr. Jenkins smiled. "I try. Now, you girls go on. I've got work to do."

We went back to the apartment. My apartment.

"You want to hang out?" I asked Wei.

"Of course. It's either stay here with you or more piano. I've already worn my fingers to the bone today."

Dee popped her head in my room. "Guess who I was just talking to."

"Maddie?"

"Nuh-uh." She beamed. "Miss Maldovar!"

"Really? School's out until after New Year's. What did she want?"

"I'm her assistant, remember?"

"Yes, but still . . ." This was the first time I could ever remember hearing of a teacher calling a student over break. "So?"

"She was wondering if I had any free time over the holidays to go with her to the Museum of Science and Industry. She wants to maybe set up a classroom visit in January."

"That sounds like fun," Wei said.

I frowned. First time I'd heard of classroom assistants doing things out of the classroom. And there was something about Miss Maldovar . . . even though I'd seen her just the one time. Her expression, maybe? No, it was the way she'd looked at me as I left Rosie's—like she knew things about me that she shouldn't know. Whatever. The huge smile on Dee's face made me swallow what I wanted to say.

"Don't be mad." Dee bit her lip and scuffed her feet, like she used to do when she had to tell Ginne she'd done something she knew was wrong.

"What did you do?" I tried to keep the irritation out of my voice, but wasn't successful.

"I told her, Miss Maldovar, about the writ." Her chin quivered.

"Dee! How could you blab our family problems to someone we hardly know?" I couldn't believe my little sister could be so stupid. We were being watched all the time, and she's volunteering information to strangers.

"I know her really well. She's been my teacher for over a month now." Fire came back in her eyes. "She thought it was awful, Nina. She said if there was anything she could do, she'd be glad to."

Uneasiness niggled at the base of my neck. That Miss Maldovar knew this about us, something indirectly related to my father, Dee's father, made me really uncomfortable. "You can thank her, but Mrs. Jenkins is going with us to the hearing. We'll be fine without your teacher's help."

"She was just being nice," Dee said. "I don't know why you don't like her."

"It's not that I don't like her. I just don't think everyone needs to know our business, that's all."

"I guess." She started to her room but turned back. "Hey, Maddie called earlier. Can I spend the night at her house?"

"Dee, isn't there enough going on right now? I don't want you taking the trans by yourself at night, and it's nearly dark out." I knew even as I heard the words coming out of my mouth that I sounded just like a mom.

Wei, who had been standing by quietly during our whole conversation, said, "Hey, Nina, I think everyone needs to get their mind off of things. Why don't we go to Soma tonight? We were going to anyway, before all this stuff happened. I actually told Derek I was staying here with you tonight, but maybe we should go. It could be fun. We could surprise him; I bet Chris would drive us, and we can drop Dee off at Maddie's."

I started to protest, but a night with my friends seemed like exactly what I needed to keep me sane. "Sounds good." The only thing that would make it better would be if Sal was there. Since I hadn't heard from him after our far-too-short conversation at the hospital, I figured there'd be a molecular chance of that happening. I knew he was on NonCon biz, like my father.

Dee went to her room to gather up things for her night at Maddie's. When I was sure she was out of earshot, I said, "I don't make the best mother, do I?"

"I think you're doing great," she said. Her PAV alarm beeped. "I almost forgot! We're supposed to meet with the Sisterhood. Do you feel up to it? If not, I'll call and postpone."

"No. No. I want to." It would be something to focus on besides my upcoming appearances with B.O.S.S. and in court.

"Let's head up to my room, we'll call from there."

Dee was busy talking to Maddie, paying me only enough attention to wave to me on my way upstairs.

XIII

"Before I click us all on together," Wei said, "I need to warn you . . . Paulette Gold is one of the Sisterhood."

"Paulette?" I bet she wanted to be in a group with me as much I did with her.

"Yeah. I couldn't help but notice the other day when I mentioned her, you were, well . . . you didn't seem to like her."

"I don't like her because I think she's after Sal," I said bluntly. "They're always together, you know. I mean, I know he's off doing something NonCon, but she's with him. Or was. At least, she was there in the background when I called him at the hospital. I don't trust her, I think she's got ulterior motives."

"You're not wrong. I know she's got this thing for him. But I also know that he doesn't think of her as anything except someone who helps him out. She's useful—with her family's connections, she can go to all kinds of places none of the rest of us can. And since Sal is a trannie whiz, her dad sets him up as a driver or mechanic. It's a perfect cover."

"So what did she say when you talked to the Sisterhood about me?"

"Uh . . . not much. Honestly, she was about as happy as you

are right now. But the other girls are thrilled. Wait until you tell them what you did today, taking those meds down to the Bureau! Nina, you even freak me out with your guts. And I am not easily freaked."

I took a deep breath and let it out. I freaked myself out sometimes. "Okay," I said. "Let's do it."

She clicked on her receiver, and three panels appeared on the wall. Paulette in one. Two girls in another. And a single girl in the third.

"Hey, everyone. This is Nina Oberon."

"Hi!" The single girl waved. "I'm Magrit. But my friends call me Mag."

I waved back.

"Brie and Dorrie here." A petite girl with blond, curly hair waved. Her arm was tucked around the waist of a tall, willowy girl whose deep brown skin contrasted beautifully with the paleness of the other. They sat back, an obvious couple.

"Hey," I said.

"I'm Paulette." Her voice was sharp as a blade. One she'd probably like to bury deep inside me, from the look she gave me. Anger shot through me, but I held it in.

She clearly knew who I was, but I didn't know if she was aware that I knew who she was. If I wanted to be in the Sisterhood, I would need to figure out how to get along with this girl. I realized, if she was here on this call, then she wasn't with Sal, wherever he was. So maybe Wei was right. Maybe she was just a necessary evil to endure, as Pops would say. Thinking of it that way made my "Hi, Paulette" sound a lot nicer than it would've otherwise.

"So," Wei said. "When we all talked, I told them about how we met, and I gave them some background on you. How you figured out where your mother had hidden that FeLS info, and that you saved my life." No details, she mouthed to me. "And they know that you're Alan Oberon's daughter."

Paulette muttered, "I still say that doesn't--"

Brie butted in. "Paulette, we discussed this to death already. And, Nina, you should know that it's not because you're Alan Oberon's daughter that we're inviting you to join the Sisterhood. Wei recommended you. We voted. You're in."

Brie, Dorrie, and Mag all nodded.

"If you want to be," Paulette said.

"Listen," I said, "if this is a big problem for you, I don't have to—"

"You're in, Nina." Wei said firmly. "Right, Paulette?"

"Sure. Whatever."

I refused to let Paulette's attitude get to me. As I looked at the other girls, I saw support and welcoming smiles.

"Tell them about today," Wei said. "Chris only gave me the bare facts, Nina. I know there's more."

The familiar warmth moved up my neck. Doing something in the heat of the moment, like rushing down to the Bureau with Pops's meds, was one thing; talking about it was completely different. I drew a deep breath and told them the whole story of my trip to the Bureau. When I was done, Mag clapped.

"I can't believe you walked into the Bureau without an appointment, and with a bag of anything, let alone unauthorized meds. You're lucky that woman only threatened you—usually they stun first and ask questions later," Mag said.

"Wow!" Dorrie said. "Weren't you scared?"

"I didn't really think about it until after I got out of there. And then I was terrified at what I'd done," I admitted.

"You've got some courage going," Brie said.

"I didn't feel very brave," I said.

"Well, courage is when you act even though you're scared to death inside."

"Foolhardy's more like it," Paulette muttered.

"Like you wouldn't do something risky to save one of your family members?" Brie asked.

"In the first place, Brie, my family members wouldn't put themselves in—"

"Paulette. Brie." Wei's voice had an edge I'd never heard before. "Calm down. Shut up."

"Look," I said. "Pops needed his medicine. It was something that had to be done. That's all. You guys do things to help the Resistance, things that need to be done. That's exactly what I did."

"Well said." Brie settled down. "Welcome to the Sisterhood, Nina."

"Yeah, welcome," Dorrie said.

"Definitely. Glad to have you." Mag chimed in.

"Right." Paulette stared straight ahead.

This wasn't going to be hearts and flowers, not with Paulette in the group. But at least I was in. That was good.

"So is now the time to talk about, you know . . . Joan?" I asked Wei.

"Yeah. They know some of the truth about FeLS, but I haven't filled them in on Joan's situation. Now's as good a time as any."

"FeLS? There's more than the sex-slavery crap?" Dorrie sat

up. "That is the most disgusting . . . Thank goodness I'm tier three and exempt. Ha! Never thought I'd ever say that."

Brie hooked her arm in Dorrie's. "Someday there won't be any tiers at all. People will be able to do whatever they want to without being held back or forced to be some way they're not."

Without trying to appear as if I was checking her out, I snuck a look at Dorrie. Sure enough. Unlike Brie's ultrachic clothes, Dorrie was wearing Sale-o-rama jeans, like me. I'd kind of assumed all the Sisterhood would be upper tier, like Wei, and obviously Paulette. On closer examination, Mag was wearing mid-tier. Not Mars 9, but not Sale either. We were a mixed bunch.

"So what's the additional info?" Paulette asked.

"You all know that Nina's mother was murdered. She'd been spying, collecting information on FeLS, details about how they forced—sorry, 'Chose'—tier-one and tier-two girls into training as sex slaves, and how the ones who didn't make it through the so-called training were shipped off to Mars to 'service' the miners. And she was killed because someone wanted the evidence she'd been gathering about FeLS."

Sympathetic murmurs came from everyone, even Paulette. I tried not to let it get to me. I'd spent the last few months steeling myself against the emotions surrounding Mom's death. I scrunched my sadness deep into my gut; no way would I break down now.

"But her killer didn't find the evidence. Nina's mom hid it, and Nina found it."

I flashed back to that last confrontation with Ed in the abandoned building. To finally finding the package of information my mom had lost her life to get from him . . .

Wei's voice broke through my cloudy thoughts. "Nina and I got the info to the Resistance, to her father, just a few weeks ago. Dad says we should be hearing an Alert on the Media soon." She humphed. "Should be interesting to see how they'll spin the fact that only a few girls entering FeLS were actually trained as diplomatic liaisons. How the rest of them were turned into toys for high-level government officials. No one, no matter if they are tier one or tier two, should ever be treated like that. I really wonder what'll happen when the truth is out?"

Echoes of "Yeah, no kidding," "About time," and "That'll set the GC back" ricocheted around the room.

"So," Paulette said, "you still have not told us about this Joan."

"Joan is the sister of one of my best friends," I said. "She was chosen for FeLS. The sex training. She couldn't take it, and when she broke, they consigned her to Mars. I don't know how, but she was rescued. By NonCons, I think. She ended up living with a group of homeless women down by the river. I recognized her one day, and I've talked with her a few times. She needs to get off the street and get some care, but she can't go to anything GC related. As far as they know, she no longer exists."

"Why doesn't she go to her family? And what makes her any different from hundreds of other girls just like her?" Paulette asked.

I stiffened. "Her family doesn't know what happened to her—they think she's still in FeLS. Do you think she can really afford to tip off the government by letting her family know where she is? Or what happened to her? And also, she's a friend of mine. And I don't know and haven't seen those 'hundreds of other girls,' but I *have* seen Joan. I know where she is, and I know she needs help.

Whether or not the Sisterhood wants to be a part of that . . . well, *I'm* going to do something, even if I have to do it alone." I set my jaw. That was it. One way or the other, Joan was going to get help.

"Nina, let me do some checking," Mag said. "My older brother might know a place she can stay. There are a few safe compounds."

"Like Rita's?" Sal's aunt had a place out in Easley Woods; we'd been there together to deliver a trannie that Sal and his brother, John, had modified for their aunt.

"Uh-huh. Except there are some specifically for women. Your friend isn't the only escapee who's messed up, and not just by FeLS. There's so much violence against women . . ."

"I'll talk to my uncle, too," Brie said. "He's pretty savvy about getting Resistance members and GC casualties to places outside the Americas, where they can't be tracked down."

"Don't worry," Dorrie said. "We'll help. Right, everyone?"

They all looked at Paulette.

"Right. I have to go. I'm helping Mom with arrangements for our big New Year's Eve party." She clicked off.

A collective sigh of relief followed her exit. "Paulette can be such a pain sometimes," Dorrie said. "Don't get me wrong. The Sisterhood needs her, and we want her, too. She gets NonCons into places none of the rest of us can, but still . . . She can cop real attitude sometimes."

"Yeah," Wei said. "We all can. Hey, Nina and I are going to Soma tonight. You guys want to meet us there?" Wei asked.

Dorrie made a face. "Can't. Family stuff for Holiday."

"I'll come," Brie said.

"Me, too." Mag nodded. "Oh, before we go. Don't forget, we have a Rogue Radio broadcast set for later this week."

"And I uploaded a schematic to the guys for vert interruptions on Michigan Avenue the day after Holiday," Dorrie said. "Thanks for the maps, Mag."

"No prob." Mag smiled. "You know me, I love making maps."

"See you guys later," Wei said. "Have fun, Dorrie."

"Right." She stuck out her tongue before clicking off.

"Mag makes maps?"

"Yeah. She has all the Audio/Video stations mapped out, and provides that information to the NonCons. They take care of the actual interruptions. Rogue Radio, however, is all ours. It's the one thing that is. It drives me crazy that we don't get to be more hands-on, but at least we have that."

"So who does what?" I asked.

"Brie and I mainly provide information. Paulette, well, she lends us all the cover of her family's top-tier Media status."

"So I noticed." I pressed my lips together, not trusting myself to say anything else.

"She also has a way of finding out all kinds of information. Because her dad's the head of Media relations, she ends up around a lot of Governing Council people. Their wives and girlfriends are really talkative, and Paulette is ultrasmooth when it comes to coaxing things out of people."

"I bet." I didn't want to think of how ultrasmooth she was, not when she was hanging around Sal.

XIV

On the way to Soma, my head was full of thoughts about Pops, Gran, and the writ. Amid all that angst, the best thing that could've happened, did. Sal called.

"I just this second got home," he said. "What are you doing? How is everyone? Where are you?"

"I'm heading to Soma with Wei. Damn, Sal, it's been an awful day. I really want to see you."

"Give me half an hour to clean up. I'll be there."

"Okay." My heart started racing. Sal was only half an hour away. I could already feel his hand curled around mine, our fingers entwined. Despite most of my life being in shambles, it was amazing that just the thought of being with Sal made me all fluttery.

"Sal?" Wei asked.

"Uh-huh. He's meeting us there."

Chris dropped us off in front of Soma and with a "See you girls later" he sped off.

"A hot date, I bet," Wei said.

Derek and his brother, Riley, were already playing. They were amazing musicians, and they focused mainly on some ancient songs from the twentieth century. The lights were dim, but Wei and I managed to find Mag and Brie at a table up front, and Paulette was there, too. Great. Nope, I stopped myself from going further down that line of thinking. No way was I going to let that top-tier snob ruin my mood. I slipped into the chair by Mag.

It would've been impossible not to notice Paulette's quick glance and smirk, probably because I was in my all-weather jeans and a T-shirt. She, of course, was ultrachic. I ignored it, turning all my attention toward Brie and Mag. "Hey, I was wondering if you guys are Creatives, like Wei? I'm trying to figure out what to get for my tattoo." The GC didn't let anyone alter the XVI tattoo on our wrists, but at least Creatives were allowed to decorate around it.

"I am, want to see my tattoo?" Brie pulled up her sleeve and exposed a dragon wrapped around her arm from elbow to hand. The XVI was inside the dragon's mouth, flames engulfing it.

"Wow!" She was ultra-feminine-looking but that obviously didn't mean she wasn't fierce, too. Wei had told me that Brie was even more accomplished at Cliste Galad than she was.

Brie giggled. Probably at my astonishment. "People are usually surprised to see it—on me, that is." Her expression turned somber. "You know, dragons symbolize evil and chaos. To me, they stand for creating chaos to stir up evil and open people's eyes to a better way."

"Nothing wrong with that," Paulette said. "Most people's eyes need opening."

"Yeah." I shouldn't have been shocked at Paulette's comment. After all, she was in the Sisterhood. But still, it seemed odd to hear that kind of NonCon talk coming from such a snobbitch top-tier. I couldn't shake my impression of her status as being a huge gap between us.

My thoughts were interrupted by a break in the music, followed by an eruption of rowdy applause from two tables of what appeared to be friends of Derek's brother, Riley. Riley was in the Early Music program at college; these guys looked like they were, too, the way they were dressed from the same era as the music. Riley joined them, and Derek loped over to our table, scooting between Wei and me.

"You're here." He grabbed Wei's hand. "I thought you were staying home."

"We changed our minds. You guys are ultra tonight." Wei poked me with her free hand, nodding her head toward the entrance. "He's here."

Faster than a veljet, I was out of my chair, across the coffeehouse, and into Sal's arms. So what if everyone in the place was staring at us?

We would've been joined at the lips for hours if someone hadn't cleared his throat right behind us, twice.

"Damn." Sal's breath on my ear tingled through my body.

Simultaneously, we looked up to see who'd interrupted us.

"Hey, man. Good to see you." Chris stuck out his hand.

Sal took one arm from around me and shook Chris's hand. "You, too."

"And not a moment too soon," Chris said. "Nina's so pretty, you'd better watch out." He waggled his eyebrows.

I wasn't sure which surprised me more, hearing a compliment

like that from Chris—I couldn't imagine his thinking of me as anything but Wei's friend—or Sal's reaction of gripping my waist a little tighter.

"Watch out?" Sal asked. "I can't take my eyes off her."

Could that be a hint of jealousy in his voice?

"Who's your friend?" Sal asked.

"This is Martinique." Chris circled his arm around the gorgeous girl next to him. "Nique, this is Nina and Sal."

The girl, who was ultragorgeous, said, "So nice to meet you. Chris was just telling me about you, Nina. I hope your grandmother gets better soon."

"Thanks."

Chris took Nique's hand. "We'll let you get back to what you were doing." He winked at Sal, who lost no time in enveloping me in his arms again. Something I thoroughly enjoyed.

However, instead of more kissing, he maneuvered us into the hallway where the restrooms were.

"What's this I hear about you going down to B.O.S.S.?" Worry wrinkled his forehead.

"Nothing." I did my best to make it sound like a trip to the grocery store. "Pops needed his meds. That's all."

"Going to B.O.S.S. headquarters with a bagful of prescriptions? You could've been arrested. Then how could I protect you? You have to be more careful."

"Careful? Protect me?" I wanted to pull away, but also I wanted to tell him exactly what I thought about being "protected." Before I could get out another word, someone brushed against us.

"Excuse me." It was Paulette.

"Paulie." Sal's voice changed, took on a lighter tone. He snuggled me under his arm. "Long time."

"Not really. You're back sooner than I expected."

"Yep."

"Did you need something?" I asked, maybe not as blandly as I'd thought.

"Just the Fems." With that, she sauntered down the hall into the girls' restroom, totally unaffected by my attitude.

"So how come she's so involved in what you do?" I tried to keep the peevishness out of my voice, but wasn't sure I was successful.

"I'll tell you later. It's nothing big. Just the way things are." He tapped the end of my nose. "You're not jealous, are you?"

"Of her?" I snorted. "Of course not." My brain was screaming, Liar.

"Good. Because she doesn't mean anything to me." He clutched my hand, and we wound our way through the crowd.

Derek and his brother were back onstage, tuning for the next set.

Martinique was directly across the table from me. She leaned in to hear something Chris was saying, and the silver highlights in her cerulean hair bathed the table in a shimmer of reflected sparkles. Running a perfectly manicured nail down his cheek, she laughed. The sound matched her twinkling highlights. I stuck my plain, unmanicured hands under the table.

"Whatcha thinking?" Sal whispered to me.

"That maybe I should dress up a little more sometimes." Immediately after the words left my mouth, I wanted to take them back.

"That's crazy." Sal kissed me behind the ear, sending shivers to all the right places on my body. "You look exactly like the girl I love."

Having only read about swooning in Ancient Lit, I understood now *exactly* what it meant. My body sort of melted against Sal, and I could've stayed there all night listening to Derek and his brother play music from a hundred years ago. But then, my PAV, and everyone else's, suddenly beeped an Alert. It was my first Alert ever, since only adults—sixteens and up—received them. And even then, they didn't happen very often.

"Citizens, please direct your attention to the nearest projection for a breaking news story."

Derek and Riley scuttled out of the way as a screen dropped down the wall behind them. Projected on the screen was Kasimir Lessig, the top man at Media. My mother had loathed him. She said he could spew lies and spread venom better than any criminal.

"Recently the Bureau of Safety and Security received information that the Governing Council's Female Liaison Specialist program, commonly referred to as FeLS, was, in fact . . ." Lessig paused for effect, and I locked eyes with Wei. This was it. The reveal. The Governing Council's scheme was finally being uncovered.

She nodded, smiling.

All eyes were back on the AV. ". . . a cover-up for a sex-slavery operation."

The insignia of FeLS appeared behind Lessig. "This information is purported to contain names, dates, audio/visual, and other damning evidence." Kasimir gave a long, meaningful look into the camera lens. His gaze piercing into every watcher. Shaking his head in disbelief, he continued, "Of course, allegations of misconduct as reprehensible . . . no . . . heinous, as this are simply unbelievable . . ." His expression changed from incredulous to severe. "However, these allegations are, even as I speak, being thoroughly investigated with the utmost diligence.

"As most of you know, FeLS was begun to assist low-tier sixteens, offering them a way out of the bottom tiers into a better life. Girls sign up for the program, and a fortunate few are chosen to attend training at the state-of-the-art FeLS station." A photo of the space station that held the training facility faded in behind Lessig. "After extensive training in the role of a FeLS liaison, the girls are assigned to specific continental and various extraterrestrial areas. Their training then focuses on the customs and conventions of that particular country or outer-space territory. Of course, due to diplomatic information to which they may be exposed, no communication with family or friends is allowed for the duration of their assignment."

He shifted positions, and the image behind him changed to a bigger-than-life-size projection of Ed. Taken completely off guard, I gripped Sal's hand, hard.

He murmured, "It's all right," and squeezed back.

"This man, Edward Chamus, is a former Bureau of Safety and Security agent." Kasimir Lessig appeared to be enjoying himself. "He was removed from active service and installed as a Chooser. It is believed that, through his position as Chooser, he lured many, possibly even hundreds, of girls to a space station replica that has been discovered in the desert outside of New Vegas City." Ed's digi was replaced by an exterior shot of a building surrounded by scrub vegetation, low mountains in the distance. "The Bureau is there at this time, collecting data from inside this compound, which was, possibly, a prison for these unfortunate girls."

If there was any real sympathy in Lessig, I wasn't hearing it. All I could imagine was the horror Joan and other girls like her must have felt, trapped in the training station. But I knew it couldn't have been the location Lessig was showing. The evidence my mom had collected had made no mention of a fake station on Earth, just the real training station in space. So what was this place?

"The Bureau suspects that Mr. Chamus was the ringleader of this vile operation. However, it has not yet been ascertained," he went on, "if Chamus was working alone. Given the broad time frame of these alleged activities, it is not unreasonable to expect that he had an accomplice. Mr. Chamus has not yet been apprehended. His whereabouts are unknown. If you have any information, call the Bureau at the number below." The pic of Ed popped up next to Lessig as B.O.S.S.'s number scrolled across the bottom of the screen. "This incredible, unbelievable breaking news story will be updated as soon as we have further information. Rest assured, the Bureau will expose the truth."

The screen went blank.

I whirled around, staring at Wei. "What the hell was that?"

"I have no idea," she said.

The AV screen disappeared, and the spotlight turned back onto Derek and Riley, who looked more like trapped river rats than musicians.

"Give us a minute, folks." Riley motioned to the lighting guy to kill the spot.

The lights went up, and Soma began buzzing with speculation. The only people not talking were at our table. I didn't know what the others were thinking, but I was grateful that only adults received Alerts. Dee wouldn't have heard any of this. Since she still believed Ed was her father, it would've crushed her.

Martinique broke the silence at our table. "Who would think something like that could happen in these times? How awful to think of those poor girls . . . All they wanted was to get out of their miserable, low-tier lives."

I cocked my head, the sweet smell of her perfume suddenly cloying. "Miserable?"

"Yes." She smiled at me as if I were a child. "How can there be anything but misery in poverty? Possibly some of those girls even considered their fate an improvement."

I looked around the table: Wei was shaking her head; Brie was wide-eyed with disbelief. And Paulette was cool, totally unreadable. Sal laid a cautioning hand on my arm, which I immediately shook off.

"Improvement?" I said. "Really?"

Martinique reached up and pushed back a few errant strands of her glistering hair. "Of course. How could anyone in tier one or two be anything but grateful for something that gets them out of their disgusting hovels and their pathetic, sludge lives."

That did it. I shoved my chair away from the table and leaned forward. "You are the reason stuff like that"—I jerked my thumb in the direction of the screen—"can happen. People are people, not sludge. Humans matter, not credits, not tiers." I stood up, furious, and barely able to control my anger anymore. "And for your information, I would give anything to be back in my 'disgusting hovel' with my mother and my best friend still alive. The only disgusting thing around here is you."

I yanked my coat off the back of the chair, which clattered to the floor. Ignoring it, I stormed out. Enough was too much.

XV

Sal and Wei followed me outside. Their faces reflected concern, but I wasn't sure either of them really understood how insulted I'd felt.

"How can Chris stand to be with that . . . that . . . Gah!" I railed. "What a clueless . . . I'd expect something like that from Paulette, but not your brother's girlfriend."

Wei opened her mouth, but before the words came out, a voice behind me said, "Don't judge what you don't know."

I spun around, face-to-face with Paulette.

My adrenaline was pumping, and I couldn't have backed down if I'd wanted to. "I know you and your kind."

"Trust me," she said. "I wouldn't be who I am if I were *that* kind." A stretch trannie pulled up in front of us. The driver got out, came around, and opened the door for Paulette. She slid into the cavernous backseat. "See you."

The three of us watched until the trannie turned the corner, out of sight. A cold blast of wind knocked any residual anger out of me. I yanked on my coat. "Guess I've ruined the evening for everyone. I'm heading home."

"Me, too," Wei said. "I'll get my jacket."

"No, you stay," I insisted. "You and Derek should have some fun. Tell him I'm sorry."

Sal grabbed my arm. "I'll take you back to Wei's house, Nina."

"It's her house, too." Wei stuffed her hands in her pockets and turned to me. "You do know that Chris doesn't feel the same as Martinique, right? She's just some girl. He has lots. I don't think he requires position statements before asking for a date."

"Maybe he should," I said.

"Well, I'll suggest it." She gave me a quick hug. "I'd better get back inside. I left Martinique in there with the girls. Brie's only got Mag to keep an eye on her. She can get pretty wound up, since Dorrie's a tier-three. I'll see you at home." She ducked back inside, and Sal and I started walking.

"You're getting pretty good at making scenes." Sal linked his arm into mine. "You know, I have some business coming up again tomorrow. But my brother took his wife out for a night on the town. How about we go to my house before I take you home?"

I'd never been to Sal's place, and it seemed like light-years since we'd had any alone time. "Cool." I chose to ignore my earlier irritation at his protective nature. We could talk that out another time.

***

Sal pulled up in front of a tall, skinny three-story house, squeezed between two taller apartment buildings. "This is it. I grew up here. Mom, Dad, and I moved into an apartment after John and Maeve got married. Dad deeded the house to John . . . just in case."

"What do you mean about 'just in case'? Did your dad know something would happen to him?"

"Come on inside." Their entry was similar to the Jenkinses', with a retinal scan rather than an auto-recognition pad. Sal closed the door behind us. "It's a total dead zone here—like the Jenkinses'. Chris did it in exchange for the work on his trannie. So you know how my dad and my mother died, on assignment for the *Global Times* over in Scotland?"

"Uh-huh." I squeezed his arm.

"The Governing Council was behind that trip, and Dad thought they were up to something. Mom insisted on going. She claimed it was because she'd never been to the Greater United Isles, but I think she had a premonition or something and wanted to be with my dad if anything happened."

In the dim hall lighting, I saw Sal's eyes glistening.

"They must have loved each other very much."

His "yeah" came out strangled.

I knew how he felt. We'd both lost our parents to the GC. Well, granted, my dad was alive, but I still hadn't met him, and he'd never been a part of my life. I had Gran and Pops, too, but that wasn't the same as a parent. Sal and I had that loss in common. I put my arms around his neck and kissed him. We stood there, wrapped in each other, until we had to breathe.

"Come on." He took my hand, leading me through the house to the stairs. "I've got the room on the top floor. You want a Sparkle or some water before we trek up there?"

"No," I said. "Just another kiss, please."

He obliged.

I wasn't sure we were even going to make it to the stairs. The next time we came up for air, he lifted me onto the first step. "All the way up. Don't stop till the stairs run out."

The staircase was narrow, so we had to go one at a time. Sal said, "I'm right here to catch you if you fall," and he touched my behind.

I play-swatted his hand away. "I think I'll make it."

It was so odd, being in Sal's house, alone with him. A few weeks ago I would have been freaked out by the very idea. But now . . . Media insists that sixteen-year-old girls are sex-obsessed sex-teens, I know it's not true. Not for me, and honestly, I think most girls are bullied into believing it's true by zines like *XVI Ways* or all the verts that show girls tempting guys in their skimpy clothes and over-the-top sexual attitudes. With Sal, I found out that having a boyfriend isn't at all the way they said it should be. I could have fun, mess around, be a teen. Just because we kissed and held each other didn't mean we were going to have sex. Although it was also true that I did think about it. Especially at times like-- Shut. Up. I told the thoughts racing around my brain.

"My room." Sal threw open the door at the top of the stairs to reveal a sparsely furnished, but incredibly neat bedroom. There was a desk and chair on one wall. An older-model Family AV in the corner and a huge bed next to the window. A digi with, I guessed, his mother and father was on the desk, along with some random text chips. And a projection of a 260G Persides transport on the wall. It looked like Mike and Derek's rooms— pretty guylike—to me.

"You could take your coat off." He tossed his on the chair. Before I got mine unbuttoned, he was in front of me.

A smile spread across my face as he took over unbuttoning the remaining buttons, then threw my coat on top of his.

His hands slipped around my waist, touching the tiniest slice of skin. I quivered down to my toes. "I'm sorry I couldn't talk when I was gone. We were . . . well, I can't tell you, but I just couldn't risk the signals getting intercepted. And the less you know—"

I put my arms over his shoulders. "I know." My lips homed in on his, soft and warm. Our tongues gently prodding and pushing, and I felt the world disappear. We must have been floating up to the stars.

His hands worked their way up my body, under my sweater. With one hand he stroked my stomach while he cupped one of my breasts in the other. No one else had ever touched me like that, and it was thrilling. My whole body was thrumming with the sensations that pulsed through me. We backed over to the bed, and he lifted me onto the covers. The cool sheets sent shivers through me when my bare skin touched them. They were warmed in an instant because my body was on fire.

Sal pulled my sweater over my head, leaving me in just my bra. He lay down beside me, his hand on one breast, kissing across my chest to the other. My half-heart charm that he'd given to me fell into a spot between them.

This wasn't what they taught in Sex Ed. And it wasn't anything my mom and I had talked about. Definitely nothing like those awful sex vids that Ed had left at our house. It all felt so good and natural. I touched Sal's face, and he rose. Struggling out of his shirt, he pressed his body against mine and kissed me, hungrily. My body took over my brain, knowing exactly what it wanted. His muscles rippled under my fingers as I ran my hands down his back. He ducked his head back down to my breasts, and a little moan escaped me. His hand went to my waist, unbuttoning the band of my jeans. Something inside my head clicked, and I pulled his hand away.

"No?"

"I can't." I bit my lip. He rolled over onto his side. I turned to him, slinging one leg over his. "Sal, I don't want to stop kissing you, touching you, being touched by you. But I'm not ready for sex. Not yet."

His breathing was fast and hard. He didn't speak until it slowed. "I'm not a sexer. And I would never force myself on you, ever. I love you, Nina."

"I love you, too." I hid my face in the crook of his neck, the smell of soap and aftershave filling my senses.

"Hey!" Someone shouted up the stairs. "You home?"

"Skivs! John!" Sal jumped off the bed.

"My clothes!" I was groping around when Sal tossed them to me.

He yanked on his shirt. "Yeah, I'm up here," he shouted back down.

Where I had been hot with passion, I was now burning with shame. What if John hadn't called up? What if he and his wife had come upstairs and found us? How something that felt so right one minute could feel so wrong the next was beyond my comprehension. There was so much I didn't know about love and sex and how it all fit together. My heart ached for my mom. If only we'd talked about things like this . . .

I reached up to smooth my hair and just felt tangles. "You got a brush?" I asked, scrambling into my clothes.

"In the bathroom," he said. "At the end of the hall. I'll wait for you." He skimmed his lips over mine. "Although I think you look beautiful right now."

I blushed and headed down the hall. He thought I looked beautiful, all messed up with my clothes askew. He didn't seem to feel any of the guilt or shame that I was feeling—and I wanted that same carefree attitude. But it was so hard. It was almost easier when I had myself convinced that the answer to the Media telling sixteens to be obsessed with sex was to turn around and reject boys, sex, and love entirely. I had thought that sex was evil, something that turned boys into monsters like Ed. But Sal had changed that, and there was no way he could know how much that meant to me. The fact that his feelings toward me were the same now as they were when we'd walked into his room. That he didn't think less of me. I wanted to feel that way, too. I just didn't know how.

XVI

"You awake?" Wei poked her head in the door.

"Uh-huh." I'd fallen asleep on the sofa the night before.

Wei sat next to me, tucking her legs up under her. "What time did you get in?"

"I dunno. Maybe eleven-thirty. Sal and I went to his house." Warmth crept up my neck.

"Really?" Wei gave a mischievous smile. "Was anyone home?"

"No." The warmth spread to my cheeks.

"Lucky you." She flopped back on the pillows. "Derek's mom is always around. We never get to be alone for long."

"John and his wife came home not long after we got there." I half smiled.

"So are you thinking about having sex with Sal?" Even though the question was frank, Wei plucked at the tassels on the edge of the throw. "It must be tough, with what happened in your past with your mom and your friend Sandy."

"Yeah," I admitted. "I think about Sal and me, a lot. But there are so many other things in my brain when thoughts of sex come up. Not just about Ed's stupid porn vids." I shuddered at the memory of his disgusting collection. "But how he raped and

killed Sandy. And had the same fate in store for me. I wish there
was some kind of memory wipe so I could forget all that stuff and
start over."

Wei touched my arm. "It's hard enough trying to figure out
how you really feel about sex with all the crap Media throws at
everyone about sex-teens . . . I can only imagine how much harder
it is with all you've been through. Honestly, I'm kind of surprised
you're even thinking about having sex."

"Me, too. It's just that . . . when Sal kisses me, touches me, my
body sort of takes on a life of its own. I forget everything except
how close I want to be to him. Do you know what I mean?"

"Uh-huh." She glanced at me. "I know exactly what you mean.
But I don't want Derek to think of me as a sex-teen."

"You?" I laughed out loud. "Of all the girls I know, you are the
last one anybody would think was a sex-teen. Besides, you know
Derek would never think of you that way. He's not that kind of
guy."

"I know. When we're together, it's like we're in our own little
bubble, and none of the rest of the world even exists. I'm pretty
sure that's the way relationships are supposed to be. Rather than
the way the Media says that it's what you're supposed to do and
that every girl should want to be ready for any guy who's, you
know, up for it." She laughed. "Sorry, I couldn't help myself."

"Punny, Wei. Very punny." A wry grin crossed my lips.

"Come upstairs for breakfast," she said.

"I have to call the hospital first and see how Gran is, and if she
can have visitors today."

"Well, come up afterward. I think Chris is making sledding
plans. It snowed a bunch last night."

After Wei left, I went to the window. The snow was beautiful, covering everything in a blanket of white. I thought about the snow and about Chris's friend Martinique. Both so beautiful—on the surface.

***

The aroma of freshly brewed coffee greeted me as I walked into the Jenkinses' kitchen. Wei's dad was at the table, sipping a cup, reading the news.

"Good morning, Nina. Did you hear the Alert last night?" Mr. Jenkins asked.

"Yeah, but where did all that stuff about Ed and the fake space station come from? It wasn't in the packet Mom had hidden."

"No, it wasn't. Lessig obviously has his own agenda about this story. I was reassigned shortly after turning in notes for the investigative team to follow up on."

Wei's dad was a Media special investigator. He worked directly under Kasimir Lessig, the man who many people thought controlled the Governing Council because of his position as head of Media. Lessig's version of the truth was what filled the news— that's what my mother had always said. No one questioned it— well, the Resistance did.

"He doesn't have the actual chips, does he?" I started feeling nervous. The real chips held the truth, and if Lessig had them, well, then maybe the only version that we'd ever hear about would be his.

"Only copies. The originals and the corroborating evidence are in a secure location. If necessary, they'll be used as a last resort."

"But they have all the information already. They can dig deeper and find the whole truth." My hand went to my charms necklace, fingering the T charm Pops had given me.

Mr. Jenkins sighed and looked straight at me. "Nina, there is the distinct possibility that Kasimir Lessig has been a recipient of more than one of these FeLS girls. They have been used to seal agreements, curry favor, and buy silence. I expect Lessig will spin his own version of the truth, whatever that is."

A slow burning sensation filled me. It wasn't fair. The truth was the truth; it needed to be heard. People needed to know that they were allowing the GC to take their daughters to be used and abused sexually. That this was not a way up and out of the lowest tiers. The image of Joan's tormented face flashed through my mind. For girls like her, the dream of something better was a nightmare.

"There will be more to the story, right? They won't let it die. They can't, right, Dad?" Wei asked.

Mr. Jenkins nodded. "The hardest part was getting it to broadcast. We fought that battle, and now that it's been on, they have to follow up. Remember, for Media, image is everything. But you should be prepared that it won't necessarily be the outcome that we'd hoped it would be." Mr. Jenkins shut down his news projection and excused himself.

My PAV beeped. It was a robotic message from the hospital.

"Nina Oberon. Yes or No."

"Yes."

"Mrs. Edith Oberon is allowed one visit, fifteen minutes in duration. Two family members in the room at one time. No visitors between eleven a.m. and one p.m. To repeat this message, say 'Repeat.'"

I clicked off. "I've got to get a hold of Dee. We can go see Gran before eleven, but only for fifteen minutes. I hope she's up."

"You want to eat first?" Wei asked.

"Nah. I'll grab a bite downstairs," I said.

"See you later for sledding?"

"Sure. I'll message you." I picked up my PAV and clicked in Dee's number.

***

Gran looked so much better than the day before. She was sitting up, smiling. Dee threw her arms around Gran's neck.

"Watch the wires." Gran laughed. "Don't know what'll happen if I come unplugged." Her eyes were sparkling.

"How are you?" I asked.

"I feel ten, no, make that twenty years younger," she said. "I don't know what that doctor did, but he's a miracle worker."

Everyone seemed to feel the same way about Dr. Silverman, everyone but me.

***

When we got back to the house, Wei's dad came out of his office. "Nina, may I see you for a minute?"

"Sure."

Dee went into our apartment, and I followed Mr. Jenkins inside. He took out his PAV receiver and clicked in a number. "Alan? Here she is." He handed me the receiver and left the room.

"Nina?"

"Dad!"

"I finally read all of the book." The sadness in his voice poured through the receiver. Dee's baby book. My mom had written messages to my dad in secret in that book.

"Mom loved you so much." It was pathetic, but the only thing I could think of to say.

"I know that." He sighed. "I never stopped loving her. To find out . . . all the sacrifices she made. That Delisa, your sister, that she's my daughter . . ." His voice cracked. I waited. "Does she know?"

"No. She thinks that Ed is her father. You know, Mom's 'boyfriend.' The source of the FeLS info. Her murderer."

"She can't know," he said. "Not yet. It's too dangerous."

My heart sank; telling Dee the truth was one thing I'd hoped for.

"Mr. Jenkins told me you're working at the Art Institute."

"For Mr. Long, he's great."

"Ah, Martin Long." Dad laughed. "A true friend. Don't be fooled by his mannerisms, Nina. He can be deadly when necessary."

It was my turn to laugh. I couldn't think of anyone less likely to be called "deadly" than Martin.

"Did you see the Alert last night?" he asked.

"Yeah. And, Dad, that's not what those chips Ginnie hid said. It wasn't just Ed; it's bigger, it's been going on the entire time FeLS has been in existence."

"Yes, I know. It involves Governing Council members, B.O.S.S. agents, people from every level of the government. And Media, which may well be the driving force behind it. Lessig will spin this story however he wants, but you don't need to worry about that. It will be taken care of. I didn't call to talk about him, Nina. I got word that my mother is in the hospital—that she had an attack. Is she going to be all right?"

"Gran is much better, I just got back from the hospital with Dee, and she looks great." At least I could give him good news. "Dr. Silverman says she has to go to rehab for a while, but then she can come home."

"As for Silverman," Dad said. "We've got a watch on him. Something there isn't right."

"That's what Mr. Jenkins said." I didn't want to bring up Pops, but I had to. "Dad, Pops got arrested by B.O.S.S. He'd been talking on the scrambler to his friends, and it ran out. I have to appear at B.O.S.S tomorrow morning. But I don't know if..." My voice trailed off. I didn't want to think about what might happen if Pops had to go into reassimilation. "I don't know what's going to happen. We're living with the Jenkinses now."

"Yes, I know." He sighed. "We're doing what we can to get him out. I also heard what you did with regard to his medications." He cleared his throat. "Nina, you can't take chances like that. It isn't safe."

"Safe? Dad, how can you talk to me about safe? After what Ginnie—my *mother*—went through for you and the Resistance, and all you've been doing since forever. 'Safe' doesn't exactly run in our family. Besides, being sixteen is daily danger, wouldn't you say?" I didn't wait for his answer. "I would have thought you'd be glad I'm not some spineless sex-teen who goes along with everything Media tells her to do." Skivs! I could hardly believe what was coming out of my mouth. Three minutes into only the second conversation I'd ever had with the father I'd never met, and I was furious and frustrated with being told not to do anything.

There was a long silence. Almost too long for me to bear.

"Nina, I can't change the past." It sounded like he was choosing his words in the same way a bomb defuser picks which wire to snip. "I wish things had been different. Much different. But the decisions made were not just mine. Your mother also had a say in how things were."

"Did she?" This was not going the way I wanted it to. Not at all. "It doesn't seem like she had much choice after you disappeared. After you left us." I clenched my fist. "And she sure as hell didn't choose to be murdered."

"You have every right to be angry--" His tone was placating, too calm. I'd had enough.

"Damn straight I do." I clicked off. Damn straight. Tears of frustration threatened, but Mr. Jenkins walked back in.

"Everything okay?"

"Fine." I forced a smile. "Just fine."

XVII

A few hours later, Dee peered around the door of my room. "You busy?"

I shuffled a clean sheet of paper over the sketch I'd been working on. I'd been reworking the drawings from the hospital. Dee didn't need to see them, to be reminded of what had happened at Metro. "Come on in."

"Sledding was ultra! You should've come." She put my all-weathers that she'd borrowed, clean and folded, on top of the dresser. "I ran these through the Laundry Queen. Thanks for letting me wear them. I would've been frozen otherwise." She snuck a look over my shoulder. "Whatcha working on?"

"Nothing much."

"You know, Nina, I've been through the same stuff you have. We both lost Mom. We both nearly lost Gran, and Pops is in custody." She walked around the chair to face me. "Whatever it is you're hiding, I wish you'd share it with me. We're pretty much all each other has anymore. Please don't treat me like a little kid."

She looked so grown up. And, she was right. But still, I didn't want to burden her with the truth. Mom had taught both of us certain things, like how to think for ourselves, not to get caught up in Media hype, to respect our bodies, and to make our own decisions. She knew how to think as well as I did. And it wasn't realistic to believe she wouldn't see the dirty side of life eventually.

The triptych from the hospital. My hand shook as I uncovered it for Dee.

Dee stared at it for what seemed an eternity.

My insides clutched. I shouldn't have showed her. It was too graphic, too real.

She gnawed her thumbnail. "That's just like it happened."

"Yeah." I clenched my teeth.

"Why doesn't Media talk about this?"

"I don't know. Maybe because if they did, they'd have to stop making girls believe that being sexy and attracting guys is the most important thing in the universe."

"Have you drawn more of these kinds of pictures?"

"Yes. But I haven't kept them. I was afraid if anyone saw them I'd get in trouble. These drawings are the way I can say what I don't have words for."

"You could be arrested for doing something like this?" She held it up, studying it more. "I guess it really makes the cops look bad."

"They *are* bad, Dee." I took it from her. "Well, maybe not bad, exactly. Just like most people, they can't stand to see the truth— the real, raw, from-your-guts truth about what's going on around us. So they stop anyone who makes too much noise about it. They should've been finding the boys who raped that woman's daughter—not shutting her up. But to everyone, it's not rape if she's a sex-teen. And if no one sees or hears, no one questions the laws that allow this stuff to happen."

"Please be careful, Nina. If you got caught . . ." Her face paled. "They'd take you away, like they did Pops. You can't let them do that. Promise me."

"Most I can promise is that I won't do anything stupid." I tucked the picture back in my drawing pad. "Now, let's go make dinner."

Neither one of us really felt like cooking, so we set the cook center to auto and let it spit out seitan burgers and tofu fries.

After dinner, Mr. Jenkins came down. "Nina, we should talk about your meeting at B.O.S.S. tomorrow."

"It's at nine," I said. "In that building where I brought Pops his meds."

"I know. I wish that Mrs. Jenkins or I were able to be there. I could probably find someone else to go with you."

"No, I can do this."

"I know you can. Still . . ." He placed his hand on my shoulder. "It should be nothing more than a formal presentation of the facts and the charges. Don't give them any more information than they ask for. Yes and no answers are good. You needn't elaborate on any points. And above all, deny that anyone else in the family knew what that scrambler was."

The hairs on my neck stood up. "I will."

He gave my shoulder a supportive squeeze. "You'll do fine."

I didn't feel fine.

***

After a mostly sleepless night, I found myself awake and perusing the clothes in my closet. B.O.S.S. noticed everything; I figured it wouldn't hurt to look a little bit older, more respectable. That wasn't going to happen with my Sale-o-rama wardrobe. Shutting the door, I went down the hall to the room where we'd put Gran and Pops's things. Not quite sure what I was looking for, I rummaged through the boxes, eventually coming to one marked GINNIE'S CLOTHES.

The first thing that hit me when I lifted the lid was the aroma of Mom. We'd boxed these things up the day after she died. In the rush to get out of the rented modular, there had been no time for doing laundry. The scent of her perfume mixed with her own personal body smell made me feel as if she was just around the corner. I buried my face in the box, tears streaming down my cheeks. I missed her so much.

It was a struggle, but I pulled myself together. Pushing aside the tearstained clothes, I retrieved a dress and sweater that I knew would fit. Mom and I were close to the same size, and I'd borrowed these same clothes for a school outing. When I was done dressing, I examined myself in the mirror. It would have to do. I didn't look top tier, and the clothes were ridiculously out-of-date, but they were from when Ginnie was a tier-five assistant. Better than my tier-two wardrobe. I knew tiers shouldn't matter, but in this case, I needed all the help I could get.

Dee was still sleeping when I slipped out the front door. If she'd hugged me and gotten a full whiff of Mom, it would have been disastrous.

Calling Wei from the trans, I asked her to check on Dee later.

"Not a problem. I could still come down there, meet you . . . I don't have to tell Dad. Chris will drive me. He's worried about you."

"I appreciate everyone's concern, but honestly, Wei, I have to learn to take care of myself. Wouldn't sisters want each other to be strong and brave?" That was the most I dared say without giving the Sisterhood away.

"You're right," she said. "Absolutely. I'll see you later."

I thought about calling Sal, but he hadn't mentioned how long the NonCon business would be. Since I hadn't heard from him yet, I knew he was probably still wrapped up in that. Besides, he wouldn't want me going to B.O.S.S. again by myself, and I'd meant what I'd said to Wei. I had to do this alone.

My PAV beeped, jarring me out of my thoughts.

"Hey, Nina, it's Chris. You got out of here so fast I didn't get a chance to tell you to knock 'em dead." He chuckled. "Not literally, of course."

"You are silly. Thanks, Chris."

"Seriously, good luck. If you want me to pick you up afterward—"

"No." I was too quick with the refusal. Chris's unexpected compliment at Soma, and a few other little things he'd done— like going out of his way to be sure I was okay after Martinique's stupid comments—had made me wonder if he was flirting with me. Don't be silly, I told myself. I was definitely not his type. "I mean, I have a couple of things to do afterward. I'll see you later. And . . . thanks for calling."

"You bet."

I clicked off. My finger slipped, and the blaring verts

surrounded me. *"Don't miss the Holiday specials!"* *"Shop Sale-o-rama, where every deal is a good deal!"* *"All-weather jeans—"* I quickly clicked off my PAV again.

Why couldn't that call have been Sal? And why had Chris's call made my heart beat a little faster? The transit pulled up in front of B.O.S.S. headquarters. Taking a deep breath, I exited the trans.

XVIII

Once I was inside, the same reception bot as before performed the obligatory weapons and ID scan. At least I knew it was coming this time. And they knew I was coming. No surprises.

The bot then directed me to a waiting room in the Yellow corridor. The room wasn't much bigger than a closet with puke-yellow walls and a frosted-glass window on one end. In the center of the room, two metal chairs were bolted to the floor, their backs to the door. I felt way too vulnerable to sit there, so I stood. Except for a large wall clock and some errant cobwebs, abandoned by any sensible spiders, the room was bare. An ancient light fixture hummed mercilessly overhead.

At forty-five minutes after the appointed time of nine, the door opened. "Follow me," a woman commanded.

Her heels tapped purposefully down the hall as we passed door after door. Each had a tiny frosted window with a number painted above it. We stopped at number 15.

"Here." She opened the door, waving me in. Then she closed it with a resounding click.

Inside, a scrawny bald man sat behind the desk, electro-notepads covering all but one corner of its surface. That spot held a name tag—LIONEL EFFINGHAM—and a fading plant of indeterminate species, not long for this world.

"Name," he barked.

"Nina Oberon."

Searching through the pads, he eventually selected one. After several swipes with his stylus, he finally looked at me.

"Sit." He motioned to the chairs in front of his desk, identical to the ones in the waiting room.

I sat. His eyes stayed glued to the pad while I glanced around the room. There was nothing to see except the man, his overloaded desk, and the plant. No emo-detectors, no scan rods, and he didn't even have the luxury of a window.

"Where is Edith Oberon?"

"She's in the hospital. She had a heart attack." Too much information.

The man's eyes darted up at mine, then back to the pad. "You must be the older granddaughter."

"Yes."

Beads of sweat rose on his forehead. "You made an unauthorized visit here?" He dabbed his face with a dingy handkerchief. "Highly unorthodox. Highly." His hand trembled as he picked up his PAV receiver. "Inquiry . . . Yes . . . Oberon . . ." That was followed by a long silence.

My palms turned moist, my shoulders quivering. Maybe those "superiors" whom the female officer had mentioned had changed their minds. Whatever composure I'd felt was rapidly dissipating, and I forced myself to concentrate on breathing, not on Mr. Effingham's sporadic monosyllabic conversation.

At the very moment I was sure my anxiety would burst out of me in some totally inappropriate way, he said, "Oh, I see. Certainly." He clicked off and, without missing a beat, picked up the pad he'd been so intent on previously. "Now, where was I? Oh, yes. Where's the other one? Says here there's another child, a girl. Where is she?"

"At home."

He patted his forehead again. "I see . . . well, then." He ran his stylus down the pad. "Herbert Oberon is charged with treason, attempting to incite actions against the Governing Council, possession of a contraband blocking device, and resisting arrest. Now, Miss Oberon"—he trained his watery eyes on me—"were you present when the aforementioned Herbert Oberon committed these acts?"

"No."

"Did you have previous knowledge of the CBD?"

"The what?" I knew he meant the scrambler, but as hard as this was on me, I had no intention of being easy on him.

"Contraband blocking device." He sighed.

"No."

"Did Mrs. Edith Oberon and or Miss, uh . . ." He snatched up another pad, scanning it quickly. "Delisa Oberon have any knowledge of this CB—contraband blocking device?" He swiped his forehead again.

"No." Only yeses or noes.

I was silently thanking Mr. Jenkins when Effingham said, "Do you want to say anything?"

"Uh, may I see my grandfather now?"

Effingham stabbed a fierce dot onto the pad. "No." Pressing a button on his desk, he barked, "Emalia."

I listened as the sound of heel clicks grew louder, then stopped. The door opened.

"This way," Emalia ordered.

Out on the sidewalk, I finally exhaled. "Well, that was fun."

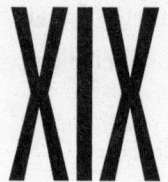

XIX

I was so busy congratulating myself on not messing anything up, I ended up on the local rather than the express trans. It stopped across the bridge from our old building, and I noticed a group of homeless women shuffling through the oasis. One glanced back at the road, and I was sure that it was Joan. As soon as we crossed the bridge, I hopped off the trans. Hurrying down the walk, I closed in on the women.

I was catching up to them when they noticed me approaching, and they scattered like a flock of startled pigeons. Joan, however, resisted the pull of her friends and waited for me to catch up.

"Joan?" I remembered how fragile her mind was and I didn't want to throw her into hysterics or trigger her trauma in any way.

"Nina. I've watched for you."

"You have?"

"Uh-huh. I've been seeing a doctor. He's helping me."

"Really?" How, I wondered, was she getting help? I glanced around. The river walk was fairly deserted, its usual state in winter. I knew there was a dead zone nearby, one that Sal had showed me months ago. "Can you come over here? We can talk." I motioned to the dead zone oasis.

"I can't stay long." Her eyes kept darting to where her companions stood, half hidden in the shadows.

"Have you been going to Metro?" I said. "Is that where your doctor is?"

"I can't go to the hospital. I'd be picked up and sent away." She pulled back her ragged coat collar, revealing the FeLS symbol tattooed on her neck. A black slash cut through the middle of it.

"What's that?"

"When a girl cracks, they do this. That way, if she escapes, she's easier to find."

"Joan, were you on a space station?" My mind was racing. Lessig's Alert and the fake space station had to be false. Joan could help prove it. "Media is reporting that they found a fake FeLS station in the desert near New Vegas City. Were you there?"

"I don't know where I was." Joan shivered. "They drugged me for the transport to Mars, I was still drugged when they rescued me."

I didn't want to probe further, to push her past her limit. I pulled off my tensalite scarf and wrapped it around her neck, not just to keep her warm but also to cover the repulsive mark. "So, a doctor is helping you?"

She nodded. "He comes here after dark with medicine, and he listens to me. He doesn't . . . touch me."

"You told him about FeLS?"

"I think he knows." She clutched my coat sleeve. "He has to. He saw my neck. But he won't tell. He promised."

I heard voices coming up the way. "Here, sit closer." I motioned her close to me. When I wrapped my arm around her shoulder, she tensed up. "I won't hurt you, Joan. I'm your friend. You know that."

"It's just"—her voice dropped almost to an unintelligible whisper—"women hurt me, too."

"That will never happen again," I whispered.

The voices passed on beyond us.

"I'd better go," Joan said. "Maybe you could . . . I . . ." She hung her head. "Seeing you reminds me of my family. I miss them . . ." She swiped her sleeve across her eyes and glanced behind her. "I've got to go."

"I'll come back." I watched her and her friends melt into the gloom between the buildings. A blast of cold air stung my bare neck. Yanking my collar up, I hunkered down, staring at the green, racing water of the Chicago River. "No one's going to hurt her again. Ever. Not if I can help it," I whispered to myself.

It was way too cold to sit by the river for long. The image of Joan's tattoo got me thinking about my need for a tattoo to surround the XVI on my wrist. I was a Creative. I could do whatever I wanted. And now I had an idea.

***

"Hey, you." Wei was standing at the top of the stairs. "Come up and tell me how it went."

"In a nano. I need to tell Dee I'm back and I have something I need to sketch first."

"Dee's up here with Chris. Bring your art stuff up here. I need to practice and you can draw while I make music."

I nodded my agreement. "Let me grab it." I hurried into the apartment, got my sketch pad and rapido, and joined Wei upstairs.

"You do know you're spending Holiday with us," Wei said. "Mom won't have it any other way. And you do not want to cross my mother."

As if on cue, Mrs. Jenkins called out from another room, "I'm not hearing any Chopin."

"See what I mean?"

Wei took out her sheet music, and I curled up with my drawing paper.

"I did what your dad said, only answered yes or no. They wouldn't let me see Pops. And on the way back"—I fiddled with my rapido—"I saw Joan. She said a doctor has been coming to see her on the sly. Giving her medicine and talking to her."

"Huh, I wonder if it's someone Dad knows about?" Wei executed what seemed to me to be a pretty difficult series of notes.

"What's that?"

"Chopin's Nocturne Number Eight."

"It sounds incredible. And it looks like it's really hard to play. I never understood how anyone could read those lines and dots."

"If you want, I'll explain it to you sometime. But it's kind of like your drawings," she said. "You make that look easy, and I can't draw at all. I got my Creative designation for music, not art. I had to get Chris to design my tattoo."

By the time she was done practicing, I had a few rough sketches of Joan and the homeless women. They practically poured out of my fingers onto the page. Real people, not faceless, worthless scum.

And I had a decent sketch of what I wanted my own tattoo to

look like. Granted, I didn't have the credits to get one yet, but if I saved from my pay each week, I might have enough by spring.

"What do you think?" I handed it to Wei.

Taking hold of my left hand, she glanced from the sketch to it several times, imagining how it would look. "This is magic! Let's make the appointment. I'll call—"

"No, I can't afford it, yet."

"Okay. Just let me know when you're ready. I'll arrange everything."

I shrugged off a twinge of jealousy. It'd take me months to save up for the tattoo. Wei probably didn't have to wait at all to get hers. She'd probably never had to wait to buy anything. I shook my head, trying to clear it. No sense in feeling bad over the way things were. If I did a good job at the Institute, and was lucky, over time I'd move up a few tiers.

Our PAVs beeped. Another Alert. "There haven't been this many Alerts since that meteor strike in the Sahara," Wei said.

She projected the Alert onto the wall.

A voice-over announcer intoned, "Stay tuned for breaking news on the FeLS scandal."

The blank screen gave way to Kasimir Lessig, seated behind a desk: Media and Governing Council insignias were prominently displayed in the background.

"Bureau of Safety and Security agents, aided by local enforcement agencies, have completed the first phase of their investigation regarding allegations about the use of the Female Liaison Specialist program as a training ground, if you will, for sex slaves." He swiveled his chair around, facing a different camera. The scene of the fake space station popped up behind him. "It is here that alleged mastermind, Ed Chamus"—a small picture of Ed popped into the lower corner of the screen—"took unsuspecting Chosens and trained them to become sex slaves for high-ranking foreign officials and corporate moguls. Furthermore"—his chair swiveled again—"Chamus did not act alone. The Bureau has recovered AV chips labeled 'Training' that show at least three different men and two women . . ."

A close-in image of one of those chips came up. The camera then cut to Lessig's face. His eyes sparkled with what I read as pleasure at being able to report on such an horrific story. "I have to say . . . in all my years of news reporting, I have never"—his eyes widened—"never seen anything as disgusting as what was being done to those young women." His lips parted slightly, and you could hear a sudden huff of breath. "I spoke earlier today with Governing Council president Xander Critchfield."

The scene changed to Lessig and Critchfield standing in front of the Justice Building on Dearborn.

"Citizens," Critchfield said. "Rest assured that the perpetrators of this horrendous scheme will be found and brought to justice. Going against the accepted mores of our society, these pathetic girls abandoned their normal, natural sex-teen lives in return for the possibility of lifting themselves out of the muck of low-tier existence. And this is how they were repaid." He shook his head, clucking his tongue. "A full accounting will be made. You have my word on it."

"Thank you, Mr. President." Lessig turned to the camera. "As further information comes forth, we will continue to provide updates to this story. News at eleven."

This was bad. They were blaming it all on Ed, which I knew

wasn't the case. Ed, who Dee still thought was her dad.

"Wei, where's Dee?"

"I think she's in the kitchen with Chris. Why?" It dawned on me that you got Alerts only if you were of age. But if Dee had been with someone getting an Alert, she could have seen the entire thing. I jumped up and ran to the kitchen, Wei hot on my heels.

Chris and Dee were at the table.

"Nina, my father wouldn't do anything like that." Her face was drawn, her jaw set. "I know he wouldn't. It has to be a mistake."

"She insisted on watching with me," Chris said. "I didn't think--"

I silenced him with a look—he should have known better. I sat down next to Dee while he and Wei quietly left.

After Dee's reaction to my triptych, I knew sugarcoating anything about Ed wouldn't work. She'd already shown she was much stronger than I'd imagined.

"Dee, Ed wasn't the nicest guy." I felt her body stiffen. "You didn't know, because Mom hid things from you. I hid things from you. Things that I saw firsthand. Remember all the times I took you to Sandy's house? Ed beat Mom up. That's how she broke her arm. That's how she got all those cuts and bruises."

"He said she was clumsy. He said that she accidentally hurt herself." She turned her tearstained face to me and said, "I believed him, Nina." Dropping her gaze, she murmured, "He's my dad."

Oh, how I ached to tell Dee that he wasn't. But her safety depended on her not knowing the truth.

Dee studied her hands for the longest time. "Does this mean I'm going to be cruel, like him?"

"What?" My jaw dropped. "Why would you think that?"

"We're studying genetics and character traits," she said. "Maybe I inherited a cruelty trait from my father."

Funny how one truth revealed opens the way for others. Still, there were some things that I just couldn't tell her.

"Character traits, and that's what cruelty is, aren't passed down through genes," I said. "Eye and hair color, how tall you'll be, and the size of your ears . . . those are decided by genetics. Who you are, how you act, the kinds of things you do . . . *you* get to make those choices. And you learn about them from the people who raise you. Mom, Gran, Pops—none of them are cruel. You couldn't possibly be."

Dee looked over at me, tears rimming her eyes. "I miss Mom so much. And Pops . . . and I wish Gran were here."

Her effort to keep from crying made my own throat ache with unshed tears. "I do, too, Deeds. I do, too." I rounded the table and put my arms around her.

She allowed the comforting, for a bit, then shook me off and stood up.

"Chris and I made Gran's green-tomato mince-pie recipe. We should try it while it's still warm, the way Pops likes it. You go get everyone while I cut the pie."

She walked to the cook center, shoulders back, head held high, reminding me so much of Ginnie. Those were the genes and the character traits Dee had inherited—those of a strong woman.

Later, Mrs. Jenkins invited Dee and me into her study. "We need to talk about Wednesday's hearing."

"Miss Maldovar's going to be there," Dee said. "She has friends at Child Protective Services and thought she might be able to help."

"Who is Miss Maldovar?" Mrs. Jenkins frowned.

"My teacher," Dee said.

"I see. Well then, I look forward to meeting her. Perhaps she *will* be of help." Mrs. Jenkins cast a puzzled look in my direction, then went on. "I wanted to share with you both the particulars on how a Writ of Unsuitability hearing is conducted. The child, the parents or guardians, and any other family members or interested parties may be present. Also the complainant, or his or her representative, which is usually Child Protective Services, will be there. We'll be called in front of a judge, who will ask questions about the case. Then the judge will hand down his or her decision."

"Will they allow us to comment?" I asked.

"We shouldn't count on that. Fortunately, Mr. Jenkins has very high standing in Media, and he's well known in the judiciary, having covered many high-profile criminal proceedings. It is helpful that you're now living with us. The judge may be more inclined to treat you favorably. However, if we get a judge who is not acquainted with Mr. Jenkins, I can't say."

I glanced over at Dee. "They can't just take her away, can they?"

"It is a possibility," Mrs. Jenkins said.

A few days ago, I would never have believed Dee's calm reaction. "Will I be allowed to come and get my things? Where will they take me?"

If Mrs. Jenkins was as surprised at my little sister's composure as I was, she didn't let on. "I truly doubt it will come to that, Dee. There are a good many points on our side. Aside from your living here now, Nina's sixteen and has a job. Her Creative designation is another boon, since they like to see ambition and the promise of moving up in tiers. There is also the fact that your mother specifically, legally designated the Oberons as your guardians; that cannot be discounted without a fight."

"I hope so," Dee said. "But if they do remove me, will you still try to get me back?" She looked at me.

"Of course, Dee! You're my sister."

"Good. Excuse me, please, I have some things I need to do."

After she left, I said, "If it were me, I don't think I'd be even half as cool as Dee is. I should make plans to get Dee out of town. My father, well, he's her father, too, could take her into hiding with him. Then she'd be safe."

"No." Mrs. Jenkins shook her head. "That's been discussed at length. If she disappeared while under threat of a writ, B.O.S.S. would search for her. Even though Ed is her presumed father, she bears the Oberon name. That alone would make the authorities suspicious. And they would most certainly seize and interrogate you. It is best that we go to court and hope that things go in our direction. You should see if Dr. Silverman will give you a statement indicating that your grandmother is recovering and will eventually be able to care for Dee. The court will already have information on your grandfather. But that cannot be helped."

I said. "What if—"

"Nina, do not torment yourself over imagined disasters. Instead, imagine the future the way you want it to be. It is always better to visualize good rather than evil."

"I can't just think my way out of this."

"No, but you can be aware of what could be and look to what you *want* things to be." She laid her hand on mine. "As we think, so we are." She brushed my hair back, looking into my eyes. "Now. Tell me about this Miss Maldovar. How does she know what's going on?"

"Dee's original teacher was in an accident of some sort, and Miss Maldovar took over. She made Dee her assistant, and Dee ended up telling her all about the writ. I've only seen her once."

"Your impression?"

"Well, I never actually met her, officially. We ran into her at Rosie's. I have to say, there's something about her that seems off. She gives me the creeps."

"Trust your intuition. But for now, having her at the hearing to tell how Dee is doing in school may be very helpful. Very helpful."

I t was nice not having to worry about school for a while. And I was able to pick up more hours at the Institute. I took a detour on my way to work, hoping to see Joan. But there was no sign of anyone, except a few early shoppers heading from the apartments up to Michigan Avenue. When I got to work, Martin was waiting for me. "My nod to the season, don't you know?" he said, handing me a steaming cup of hot cocoa with a peppermint-stick stirrer poking out the top.

That one small gesture reminded me of Holidays with Ginnie. Hot cocoa was a tradition. I felt like laughing and crying all at once. But what I did was thank him, and then I took myself and my cup to the storeroom. Perched on the edge of my chair, I verified artwork against catalog numbers and descriptions. It wasn't the most fun in the galaxy, but I loved the feeling of being in the midst of all this amazing artwork. And I was learning lots about how artists like to describe their work. Some were so esoteric—on purpose, or so it seemed—and it only made them sound snobby and affected to me. Like ultrafamous, university-taught Lars Estagean, whose artist statement was so out there that it was totally incomprehensible to me. While Stefan B, a recently discovered "street artist," came across as honest and unassuming. His simple statement, "It feels phenomenal to be able to take what I see and turn my feelings about it into a truthful portrayal of what's there," was exactly how I felt about my own artwork; it was nothing fancy, but it was honest.

I hadn't been working all that long when Martin and Percy came in. I'd never actually met Percy face-to-face, only on vid calls.

"Pers, allow me to present the fabulous Miss Nina Oberon. Isn't she even lovelier in person?" Martin gushed.

Percy shook my hand. "Beautiful, Marty. Absolutely beautiful. The apple didn't fall far from the tree. Your mother was absolute perfection."

My cheeks blushed hot. "Thank you." I hadn't realized they'd known Ginnie, too.

"You are coming to the party, aren't you?" He didn't miss my puzzlement. "She is coming, isn't she?" His gaze bounced over to Martin, then back to me. "You have to come, you know." To Martin, "She simply *has* to."

"What party?" I asked.

"The New Year's bash at the Golds," Percy said. "Everyone in the universe will be there. Which means, you *must* be there, because the universe *has* to meet you."

"Gold, like Paulette Gold?" My eyebrows shot up.

"That's the daughter. Right, Marty?" Percy continued talking, wiping out any response Martin might have made. "She's a bit of a swagger, but not a bad girl. You know her? Of course you do, or you wouldn't have asked."

"Percy." Martin grasped his arm. "We'll take Nina to the party. For now, I merely wanted to introduce you in person and to tell Nina that she could go home." He smiled at me. "No more work until after Holiday. Oh." He dug into his pocket. "Here's a free hire-trannie ticket. Go home in style." He hugged me. "I hope your grandmother is feeling better, and here's hoping for good news about your grandfather. Happy Holiday, Nina."

"Yes, dear." Percy hugged me, too. "Happy Holiday. Lord knows you deserve one." He gave me a little peck on the cheek.

The scent of spicy aftershave lingered long after the door closed. I stared at the ticket. I'd been in a hire trannie only once, and then only as an escape. This time, however, I wouldn't be running away from Ed. I'll pretend I'm upper tier, I thought. It will be fun, even if only for a few minutes.

***

Stuck in traffic, I stared out the window at all the Holiday lights on Galaxy Mile, the part of Michigan Avenue that had all the ultrachic, top-tier shops. Holiday verts were coming fast and furious, competing for shoppers' attention.

"Her eyes will light up as bright as the diamonds in this Urban-Retro, twenty-carat-gold mail necklace." "Give your Holiday Pre a glimpse into the ultra world of XVI with a XVI Ways Day Spa gift certificate." "Surprise Dad this Holiday with an all-weather Verolux chronos."

We were sitting in front of Mars 9, the ultra shop for teens. Their display scene was a party. I clicked my PAV to tune out the verts and pressed my nose to the glass. A girl mannibot drifted through the crowd in a scintillating, strapless gown. The scene was enthralling. A longing to look that nice, just once, seared through me, leaving behind a burning hole in my chest.

I would *never* be that girl.

I shut my eyes and didn't open them until I felt the vehicle lurch forward. Paulette's upper-tier party. My Sale-o-rama life. There was no way I could ever go to that party, no matter what Martin and Percy said.

I thought about Sal. About us. I hadn't spoken to him in a while. I knew he was on NonCon business. I hadn't gotten so much as a message. I shouldn't be surprised, I told myself. But still.

Finally, the trannie pulled up to the house.

Chris was on his way out as I was going in. "You okay?"

"Yeah. Sure." I didn't even try to hide my low spirits.

He touched my arm. "You want to talk?"

Our eyes connected, and suddenly I did want to talk—to him. "I, uh . . . no. Is Wei home?" What was I thinking? Sal was who I should be commiserating with, not Chris.

"She's upstairs." He gave my arm a squeeze. "Whatever it is, Nina, it'll get better."

He left and I closed the door, confused. The more I saw of Chris, the more I liked him. And lately it seemed that he liked me—more. His interactions with me sometimes seemed flirty or, like now, attentive and filled with concern. Sure, I told myself, it's perfectly normal to want to share my worries with someone who cares. It's just that that someone should be Sal.

"Hey, you!" Wei came traipsing down the stairs. "I saw you through the window. What's up with the hire trannie?"

I told her everything—except my near-breakdown in front of Mars 9.

"Paulette's party? Lucky you! Mom and Dad had another commitment, so they won't be there, but . . . yeah. You should definitely go."

I said, "Maybe," even though I knew it was the last thing I would ever do.

XXII

I woke up the next morning surprised I'd slept so soundly, especially considering what was in store for the day. Dee was up before the alarm and in my room, fretting. She fidgeted on the corner of my bed. "What should I wear?"

"The nicest clothes you've got," I said. "Your black pants and your red sweater?"

"Sweater's too small." She checked out my room. "What are you wearing?"

"The same thing I wore when I went to B.O.S.S. headquarters to see about Pops."

"What was that? You left before I was up."

"Some of Mom's clothes. I felt close to her, like she was there watching over me."

"You think anything of hers might fit me?"

"Let's go see. They're in Gran's room."

Five minutes later, we'd found the perfect asteroid-blue sweater for her to wear. It was the tiniest bit big, but nothing a couple of well-placed pins couldn't fix.

"It smells like Mom." Her eyes got misty.

"Don't be sad, Deeds. Think of it like she's right here with you."

By the time we met Mrs. Jenkins on the stairs, we both looked, if not tier five, at least four. And, neither of us had cried, on the outside.

First stop was Metro Hospital. Dr. Silverman had left a transcribed, notarized statement about Gran's recovery and general good health. At least that was going in our favor.

When we got to the Hall of Justice, Dee slipped her hand into mine.

"It will be fine," I whispered.

Simply standing outside the Hall was intimidating. Instead of the sleek, modern fronts of many of the surrounding buildings, it was old. The walls were row after row of glass, going up at least thirty stories. A balance scale was projected on the entire surface of the Dearborn Street side.

Balance. Right. The balance is all on their side, I thought. Doesn't matter how many times they tell us we are free. It's their version of free; I was guessing it was nowhere near my father's version, and it definitely wasn't mine.

"We're in courtroom seven B." Mrs. Jenkins hurried us inside. "We don't want to be late."

With my free hand, I pulled out my charms necklace, touching the number 7 that Gran had given me—"For completeness." Surely it was no coincidence that we were in courtroom seven. It was my lucky number. I squeezed the charm.

We had no problem clearing the scanners flanking the doors. Mrs. Jenkins's heels clicked purposefully as we made our way through the expansive lobby to the information desk. I was surprised at the number of actual people, rather than bots, who worked here, although the man who directed us was as impassive as any Hal at school.

Outside the courtroom, a uniformed officer guarded the door. He sent us to a room across the hall. "Wait there until you're summoned."

Before we even entered the room, I heard a familiar whirring noise.

"Mrs. Marchant!"

"Yes, Miss Oberon. That is who I am." She glided over to us. "This must be your sister, Delisa. Good morning." She extended her hand. "I am Mrs. Marchant, the principal at Nina's school."

"Hello." Dee's eyes swept across the transchair, but she made no comment.

"This is Mrs. Jenkins," I said. "She's—"

"Yes, I know Mrs. Jenkins well." A deep-throated laugh erupted. "We've met on more than one occasion regarding Wei."

Duh. The first day I met Wei, Mr. Haldewick had threatened to send her to Mrs. Marchant's office. She did like to create scenes.

"So nice to see you again." Mrs. Jenkins's eyes twinkled.

"I heard about Nina's situation," Mrs. Marchant said. "It seemed to me that a character witness might be a good thing. I didn't care for the way CPS treated one of my students, in my school, in my office." There was fire in her eyes.

The door squeaked behind us.

"Miss Maldovar!" Dee broke into a smile. "You came."

"I told you I would." She cupped Dee's chin in her hand. "You look worried. Don't worry. Everything will be fine. Why don't you introduce me to your sister and ..." She glanced at the three of us.

"Oh, this is Mrs. Jenkins. It's her house we're living in."

Miss Maldovar approached, smiling. "Mrs. Jenkins." She held out a gloved hand. "What a wonderful thing your family's done, taking in Dee and her sister." After they shook. Miss Maldovar turned to me. "You are, of course, Nina. I've heard so much about you. Your sister quite looks up to you."

"Thank you. It's very nice of you to come," I said. "But you needn't have, especially at Holiday time. We'll be fine."

Miss Maldovar's smile changed to a look of warm concern. "I'm sure you will be. But as I told Dee, I have many years of dealing with Child Protective Services and even know some of the judges who hear these cases. Perhaps I may be of assistance. I hope you won't mind if I at least observe."

Mrs. Marchant cleared her throat.

"Excuse me." I stepped back. "This is Mrs. Marchant, the principal of my school."

Miss Maldovar extended her hand. "What a pleasure to meet another educator."

Mrs. Marchant nodded. "It would appear that the school system is concerned about its pupils. That would make a good headline, wouldn't it?" Her chair skimmed backward, and she set her gaze on Miss Maldovar. "You haven't been at Dickens for long. Where were you before that?"

"Overseas at a private institution. I'm substituting while I decide if I want to stay in the Americas or go back to the European States."

The officer from the hall stuck his head in. "Oberon?"

"Yes." I tensed.

"They're ready for your case. Please proceed to the front of the courtroom."

Rows of straight-backed, worn wooden seats flanked the center aisle. The place was certainly not built for comfort. Miss Maldovar took a seat halfway up, and Mrs. Marchant whirred over near the wall. We installed ourselves at one of the two tables in front of the judge's bench—the one marked DEFENDANT.

The doors opened again, and in walked Crow Face and Songbird. They were accompanied by a tall, lanky man clutching an oversize digi-pad in his bony hands.

They'd barely had time to sit at the Prosecution table before the court officer said, "All rise. The Honorable Judge Gordon Hughes residing."

A short man with dark curly hair entered through a door behind the bench and sat.

"All be seated," the officer said. "Court is now in session."

Judge Hughes busied himself with reading something. There were voices behind me. I strained to hear what was being said. All I could make out was Miss Maldovar asking one of the officers, "Where is Judge Patton?" The only part of the officer's reply I could hear was "emergency." Had Miss Maldovar expected there to be a certain judge?

The judge raised his head. "All interested parties, please identify yourselves. We'll start here." He pointed directly at me.

"I'm Nina Oberon. This is my sister, Delisa, and our friend Mrs. Jenkins."

"Where are Edith and Herbert Oberon?"

"Pops—I mean, Herbert—is, uh . . . he's in jail, and Edith is in the hospital. I have a paper here that says she's going to be fine." I held out the doctor's statement.

"Bailiff." Judge Hughes motioned the court officer to bring him Dr. Silverman's statement. While he studied it, he said, "Mrs. Jenkins, what is your interest in this case?"

"As friends of the family, my husband and I have opened up our home to the Oberons. They are now living in an apartment in our building."

"Your husband is . . . ?"

"Jonathan Jenkins."

"Jonathan Jenkins, senior Media investigative correspondent?"

"Yes, Your Honor."

"Interesting." He laid down the paper and looked directly at me. "Nina Oberon, are you of age?"

"Yes, Your Honor." I held out my wrist, showing the XVI.

"Your Honor, if I may speak." Crow Face stood.

The judge narrowed his eyes. "When I am ready, I will ask for your input, Miss . . . ?"

"Griswold," Crow Face answered.

"And you are . . ."

"Child Protective Services. You see, Your Honor—"

"Just answer the questions I ask. When I want more from you, you'll be the first to know." He turned to Songbird. "And you?"

"Angie Page, Child Protective Services, junior officer."

"Thank you, Miss Page. Sir?"

"CPS officer Bolton, Your Honor."

The judge nodded as his eyes scanned the courtroom. They lit on Mrs. Marchant. "Caroline? Caroline Marchant? Is that you?"

Mrs. Marchant nodded, her eyes twinkling. "Yes, Your Honor."

"I'll be damned. I haven't seen you since, well . . ." His voice trailed off. "Now is not the time, nor the place. To what do I owe the honor of having you in my courtroom?"

"I'm here on behalf of the Oberon girls," she said. "I wanted to be certain justice was served. With you on the bench, I'm sure it will be."

I couldn't help but notice her eyes cut in Miss Maldovar's direction.

"Thank you for that vote of confidence." He scribbled something on a piece of paper, then looked behind us. "And you, ma'am?"

Miss Maldovar stood. "I am Delisa's teacher, Adana Maldovar. Like Mrs. Marchant, I am here for the girls."

"Thank you. You may be seated." He turned to the Prosecution table. "Now, Miss Griswold, what are the specifics in this case?"

"Herbert Oberon was arrested for being a subversive. He's the father of the infamous, late Alan Oberon. That ne'er-do-well who pumped up the Resistance with his following of nonconformists. The law states that no child will be allowed to stay in the care and under the influence of a known—"

"I am well aware of the law, and hardly need you to remind me of it."

"Yes, Your Honor." Crow Face at least had the intelligence to appear contrite, which I'm sure was all for show.

"Who brought this to the attention of CPS?"

"Anonymous."

"Of course." He turned away from Crow Face. "Miss Maldovar, please approach."

She came down the aisle to the judge's bench.

"How has the child been in school? Problems? Poor performance?"

"On the contrary," Miss Maldovar said. "She's quite well adjusted, given the horrible circumstances of her recent life—her mother's death." She clucked her tongue sympathetically. "And she's in the top percentile of students. Very bright. I've appointed her my classroom assistant." She lowered her voice. "She's a delightful child. I think this writ business is ridiculous. Some busybody with a grudge against the Oberons, perhaps? Alan Oberon, whatever he may have been, has not been an influence in Delisa's life. She's not even his biological daughter."

The blood drained from my face. I hadn't thought that would come up. If they did a DNA scan on Dee, they'd know the truth.

"Of course," Miss Maldovar continued, "with Herbert Oberon in B.O.S.S. custody he is not caring for nor influencing her. And Edith Oberon has been charged with nothing that I'm aware of."

Crow Face burst out, "But she's—"

The judge held up a silencing hand. "Has Mrs. Oberon been charged with anything?"

"No." Crow Face looked downright disappointed.

If everything hadn't been so serious, I would've laughed at her discomfiture. I was rather enjoying seeing her be treated the way she'd treated me.

"Thank you, Miss Maldovar. Mrs. Marchant. Do you mind?" The judge indicated the space in front of his bench.

Mrs. Marchant's transchair skimmed to the center of the room.

"What about Nina Oberon?"

"Nina's a good student. A Creative with a part-time job at the Art Institute, which hasn't interfered with her schoolwork. I can vouch for her integrity and her responsibility."

"Thank you." A look of almost desperate tenderness crossed the judge's face. "Bailiff."

The officer went to the bench. The judge whispered something to him and handed him a sheet of paper. The bailiff gave the sheet of paper to Mrs. Marchant, who had returned to her spot by the wall. I tried to catch her expression, but the judge rapped his gavel and all eyes were on the bench.

"It is the finding of this court that there is nothing defensible in the writ as it stands. Delisa Oberon is currently to stay in the custody of her grandmother, Edith Oberon, and her of-age sister, Nina Oberon. Should Herbert Oberon be released from incarceration, the court will ascertain if, at that point, he is legally being considered a subversive. If so, this case will be revisited. But for now, case closed." He struck his gavel on its block.

"All rise," the bailiff intoned, and the judge exited the courtroom.

I pulled Dee into a huge hug. Mrs. Jenkins put her arms around both our shoulders. With my eyes closed, and the smell of Mom on Dee's clothes, I could imagine Mrs. Jenkins was Ginnie. Family. Together.

The spell was broken when Miss Maldovar and Mrs. Marchant joined us at the Defense table.

"I'm so glad it turned out in your favor," Miss Maldovar said. "I hope I was of some help."

"You were," Dee said. "And, Mrs. Marchant, thank you so much for saying all those things about Nina."

"They're true," Mrs. Marchant said. "She's an excellent role model. Now, if you'll excuse me." She glided past us, exiting through the same door the judge had used.

Crow Face noisily pushed back her chair and huffed out of the courtroom. Songbird ducked her head, giving me the slightest of smiles. The nondescript man followed them both.

We'd won, and Dee could stay with us, her family. I couldn't help but wonder who'd actually filed the writ and how this outcome would make him or her feel.

XXIII

On the way home we stopped at Metro. Gran's spirits lifted with the news that the writ had been denied. Dr. Silverman was moving her to Edgewater Rehabilitation Center after Holiday, and hopefully home shortly thereafter. The one thing she didn't bring up was Pops. Which was probably for the best. If she got all worked up again, Silverman might make her stay in the hospital longer, and none of us wanted that.

As we were leaving, Gran said, "Call Harriet and let her know what's going on. They've only let me talk to her twice," Gran said. "Make sure she won't be alone on Holiday, what with her son, Johnny, being taken away by B.O.S.S."

***

When we got home, Chris and Wei were waiting for us. After congratulations on the outcome of the hearing, Chris spirited Dee away to the grocery for Holiday food supplies. She was becoming quite the chef under his tutelage. Wei took me to her room for a PAV meeting with the Sisterhood. Everyone was on the call except for Dorrie.

"How'd the hearing go?" Brie asked.

"The judge dismissed the writ."

"Awesome. Did they ever figure out who filed it?" Brie asked. "That was ultracruel. Your poor grandmother."

"It was filed anonymously," I said. "It's what caused Gran to have the heart attack, that and Pops's arrest by B.O.S.S."

"My grandparents' doctor goes to their house once a month to do a routine health scan. All elderly people should do that," Paulette said.

"Yeah, well, not everyone has a personal doctor, or the credits to hire one. And when you've only got one medical option, that isn't going to happen. Can we stop talking about my family now?"

"Sure," Wei said. "So what's up? And where's Dorrie?"

"Today's the day," Brie said.

"Rogue?" Mag said.

"Uh-huh. Dorrie's recording right now. It'll be on at six tonight."

"So wait, how does Rogue Radio work?" I asked.

"Each of us gets a turn at putting together a broadcast. After it's recorded, Dorrie hacks into the signals of three obsolete communication satellites and programs them to play at a set time on a specific frequency. We've done some vid interruptions, too."

"Wait a nano! Did you guys do the clips of the Fems' rally that interrupted that *XVI Ways* fashion show?" I said. "That was ultra!"

"Sure enough," Brie said. "Dorrie loves interruptions. She's got her PAV programmed to hit those satellites from anywhere at any time."

"I have to admit, I've only ever heard Rogue Radio by accident," I said.

"Chris can set up the channel on your PAV," Wei said.

"There'll be an impromptu vert interruption this afternoon,"

Paulette said. "Just in time to hit all the last-minute Holiday shoppers. If you want some free entertainment, go down to State or Michigan. Should be fun."

"I would, but all my shopping's done," Brie said. "And I sure don't want to be part of the mob that's doing the last-minute routine."

Mag and Wei nodded. I did, too, although in reality I hadn't bought one single present. Everyone was getting something I'd made or drawn. Sometimes it really sucked being low tier. Really.

"Sorry your parents can't make the New Year's party, Wei. Lots of top-tier people will be there," Paulette said. "Mom hinted that even Kasimir Lessig might attend."

"That jerk?" Brie asked. "Who'd want to be in the same room as him?"

Wei passed me a note. *You going to tell her about your invite?*

I shook my head.

"You guys been listening to the Alerts?" Mag asked. "Do you believe there's a fake space station out west?"

"I don't," I said. "Although Ed used to take a lot of trips. I suppose he might have been doing something like that."

"Ed? Ed Chamus?" Mag gasped. "You know that guy?"

Skivs! I'd forgotten that they didn't know about my connection with Ed. About my killing him. About anything.

"What gives, Nina?" Paulette's steely eyes bored into me.

"Yeah, I knew . . . know him. He's my sister's father." I nearly choked on the words.

After what seemed an eternity of silence, Paulette said, "Well, if he did what B.O.S.S. is after him for, he's as good as dead. My guess is he'll be killed while they're apprehending him. The GC can't afford to let him reveal who gave him his orders. He didn't look smart enough to have figured out a scheme like that on his own."

I couldn't believe she hadn't ripped me for Ed being Dee's dad—even though he really wasn't—which, of course, I couldn't say. To be safe, I changed the subject. "I saw my friend Joan on Monday. Some doctor's been treating her on the sly. She seemed a lot better. Has anyone thought any more about what we could do to help her?"

"We'll figure something out," Mag said. "It's tough to plan anything during Holiday because so many people have family obligations. However, we'll come up with the right plan. And I bet we can get her out of town ourselves. Don't you guys think so?"

Wei's eyes lit up. Brie did a slow, affirmative nod. We all looked at Paulette.

"Are you willing to plan a daring rescue, Paulette?" Wei asked, teasingly.

"Only if it's after New Year's. There's no way I can leave my mother in the lurch with this party." She set her jaw. "After that, I'm game. No reason the guys should have all the fun."

My eyebrow shot up. Paulette was a constant surprise. Now she's up for helping a homeless girl? It stood to reason that she must believe some of the same things as the rest of us, since she *is* in the Sisterhood. But this?

XXIV

I left Dee in the kitchen, absorbed in her newfound passion for cooking, and headed over to Harriet's. I thought a visit would be better than a call.

On the way over, I called B.O.S.S. headquarters, to see if maybe I could get some information about Pops, or at least leave a message for them to give to him. It was Holiday, after all. The only two things they confirmed were that he was there and that he wasn't allowed visitors.

When I got to Gran and Pops's old building, I automatically put my hand on the auto-recognition pad. When nothing happened, I remembered I didn't live there anymore.

Pressing D14, I said, "Nina Oberon for Harriet Pace."

In a moment, her face popped up on the monitor.

"Lord! Nina? Come in."

When I got off the elport, Harriet was standing outside her door. "How is Edith? I've been worried sick about her. I heard from her only once. The hospital won't tell me anything, and this darn sciatica's kept me laid up." She latched onto my arm, ushering me into her apartment. "I've been so worried about her."

It was almost nice to sit and talk with Harriet for a while. Almost like our old life. Two cups of tea and several cookies later, I left. But not until Harriet had assured me she was having Holiday dinner with the couple in D17. I was glad she wouldn't be alone.

I headed out and walked along the riverfront, in the direction of Michigan Avenue. I was hoping to see Joan, but there was no sign of her or the homeless women she had been hanging out with. Heading up Illinois Street, I cut east. At Rush Street, I noticed an ultra single trannie idling at the light. The driver was Dr. Silverman. Before I could make up my mind to wave or not, the light changed and he speeded off. After what Mr. Jenkins had said about Silverman's demotion to Metro Hospital, I wondered how he could afford that kind of transit. Maybe he'd made a ton of credits when he was doing research.

Any thoughts I had of the doctor disappeared as soon as I turned the corner onto Michigan Avenue. It was a virtual fairyland of twinkling lights and Holiday music—if you blocked out the verts. I clicked on my PAV to music only and ambled down the street. The decorations and the music were breathtakingly beautiful. But it wasn't long before I was paying more attention to the sour faces of the people jostling past me, laden with bags and boxes. They weren't happy; they were stressed. The only smiling people were the few who, like me, were without packages—strolling slowly down the sidewalk, taking in the sights.

I was standing in front of Yum's candy shop, watching marzipan ballerinas twirling to the strains of *The Nutcracker*, when the vert interruption hit.

Trannies screeched to a halt. Shoppers' packages went flying as people bumped into each other, confused by the silence. It would've been more comical, except for the fear on the faces of little kids, clutching their parents' hands.

"Once upon a time, Holiday meant more than a buying frenzy. It was a time for family and friends and compassion for those less fortunate. The spirit of selflessness, generosity, and charity were foremost in a man's heart. Search your own hearts, people. Is the homeless person, freezing in the harsh winter, less worthy of—"

It was my dad's voice. Hearing him made me think back to our last conversation, when I'd clicked off on him. Suddenly, a high-pitched electronic screech cut off the speaker. Everyone, myself included, clapped their hands over their ears. Within seconds, a repair trannie flew by, heading to the Media station at the corner of Michigan and Erie. Moments after they arrived, Holiday music was flowing and verts filled the air. I clicked off my PAV to catch snippets of conversation.

An older man said to his companion, "I remember when I was a kid, we'd volunteer at the Shelter and Food works up in Rogers Park. Felt pretty good."

"Hush," the woman said. "Someone might hear you and think you agreed with that . . . that . . . subversive propaganda." She glanced around nervously.

"Maybe I should," he said.

She yanked him away. "We've got grandkids to think of . . ."

I continued up Michigan, purposely avoiding Mars 9, and took a left at the Water Tower. A trannie spun out of an alley, nearly knocking me over. When I glanced down the alley to see if anyone else was going to barrel out and flatten me, I saw a poster stuck on the wall. It was a rough drawing of a homeless man being stunned by a cop. Subversive art. Absolutely illegal . . . and thoroughly cool. Had the person in the speeding trannie posted it? How long would it stay there before the authorities tore it down? An idea began formulating in my brain. By the time I got home, I had a full-blown plan.

***

"So," I said to Wei, "we could reproduce my drawings and post them all over the city."

"Or," she said, "we can do a vid interruption made up of your pics. That would be ultra-ultra! We can call the others and see what they think. By the way, Derek's coming over tonight to listen to Rogue Radio. I heard Sal's back from his business. Why don't we get him and Mike to come over, too?"

"Good idea!" I hadn't gotten a message from Sal, but Wei knew he was back. The bubble of doubt crept up my throat, but I tamped it back down. "Oh, by the way, the vert interruption was great. It was weird to hear my dad talking."

"It was from an old debate he gave. He's got such a compelling voice," Wei said. "People listen to him."

"Just not enough of them," I said ruefully. Of course, I hadn't listened too well when we'd talked. He might be persuasive with the masses, but, as his abandoned daughter, I might need a little extra convincing of his sincerity, at least where I was concerned.

I messaged Sal and Mike, both of whom said they were coming over. Now I needed to figure out how to tell Dee about Rogue Radio without telling her too much about all the rest of our activities.

"So everyone's coming over tonight," I said, walking into her room, where she was watching a vid on her PAV.

"Really? How come?"

"We're going to listen to Rogue Radio." I waited for the anticipated barrage of questions.

"Cool. Chris was telling me about that. He said the music was tons better than anything Media produces. Is he coming, too?"

"I didn't ask him. He probably has a date or something." I was surprised that Dee was so accepting of Rogue Radio, but I guess coming from Chris, it softened things.

"Nuh-uh. He told me he was through with dating. That his last girlfriend was kind of a jerk and he'd rather be teaching me to cook than going out with someone like her again. He's so nice. And really cute, don't you think?"

"Yeah, I guess." My little sister appeared to have the beginnings of a raging crush on Chris. I figured he could handle that, because he really *was* a nice person. And cute, too. Why was I thinking that? "Go ahead and ask him if you want," I said.

While she was upstairs, I put the finishing touches on pictures I'd drawn for Wei and her family for Holiday. I wished I'd had credits to buy them something instead. But, I told myself, these were from the heart. Like the vert interruption had mentioned—Holiday was supposed to be about more than expensive presents.

***

I was sandwiched between Sal and Chris on the sofa, while Derek and Wei were sharing Pops's chair. Dee sprawled on the floor on a pile of pillows.

"Smells like ginger," Derek said, sniffing the back of the chair.

"That's Pops's chair. Candied ginger's his favorite thing,"

Dee said. To Wei, she said, "Did you know your mother got him hooked on it when she was in high school? She and your dad were friends with our mom and Nina's dad. They even went to grade school together."

"That practically makes us family, then," Chris said.

His thigh was pressed against mine, and I found it more than a little distracting. Especially when he flashed one of his killer smiles at me. I pressed myself closer to Sal and squeezed his hand.

"Missed you, too," he whispered.

"Shhhh," Wei said. "It's starting."

Dorrie's voice came through loud and clear. "Tonight we're going all the way back to the sixties—the *nineteen* sixties, that is. We'll be hearing from ultracool Bob Dylan, Neil Young, and Joan Baez. After a quick trip around that decade, we'll leap forward to the two thousands to hear from Ansley Garnett, Claudette Lucier, and Little Joe Andersen. Wrapping up tonight's broadcast will be the latest from Chicago's own Beppo Wills. But you didn't tune in to listen to me, so without wasting another nano, let's get something happening here with Buffalo Springfield's 'For What It's Worth.'"

At the end of the program, Dorrie said, "There you have it, guys and fems—a sampling of some music that's changed the world. Music can do that, you know. Until next time, keep your profile low and your scanners on. When you least expect it, Rogue Radio will return."

"Damn. I love that ancient stuff," Derek said. "Dylan was a genius, and so was Neil Young. Man, I wish I had my guitar, the show gave me some great ideas for songs."

"You could use the piano upstairs," Wei said.

"Brilliant. Let's go."

"You don't mind, do you, Nina?"

"Of course not." Maybe this would translate into some alone time for Sal and me. Although I didn't see how, with Dee and Chris planted firmly in their seats.

"Hey, Dee," Chris said. "Can we talk Holiday menu for a sec?"

"Sure!"

They disappeared into the kitchen.

Sal immediately pulled me into an embrace. "I have been wanting to do this all night." His lips were soft and warm on mine.

"Dee and Chris will walk in on us," I said, when we came up for air.

"Too bad." He kissed me again. "I missed you, Nina Oberon."

I leaned into him, kissing back. "I missed you, too, Sal."

"Nina!" Wei came through the door. "What are you guys up to?"

"Decorating," Dee stood back, hands on hips. "What do you think?"

Wei surveyed the Holiday decorations that Dee had insisted on putting up. "I think it looks ultra. I really like the antique Santas around the poinsettia. Is that silk?"

"Uh-huh," Dee said. "Gran's had it since before I was born."

"And the star lights around the doorway—ultracool." Wei nodded her approval. "Listen, would you mind going upstairs to help my mom? She's doing some baking and needs a hand— preferably not mine." Wei accompanied Dee to the kitchen door and whispered something to her.

The cook center timer went off. "Cookies are done," I said. "You go on, Dee. I'll get them. What was that about?" I asked Wei.

"Nothing. Don't you know not to ask questions around Holiday?" Her eyes latched onto the cookies. "Mmmm, those smell delicious!"

It would've been impossible to resist at least one, okay two, cookies each. Wei and I were just washing down the last bite with nut milk when Chris came in. "Let's go."

"Come on, Nina." Wei grabbed my arm. "We've got a surprise for you. Get your coat."

We ended up on the south side of Chicago, in a neighborhood that reminded me of where I'd taken refuge when I'd escaped from Ed's kidnapping attempt. Preferring not to think about that, I said, "Where are we going?"

"Right here." Chris pulled up in front of a grimy, boarded-up storefront. A sign hanging on the side of the building said LITTLE BLUES TATTOOS, with an arrow pointing down the alley.

My shoulders shivered, not from the cold. "You're not . . . are you?"

"It was Chris's idea," Wei said. "He really wants you to have your tat."

He shrugged and smiled. "You deserve it."

"But . . . it's too expensive. I can't let you—"

"You can't stop us," Wei said. "Come on. Don't want to be late for your appointment, do you?"

Chris punched a code into the door at the top of the stairs and held it open for Wei and me.

A guy appeared, inked from his fingers to the top of his head and, from the designs that disappeared under his shirtsleeves, probably a lot of other spots.

"Chris. Long time!"

"Colin. How are you doing?"

"Good. Real good. Is this the girl you told me about? Nina, isn't it?" Colin shook my hand. "I'll have to scan your designation before I can do anything around your XVI." He grimaced. "It's the law." He scanned my ID. "Creative in art. Awesome. Wei says you did your own sketch."

Wei produced my drawing from her coat pocket. "Dee took it to Chris," she said when I looked at her, mouth agape. "What do you think, Colin?" She spread it on the counter.

My stomach went all butterflies, waiting for his assessment. After all, he was a professional artist. I certainly wasn't.

"You're good," he said. "This is impressive."

"Thank you!" I relaxed the tiniest bit. "I wanted it to be more than just a distraction around the XVI."

"Mission accomplished. You've got completeness, love, and truth. Heavy on the truth. Nice."

I blushed. "Is it going to hurt, much?" The government tattooist had been just to the right of sadistic when she'd done the XVI on my wrist.

"Nah," he said. "I've got zone-out chips. You'll be fine."

"Mom has good salves, too, for when that wears off," Wei said.

"Well, let's get started." Colin drew the curtain behind him, inviting me into the back room.

I glanced over my shoulder at Wei and Chris. "We'll wait." Wei smiled reassuringly.

I followed him.

An hour later, Colin leaned back. "Well, what do you think?" he asked.

I flipped between my wrist and the back of my hand. Three "truth"s in cursive circled the XVI, latching onto each other like serpents. Curlicues snaked around to the back of my hand and became a stylized pond, where six small lotus flowers floated around a fully opened seventh that was poised on a long stalk. Antique print spelled out L O V E, one letter per finger above my knuckles.

I threw my arms around Colin's neck. "It's perfect! Just perfect!"

***

"Let me see again." Wei was in the backseat of the trannie with me, admiring my tattoo. "This is ultra-ultra. It's magic. Hell, yeah! The other girls will be crazy about this."

"I don't know how to thank you guys."

"No thanks needed." Chris's eyes met mine in the rearview. "I wanted you to have it. It fits you perfectly."

I felt my neck redden. "Thanks anyway," I said quietly to Wei.

***

Later on, Chris dropped off Dee and me for a brief visit with Gran.

"I am so glad you're here." Gran was sitting up in bed, still attached to the monitor, but it sounded strong. "What's this?" She snatched my hand. "Oh! Nina! It's beautiful." Her eyes misted. "You designed this, didn't you?"

"I did." My chest swelled with pride. Dee smiled at me, too.

"Ginnie was right to put you in those art classes. You have real talent."

I dared not tell her the ideas I had for using that talent.

"Oh, girls, I'm so happy. With everything—" Her voice cut off, and her eyes got watery.

"I know Gran. At least this part is okay," I said, hugging her close. "I wish we could stay longer, but they won't let us stay past the allotted time. Even though it's Holiday Eve. I love you."

"I love you, too, Gran," Dee said.

"I love you both, girls, more than you know." She clutched Dee's hand tight.

I leaned down and kissed Gran on the forehead. "I love you. I can't wait until you're home again. Happy Holiday."

***

I was hoping for a repeat of the night before, with all my friends, except we were going to watch Holiday vids instead of listening to Rogue Radio. Chris had gone out with some friends. And Sal's NonCon duties had called him away, again. He didn't know how long he'd be gone. Again. It wasn't fair. I'd seen my boyfriend for a nanosecond the last few days.

At least everyone else was there. It was almost like old times for me, hanging with Derek and Mike again. And Dee and Wei, too.

The warm apple pie in the kitchen was the fruit of Dee's latest labor. I was really impressed with her cooking. She was getting good—really good. She was also beat and fell asleep halfway through the second vid. Snuggled up together on the couch, Derek and Wei were not paying attention to anyone else. That left Mike and me munching on pie and watching *Joy on Mercury Way*.

"That's a good one," I said when it ended. "Let me find *Home for Holiday*."

Out of the blue, Mike said, "I've been meaning to ask you something about this whole FeLS scandal."

I froze. I hadn't expected this from Mike. But I should have. Joan was his sister.

"Do you think Joan was involved with that somehow? I mean, her two years were up a while ago. And we've never heard from her."

"I don't know," I hedged. "Maybe she got a job in one of the countries she was sent to. Sometimes girls . . ." Knowing what I

Julia Karr

knew, it was hard to come up with any kind of excuse.

"Joan isn't like that. Mom hasn't heard from her since a week after she left. It kills her. Especially at Holiday." He fiddled with the fork on his empty plate. "I miss her, too."

I felt awful keeping what I knew from Mike. It wasn't like he had a lot in his life. And he and Joan had been really close before she left. Like I'd done with Mom, after Ed beat her up, Joan had taken care of Mike after his dad's beatings. I longed to tell him about her, but his knowing the truth would put Joan in danger, and Mike, too. Especially if he saw the conditions she was forced to live in. I knew Mike, I knew what he'd do—rush in first, think later, and probably get himself arrested, or worse.

"I'm sure if she's heard about the investigation, she'll be in touch. I bet a lot of girls who haven't contacted their families will now."

"I sure hope so."

I said, "Me, too." Even though I knew she wouldn't be contacting anyone, at least not for a while.

XXVI

I'd expected Dee to be the one bounding out of bed at five a.m., not me. Although I didn't exactly bound. Even my usual burrowing under the covers couldn't coax more sleep, so I got up, went to the kitchen, and started our usual Holiday morning routine—fresh cinnamon rolls, coffee, and orange juice.

Dee padded into the kitchen as I was taking the rolls out of the cook center. "It smells just like Holiday." She sighed. "I wish Mom was here."

"Me, too." I filled a cup with coffee and stirred in two spoonfuls of sugar. Making the cinnamon rolls might not have been my best idea. Ginnie had always done it, though. I didn't want the day to be sad, but maybe that was just wishful thinking. How could it not be without her. Without Gran and Pops.

"What are you doing?" Dee asked. "You hate coffee."

"I'm learning to like it." I took a sip of the murky brew and promptly spat it into the sink.

Dee laughed. That was a better start to the morning.

"Let's go see if any presents miraculously appeared," Dee said.

I knew there would be one for Dee, from me.

"Lookie here." She sounded just like Pops. "A present for Little

Bit." She handed me a thin rectangular box, wrapped in silver paper with a gold bow on top.

"Lookie there." I'd hidden her present behind Gran's poinsettia. "Something for Deedles."

She retrieved a loose roll of paper with a ribbon tied around it. "I hope Pops is okay. Did you call?"

"Yeah. They won't let him have visitors." I didn't want Dee to start crying, or me either, for that matter. "I wonder what this could possibly be?" I held up the present she'd given me. "It's definitely not alive." Shaking it, I said, "No small parts. Hmmm . . ." I studied it. "I wonder what it—"

"Open it already!"

"You think?" I teased the ribbon loose and unsealed the paper. Inside was an animated digi of Ginnie and me. "Oh, Dee! It's ultra! How on earth did you do this?"

"Chris helped. He's so great."

Yeah, I thought, he is pretty great. First my tattoo, well, first helping us move and everything else he'd done since then . . . and how sweet he was.

"So what is this? A telescope?" She held the roll to her eye. "Nuh-uh. A straw?" She tried to get her mouth around it. "No way."

"Dee!"

"Yes, ma'am!" Untying the ribbon, she unrolled the paper to reveal a drawing of her at five years old, sitting in Mom's lap. They were reading a real book. She sucked in her breath. "It's the most beautiful thing I've ever seen." Her cheeks glistened. "This is the best present ever."

We finished off breakfast and had just settled in front of the FAV to watch *Home for Holiday*, since Dee'd slept through it last night and I could watch it a million times, when Dee's PAV beeped.

After a brief conversation, she clicked off and said, "That was Miss Maldovar. She's going to bring by some presents at ten."

"She is?"

Dee got up. "Yep. You think she'd like it if I made her cookies?"

"I'm sure she'll like anything you do." I did not understand this woman's big interest in Dee. Was it just a tender heart toward a girl who'd lost her mother? I was not likely to figure it out in the next few hours, so I turned on the FAV and zoned out on my favorite vid.

I kept an eye out for Miss Maldovar, not wanting her arrival to bother the Jenkinses. When a hire trannie pulled up, Dee was in the kitchen, so I ran to the front door. She came in, followed by the driver, who was loaded down with bags and boxes. He deposited the packages inside, and I couldn't help but notice his face when she tipped him. His Holiday was made.

"It smells wonderful in here," she said. "Who's the baker?"

"Dee. She's making some of our grandmother's Holiday recipes."

"I'm not surprised. She's so smart." She shrugged off her coat and threw it over the back of Pops's chair. "I hope you don't mind that I got a few presents for Dee. I know how difficult it must be for you with all the family issues you've had. I'm sure finding credits for presents was not high on your list of priorities."

"That's very nice of you." Something about the way she talked to me raised my hackles. The woman was a definite trigger for my danger radar—especially with the obscene number of presents she'd brought. One or two would've been normal; this was excess to the outer limits. "You really didn't need to do anything."

"I know. However, I wanted to. Dee's been such a big help to me so far. And as the semester progresses, I'm sure she'll continue to shine as my assistant." She glanced at the mountain of gifts. "I might have gone a little overboard, but it was so much fun buying for a Pre."

Dee came in from the kitchen. "Miss Maldovar!" She wiped her floury hands on the apron she was wearing, then she noticed the presents. "Those are for me?"

"Nearly all of them," Miss Maldovar said. "I did buy a few things for your sister." She flashed me an all-teeth, no-eye-crinkles smile. "I didn't want you to feel left out."

"Thanks." I should have been curious, and maybe I was a little, but mostly I wanted to know what was behind her generosity. "Would you like some coffee? Maybe some cookies?"

"Cookies for sure!"

Dee brought in a plate of cookies and set it on the table. Miss Maldovar watched as Dee unwrapped what ended up being an entire wardrobe of clothes and accessories from Mars 9. It must have cost Miss Maldovar a fortune.

She had gotten me a beautiful ultrachic sweater, TT brand all-weathers, and a gift certificate for two hundred credits at Mars 9. More than I could possibly have imagined.

Dee was modeling her new clothes for us when Wei came downstairs. It was her first introduction to Miss Maldovar, who was as smooth with Wei as she was with me.

"Mom sent me down to tell you that dinner's in an hour," Wei said. "And Chris was wondering if Dee would mind helping him with your grandmother's pie recipe."

"Let me change." Dee snatched up her new outfits. "I'll be right back."

"Are you spending Holiday with your family?" Wei asked Miss Maldovar.

"No," she said. "My parents are no longer with us, and my brother is out of the country."

"Oh, that's too bad." She frowned. "Tell Dee to come on up." As she opened the door, she motioned me over and whispered, "Do you mind if I ask Mom if she can stay for dinner? There's more than enough food, and it's kind of sad that she's alone."

"I guess not." I glanced over at Miss Maldovar, who was engrossed in her PAV receiver. "I don't trust her, but she's been more than nice to Dee and me. It can't hurt, right?"

"I'll call you right back." Wei rushed up the stairs, taking them two at a time. Practically before I sat back down, my PAV beeped. "Mom says ask her."

"Would you like to join us at the Jenkinses' for Holiday dinner?" I asked. "Mrs. Jenkins would love it if you could."

"What?" Dee came into the room. "Are you going to have dinner with us? That would be beyond ultra!"

"I guess it's settled, then," Miss Maldovar said. "Please, tell Mrs. Jenkins I'd love to join all of you."

"We'll come up in a few," I said to Dee. "I don't want to be in the way." And, as uncomfortable as I was around Maldovar, I thought maybe a bit of time alone with her might give me a clue as to why.

After Dee left, Miss Maldovar said, "I used to love Holiday. Up until I was a Pre, my parents would always buy my brother and me matching sweaters. After twelve, though, you don't necessarily want to look like your twin." She gave a wistful laugh. "Teddy and I were always close, though."

"You have a twin?" I said. "I've never met twins. Do you look alike?"

"No. We're fraternal."

"Does he live in Chicago?"

"No. He lives in the suburbs."

I hated small talk, but I kept on chatting. Something told me there was more to Miss Maldovar's story. I wasn't sure what, but I wanted to find out. "Do you see him often?"

"I used to, but I haven't seen him in a while." A disturbance crossed her face, so quickly I might have missed it if I hadn't been looking closely.

"I bet you miss him. I would be lost without Dee."

She gave me the oddest look. "I do miss him. Although as siblings grow older, they are not always as connected as when they were young."

I was running out of things to say. "Thank you again for coming to the hearing and giving us your support."

"I was glad to do what I could to assist Dee. Families should never be torn apart."

The ensuing silence lasted for what seemed like forever, until Dee walked in. "I want to wear one of my new outfits for dinner." She beamed at Miss Maldovar. "And I almost forgot the Holiday bread I made yesterday. It's my present to the Jenkinses."

Following her lead, I changed into my new TTs and the sweater, and upstairs we all went.

***

Dee and Chris's dinner was delicious. There was seitan roast stuffed with a nut-and-veggie mixture, mashed potatoes, the most delicious gravy (I'd never tell Gran it was better than hers, but it was!), fruit sauces, and a whole tableful of exotic foods I'd never heard of. And to top it off, Chris had baked two pies—cherry and Gran's green-tomato mince pie.

It was the first time I'd ever met Wei's older sister, Angie, and her husband, Leo. Angie and Leo were originally supposed to have our apartment, but they had turned it down. It didn't surprise me, now that I'd met them. They were so different from the rest of the Jenkins family. It was obvious that Angie didn't fit in with her family.

"We're going to Leo's parents' at four." Angie picked at her food.

While Miss Maldovar engaged Leo in small talk, Angie, who was sitting next to me, said, "Nice sweater."

"Thanks."

"And your sister"—she nodded toward Dee—"good taste. She looks like a *XVI Ways* vert."

Angie was right. Dee did look exactly like a Pre was supposed to, which bothered me. But she loved the clothes. Just because she was dressed that way didn't mean she thought like a Pre, or was going to act like one. People like Wei wore ultrachic, and she was about as far from being a snob or a sex-teen as anyone I knew.

As full as I was, my belly felt suddenly empty. You can't figure out who's who by appearances. No matter how much the government or the Media, or even your friends, say you can. You can't know who a person is unless you get to know him or her. *That* was the truth.

Wei snapped me out of my philosophical reverie. "You could take some of this food to your grandmother, if you want. Please?" She bent toward me conspiratorially. "Or we'll be eating leftovers till New Year's."

XXVII

After dinner, Angie and Leo offered to give Miss Maldovar a ride home on their way to Leo's folks. Wei sent Dee and me downstairs with bags of leftovers.

Dee and I made a quick visit to Gran with some of the food. She was in good spirits and ready to move to the rehab center. We didn't stay long because Maddie's mom was bringing her, and most of her Holiday bounty, over for the afternoon.

After Maddie arrived, I filled two bags with the rest of the leftovers Wei had insisted I take. My plan was to give them to Joan and the other homeless women. Chris was coming in as I was leaving. "You want a ride wherever you're going?" he asked. "That's a lot of stuff to carry on the transit."

"No thanks."

"You sure? I don't mind."

"I'm sure."

"Well, have fun." He held the door for me.

I was as eager to carry out my tasks alone as I was to stay away from Chris's twinkling eyes and ultra smile. Whenever I was with him, I felt a freedom I couldn't quite explain. He didn't try to save me or do things for me; instead, he treated me like I was equal to

Julia Karr

the tasks in front of me. That made me feel powerful. It was nice to know someone trusted me to take care of myself.

The bags full of food bumped against the transit steps as I got off in front of our old apartment building. I lugged them along the riverfront. There was no sign of life, except for me. Clouds scuttled across the bleak, winter sky, and a brisk wind swept down the choppy waters. My arms were killing me. Stopping at the DZ oasis, I pulled my coat collar tighter. "Maybe I'll use those credits at Mars 9 to get a new scarf." I'd taken one of Ginnie's from among her things, but it was too thin to provide much protection from the Chicago winds. I hoped my old scarf was keeping Joan warm.

No sooner had I thought that than I caught movement between two buildings. Grabbing the bags, I headed across the street, slipping into the shadows along with the homeless women. "Joan?"

She separated herself from the group and drew near to me. A gust of wind blew her hair back, and I noticed her neck was bare. "Where's the scarf I gave you?"

She flipped the collar of her tattered coat up and shook her head. "Why are you here?"

"Today's Holiday."

The other women circled around us. I felt, more than saw, their eyes rake over me. "She's the one that keeps coming around," said the woman who'd acted as Joan's protector earlier. "Get us in trouble with the checkerheads for sure."

I gave Joan a questioning look, but she cast her eyes down, toeing the snow with her worn shoes.

"I brought some food." I held out one of the bags to Joan. She stuck her hand inside and pulled out a container of leftover roast and potatoes. The woman who seemed to be in charge snatched it away from her.

"Trying to poison us?" She waved the container in front of me.

My mouth fell open. "Why would I do that? I'm Joan's friend."

"Homeless got no friends. Cleanup Committee sent you, didn't they? Been trying to get rid of us for months. Don't like us dirtying up their precious waterfront park." She swung her arm in the direction of the river. It was then I noticed my scarf around her neck.

"What are you doing with—"

Joan touched my arm. "I gave it to Svette," she whispered.

"Look." I pulled a plasticene fork from inside the bag, popped the lid off the container, and took a bite. "See? It's not poisoned."

That was enough to do it. The women swarmed over the food. Not bothering with utensils, they silently wolfed it down.

"I'll bring more soon," I said.

"You'll get caught," Joan said. "If the police see you doing this, they'll arrest you."

"They don't care," I said with much more confidence than I felt. Could I get arrested for feeding homeless? I supposed it was possible.

The women dispersed into the shadows, and I gathered up the bags and empty containers.

"You there," a voice called me to a halt.

I turned around and found myself face-to-face with a Chicago policewoman.

"Yes, Officer?" I kept my voice as steady as I could. After what Joan had said, I was terrified.

"ID." Her voice was sharp as the cold that cut through me.

She wanded my outstretched hand.

"The address on your ID is incorrect. You no longer live there." She jerked a thumb toward our old apartment building. "You were evicted."

"Yes, ma'am." At least my voice wasn't quivering as bad as my insides were. Had she been watching me? Did she know about the food? Was I going to be arrested?

"What's in the bag?"

"Empty food containers," I said.

She gave a cursory glance to the empty bags before focusing more of her attention on the surrounding neighborhood. "Robbery earlier. A deserted riverfront's no place to be hanging out alone. I suggest you go home. And see that you get that address fixed. If it wasn't Holiday, I'd give you a citation."

Lucky me.

***

After Maddie left, Dee and I spent the rest of the evening putting together outfits with the clothing and accessories that Miss Maldovar had given to Dee. By the time we were through, it was long past Dee's usual bedtime, and I was exhausted, too.

I was nearly asleep when Sal called. "Wish I was there with you right now."

The mere sound of his voice sent tingles through my body. "Isn't there some way that I can go with you when you do whatever it is you and John do?" I asked.

"Absolutely not. What we're doing is, well . . . dangerous."

"Isn't everything related to the Resistance dangerous?" The

warm feeling I'd had melted away. "Just because I'm a girl doesn't mean I'm helpless."

"I know that. But, well, in some ways you are. I mean, the whole Ed thing . . ." His voice trailed off.

I was warm again—actually downright hot—but with anger. "I didn't have a choice. Wei needed help. There wasn't anyone else to call."

"That's what I mean. Besides, how could you have moved his body, huh? Deadweight. It took two hulking guys to—"

"So? It might have taken three or four girls to do the same, but we could've done it. Girls are just as capable . . . Take my mom— she was a NonCon. She managed to get all that information about FeLS and—"

"Look at what happened to her."

I drew in a sharp breath. "How. Dare. You," I clicked off before he could say another word. If it hadn't been for Dee asleep in the next room and the Jenkinses overhead, I would've screamed. Could Sal not see that I was just as capable as he was in fighting for what was right? My mother's sacrifice for the cause was no less valid or less important than some guy's. Men were killed just as easily as women. Murder was not gender-specific.

Wrestling my way out of the tangle of blankets, I stumbled out of bed and over to the window. The moon cast tree shadows on the snowy ground, and I stared at them until my feet were frozen. Crawling back into the bed, I couldn't turn off the thoughts.

My dad had been the one to go underground, leaving my mother and me supposedly out of danger. While he was fighting from the relative safety of secret hideouts—like Aunt Rita's place—

Ginnie had put herself in danger every moment of every day. And not just to keep my father's secret safe, but to discover the truth about FeLS. With Ed as her only connection to the truth, she had endured beatings and abuse whenever he felt like it. She dropped down tiers for the cause—she had been a tier-five once and had died a tier-two.

My anger at Sal spread like the latest vert campaign, covering every man I knew, including my long-lost father; finally, I drifted off into a fitful sleep

XXVIII

There was nothing like an Alert with breakfast. For months, the country had gone without any at all, but now we were at the third in less than a week. The FeLS news was big. Since Dee had already seen the one about Ed, I included her. We sat in the kitchen, watching a projected Kasimir Lessig on the wall.

"Investigators are closing in on the mystery woman believed to be Edward Chamus's accomplice. Although her identity is still unknown, the wife of the missing man has been cleared of any wrongdoing."

Lessig swung around to face the camera full on.

"In related news, several girls who were abused at the fraudulent FeLS training station have come forward."

Images of girls—their blank, expressionless stares interspersed with the haunted terror that I'd seen in Joan's eyes—flashed on the wall.

"These unfortunate young women are even now on a transport to a safe facility on the Dark Side, where they will be assessed and treated for the traumas they've endured. After a time, they will, hopefully, be ready to return to mainstream society." A number ran across the projection, under Lessig's face. "Some of these girls were so terribly damaged that they fled in terror when authorities approached them. To facilitate the assistance and aid of these poor girls, the Governing Council is offering an unprecedented fifty thousand credits for information leading to the procurement of any girl who was subjected to the illegal training and has somehow managed to escape the clutches of the alleged perpetrator, Edward Chamus."

As he repeated the number and calling instructions, Dee leaped up. "Fifty thousand? You don't know any girls that happened to, do you? That's a megaton of credits. Just think, you'd be helping some poor girl, and we'd be up-tiered."

"Dee, did you not hear what Lessig said?" I shut off the projection.

"Yeah." Dee cocked her head. "He said they're going to help any girls who were sent to that fake FeLS training."

"No, they're taking those girls to some secret location on the Dark Side. When they come back, they will have been reassimilated. There won't be *anyone* left to tell the truth about who was involved in the training, or who those girls were given to afterward. You could tell just by looking at them that they'd already been drugged."

"Really? You don't think the GC wants to know who all's involved?"

"Exactly." I pressed my lips together. The time for telling Dee about the Resistance was getting closer. "I'd bet even some of the top men in the GC are involved."

"What about that woman they're talking about?" Dee's forehead wrinkled. "I don't understand how a woman could let men do ... that ... to girls who were supposed to be virgins. Who thought they were ..." A look of horror crossed her face. "I have to apply for FeLS when I turn fifteen. What if all this stuff is still happening then?"

"Deeds, I've got a job. I'll have plenty of credits by then to buy out your contract. Don't worry. There may not even be a FeLS program in four years. Which reminds me, what do you want for your birthday? It's coming up pretty soon."

She braved a smile. "I don't want anything. Except maybe for Gran and Pops to be home. I miss them."

"Me, too."

***

Later that morning, Dee was poring over Gran's cook center cards, while I stayed in my room drawing. I was working on a series of pictures of homeless people whom I'd seen over the years.

One was of a man, frozen on the street. An image I wasn't likely to forget, ever. I'd been all of eight and in the city with Mom, Ed, and Dee. Mom and Dee were shopping, and Ed had taken me with him to pick up some vids. The homeless guy was lying just inside an alley entrance. Ed dragged me over to show him to me. "*This* is what happens when you don't follow the rules," he growled.

The man's head was stuck to the sidewalk in ice. His sightless eyes stared up at the snow pelting down on him. He was dead. I'd puked on Ed's shoes, which really pissed him off. That night he sent me to Sandy's with Dee. Next day, Mom had a black eye.

I looked at the drawings, people of all ages, and reached for my PAV.

"Hey, Dorrie, it's Nina. Can we talk about Rogue Radio and vid interruptions?"

***

Dorrie lived in an apartment with her dad. Her mom had run off to New York with a maintenance guy. Dorrie had never heard from her again. I guessed that was probably for the best. She and her dad looked like they were doing all right. They were tier three; he was a production grower at the Chicago Botanical Gardens, and their apartment was full of plants. He was also a NonCon.

"So"—I handed her a tube of my drawings—"here they are. You think you can do something with them?"

She spread out the pictures and studied them, scrunching up her mouth and tipping her head from one side to the other. "Hang on. Let me get my recorder."

Half an hour later, she had recorded all the images and was already selecting music to go along with the program she was imagining.

"This will be brilliant, Nina. I don't get to do nearly enough vid interruptions. I'm thinking right in the middle of *Vacation Destinations of the Ultra-Riche*. What do you think?"

"Perfect."

On the way home, I hatched up a further plan and called Wei. "Can you meet me in fifteen minutes downstairs?"

When I walked in, Wei had Dee in a headlock on the living room floor.

"What are you guys doing?"

"I was teaching Dee some Cliste Galad moves. She asked . . ."

"I'm going to learn it." Dee stood up. "I need to get back to the kitchen. Chili tonight."

"Dee is so cool," Wei said. "It won't be long before you have to tell her about the Resistance. She'll figure it out if you don't. Or she'll accidentally let something slip."

"I know," I said. "I'm not exactly sure how to tell her. I'll figure it out. Listen, come to my room."

I unrolled the drawings on my bed. "What do you think?"

"Like I said before, your sketches are as powerful as your dad's speeches."

"Well, what would you think if we, as Pops used to say, 'painted the town,' so to speak?"

"What are you talking about?"

I told her about Dorrie creating a vid interruption. "She's going to broadcast it during that show about ultrarich vacationers. I was thinking, what if we posted these around town? We'd have to do it after dark."

"And we'd need a getaway trannie. I wish I could drive." She drew her fingers across her chin. "I'd say Sal or Chris, but I don't want them to be part of this. This is for the Sisterhood."

"Yeah," I agreed. I thought back to how I had left things with Sal the night before. He hadn't tried to call me, and there were no messages on my PAV either.

"What about Paulette? Would you hate that?"

Yes. But I didn't say so. "Not if you promise *not* to talk about Sal. Or her party."

"I promise." Wei held up her hand. "So, what's going on with Sal. You're mad at him, huh?"

I gave her the short version of my previous night's conversation with Sal.

"Guys can be so ridiculous when it comes to realizing that girls are just as capable as they are. And women are as good of fighters as men. Fems *did* have control of the country for nearly fifty years."

"Yeah, I know." I didn't mention that the Fem government had been completely swallowed up, without any kind of fight, by the Governing Council.

Mom had said that Media influence undermined the effectiveness of the Fems by implying they hated men. It didn't matter that many of the Fem leaders were wives and mothers. Media began broadcasting subtle anti-Fems messages, combined with bombardments of verts glorifying the sexualization of women and teen girls and implying that the only strength women had was in their sexuality. Eventually, the tide turned, and the GC took over and partnered with Media. Leaving women and girls as mere sex objects.

"Nina, Sal can be reasoned with," Wei said. "I'm sure it's because he's so crazy about you that he worries something will happen to you. That's the excuse my dad uses, at least."

"What about your mom? Doesn't he worry about her?"

"Do you think my mother would let anyone stop her from doing anything she wants?"

Knowing Mrs. Jenkins, I chuckled. "Nope."

"Dad's figured that out, too." She shifted to face me. "So have you tried calling Sal?"

"No, and I'm not going to. I don't know what I'd say to him. I hate that he's out there, doing NonCon whatever and is in danger of being discovered, and we left everything so badly."

"So call him. Now."

I thought about it. It didn't matter how angry I was, I loved Sal. I didn't want it to end; I just wanted him to understand how I felt. I picked up my PAV, then put it down.

Finally, I picked it up again and sent him a message: "Sorry I got mad. I love you."

I turned to Wei. "You want to call Paulette?"

After a short PAV conversation, Wei said, "Eight o'clock tonight. I'd better get upstairs and practice piano. See you later. Wear black."

XXIX

"I'm going out with some friends for a bit," I told Dee.

"No problem," she said. "Miss Maldovar sent me a message to call her when I could. She wants to talk about the first week back after break."

What was it about that woman that bothered me? I went out into the foyer to wait for Wei, and called Dorrie. "Can you find out information on people, like family backgrounds and such?"

"Sure," Dorrie said. "It might take a while, but it can be done. Who is it?"

"Adana Maldovar," I said. "My sister Dee's teacher."

"I'll see what I can find. By the way, I showed Brie what we worked on. She's impressed."

I was glad she hadn't asked me why I wanted the info, because I wouldn't have been able to come up with a good answer. But there was something, of that I was sure.

Thank goodness Paulette didn't show up in her dad's stretch transit. I was surprised that the trannie she had was so unassuming.

"What exactly are we doing?" Paulette asked. "All you said was that we had a mission."

"Can we talk in here?" Wei asked.

"Yeah. Sal took care of this one. We use it a lot."

I held my tongue. Sal had told me he wasn't interested in her—that should be good enough. Of course, the little voice in my head insisted, that was before you told him off and hung up on him. I didn't have time to listen to that—what we were planning was important.

"We're doing a little art show." Wei uncovered the copies of my drawings that she'd made. "You drive, I'll be the lookout, and Nina will post her sketches."

"This should be fun." Paulette eased the trannie into gear. "Where to first?"

"State Street," Wei said. "Mag gave me seven locations where she knows the surveillance cameras are down."

Our first stop was on State Street, near the Chicago Omniplex. Paulette pulled into the alley, and Wei and I hopped out. I secured two posters, one facing north, one south; Wei watched out for passersby. That one was easy.

We nearly got caught on Oak Street when a doorman told Paulette she couldn't park where she'd stopped. I had to admit, though, she was smoother than smooth. Not only did she talk him into allowing her to stay, but he said if she ever needed free parking downtown while he was on duty, he'd find her a spot in the hotel lot. I was sure I saw her give him a tip card, too.

The other five stops were quick and easy. After the last one, we drove back by the first location to see if they were still there. They were. And they'd drawn a crowd. We didn't dare go by the one on Oak, for fear the doorman might recognize Paulette's trannie. A Media van was stopped at the third one—which was across from the Justice Building. The crew was taking pictures.

"I'd say you've made an impression," Wei said.

"Looks like she'll also make the news at eleven," Paulette said.

"Except no one will know it's me," I said. "And that's a good thing."

"Yeah, well," Paulette said. "It's late. I have to get home. Last-minute party arrangements."

Wei glanced back at me. I shook my head. Paulette didn't need to know that I'd been invited. And Wei didn't need to know that I had no intention of going.

***

Next morning Dee insisted that I go to Mars 9. "They have tons of stuff on their sale racks, Nina. I know you can find something ultra!"

"You want to come with me?" Maybe some of her excitement would rub off on me.

"No. I promised Miss Maldovar that I'd do some research on the Museum of Science and Industry. We're taking a field trip there in February." She picked up her cup of cocoa and trotted back to her room. "Get something cute!" she called out before she shut her door.

"Great." I trudged back to my room and grabbed the gift certificate. "I'm not going to that stupid party," I muttered. "I'm getting a new scarf."

Just then my PAV beeped.

"Nina, it's Martin. Percy will not leave me alone until I confirm that you are coming to the party, don't you know? He's absolutely smitten with you. I should be so jealous. But I'm smitten, too. Are you coming?"

"Martin, I . . . I don't think it's a good idea. I don't think it's the kind of thing for me. I'm only tier—"

"Nonsense, Nina. You are a *Creative*. And you are my assistant. And as such, you need to learn to associate with these people, like it or not. But listen, if you don't have anything to wear, I'd love to take care of that. We could go shopping at—"

"No, please. I've got a gift credit at Mars 9. I was just going shopping. I'm sure I can find something perfect there." Martin was right, if I was going to do anything in the art world, I was going to have to do things like this. I was going to Paulette's whether I wanted to or not. And I was definitely on the "not" side of things.

"Fabulous! I'm off to tell Percy. See you at work tomorrow. Hugs and smooches."

As I was pulling on my coat, I thought about my scarf, which made me think of Joan, which made me think of food. It was one thing to give to the homeless on Holiday, but people needed to eat every day. I made a detour into the kitchen and threw together a dozen nut butter sandwiches. It wasn't much, but it wasn't rotten garbage either.

***

I got off the transit at my old stop, thoroughly checking for any sign of that lady cop before ducking behind the buildings. I'd walked the whole length of the alley and was about to give up when I heard some female voices around a corner.

"I heard it myself. They're offering fifty thousand for any escaped FeLS. We could get into one of those welfare dorms, you and me," an eager voice said.

"We are not turning in anyone. Period. Understand?" The responding voice was threatening.

"Okay. I was only tryin' to help."

"It's not help if you turn on your own."

I couldn't hear the muttered reply. Their footsteps crunched on the snow, coming closer. I spun around the corner, out onto the street. As soon as they passed between the buildings, they saw me. One of the women was Svette. She motioned me over.

"I brought you more food," I said. "It's just leftovers, but—"

"Better'n nothing." The second woman snatched the food from my hands.

It was impossible for me to tell which of the two had wanted to turn Joan in.

Svette squinted one eye at me. "You're being nice to us 'cause of Joan? Why? What d'ya want?"

"Joan's a friend. I help my friends when I can." I backed away. "Tell her I'll see her soon." With that, I hurried off. I was pretty sure the cold had nothing to do with the chill that ran down my spine. With that "reward" for escaped FeLS, Joan was in danger. The Sisterhood had to do something. And soon.

***

Mars 9's Holiday scenes still played in the windows. Girl mannibots pranced around in skintight pleather pants and faux-shearling jackets over skimpy tops that left nothing to the imagination. I could almost hear Gran admonishing one of these "girls" to "cover up, before you freeze to death . . . or worse."

My heart skipped a beat when a real, live person opened the door wide, welcoming me in. I hesitated for an overlong moment.

Even with the gift credit in my pocket, I felt like a fraud. Two top-T's came up behind me.

"Are you going in or just gawking, sludge?" They pushed past me.

The man holding the door flashed me an apologetic smile. "Won't you come in? We have megasales going on right now. It's the best time to find exactly what you didn't get for Holiday."

I muttered a thank-you and scurried past him, not stopping to look at anything until I was deep in the store. Shoes. I was surrounded by every kind of ultrachic shoe a girl could want. On my right were sweaters. Spying the one Miss Maldovar had given me, I couldn't resist. I checked the price. Damn! How could a teacher afford even one gift from here, let alone the massive piles of clothes she'd gotten for Dee? She must be doing something besides teaching, I thought. Maybe she pushes animal flesh. The thought of Miss Maldovar, doling out packages of meat from the chiller in her home, made my stomach turn.

"May I help you?" I was accosted by a salesclerk who was dressed ten times more fashionably than I could ever hope to be. "Our sale racks are in the basement. That way." Her nose wrinkled, her comet-red nail pointing the way. Even the people who sell to top-tiers look down on everyone below their customers.

"I'm shopping for a party dress." I wished I'd worn my new sweater. Even if I didn't have enough credits to look at anything full priced, I was not going to let this jerk of a salesgirl make me feel like, well, like what those girls had called me—a sludge.

She arched a brow. "Evening gowns are on the second floor. Elport is there and elsteir over there." Giving me one last derisive look, she stalked off to pounce on a more worthy customer.

Convinced that she was still watching me, I took the elsteir up, and then, without so much at a glance at clothes I'd never be able to afford, I took the elport to the basement. A knot of high school girls were picking over the dress remains, pulling them off the rack and making fun of either the quality or how "ridiculously expired" they were. When I glanced at the sale tag on one that didn't look too terribly dated, I nearly passed out.

I slunk out of the store, defeated.

"You can't wear that, Nina." Dee dropped onto my bed. "Isn't there something just a little more ultra in Mom's clothes?"

I shut the closet door. "The only thing close to ultra is older than me—too old to be chic and too new to be vintage. I won't go."

"You have to go to this party. You told me you promised your boss." When I'd gotten home from shopping, I told Dee my plans for New Year's.

"I did. But I'll have to tell him I don't have anything to wear. And . . . I'm not taking any credits from him to buy a dress. It wouldn't be right."

"What wouldn't be right?" Wei walked into the room.

I told her about not being able to find a dress I could afford at Mars 9. "So I'll just not go." I shrugged. I didn't really mind missing the party. I did, however, hate to disappoint Martin and Percy.

"Oh, yes, you will. Come on." She latched onto my arm. "You, too." She hauled Dee off the bed and dragged both of us up to her room.

Sitting on Wei's bed, I said, "I can't fit into your clothes. We're not built the same."

She twisted her mouth over to one side as she studied me. "Wait right here."

A few minutes later she returned, her arms full of dresses.

Dee's mouth fell open. "Those are beautiful!"

"They're Mom's." She laid the clothes on the bed. "Borrow anything that fits. And get this . . . Mom's offered to fix your hair. I'm telling you. You're getting the ultra-ultra Jenkins treatment. She is a galactic genius when it comes to styling. You will look light-years beyond ultrachic."

"Like Cinderella—the one with the fairy-tale ending," I said.

After trying on every single dress, I decided on a red silk Asian-inspired gown embroidered with a crane and lotus flowers.

"That's Mandarin style," Wei said. "Very traditional. Fits you perfectly, and it matches your tattoo."

Twisting my wrist back and forth in front of the dress, I studied the reflection in the mirror. "Almost like it was made for me."

"Wait till Mom's done with the hair and makeup. You'll be more ultrachic than Paulette. And that's not easy to do."

Mrs. Jenkins tapped at the door. "May I come in?"

"Look at Nina," Dee said. "She's beautiful!"

"Yes, she is." Mrs. Jenkins ran her fingers through my hair. "I think a few twists, like so . . ." She deftly coiled a lock atop my head.

"Here." Wei handed her mom a couple of two-pronged lacquered sticks.

Mrs. Jenkins secured the twist with the sticks. Then she feathered out a few strands on either side of my face and arranged my bangs. "There." She stepped aside so I could see my reflection. "What do you think?"

"I love it!" I turned my head to different angles. "But it doesn't look like me."

"Yes, it does. It's you in this dress and these ornaments. There are many different ways to look and to be. The essential Nina is still inside. It's only when we allow the outer trappings to dictate our inner feelings that we lose sight of ourselves."

"Nothing from Mars 9 would look that good," Dee said. "You're an original."

I studied myself in the mirror. Original. A smile nudged the corners of my mouth. Even ultrachic wasn't original.

"I'm going up to my greenhouse to water and prune the herbs," Mrs. Jenkins said. "Would you like to help me, Dee?"

The door closed behind them, and Wei said, "Your sister is so great. Between Chris's cooking lessons and my mom's herbals, she'll know how to do all those things that I'm afraid I've disappointed my mother by not wanting to learn."

"Dee loves to do things with her hands," I said. "I have to figure out something she can do to get her Creative designation. She doesn't like to draw."

"Cooking," Wei said. "She's a natural chef. And with Chris's tutoring, she'd pass with flying colors!"

"You are brilliant. Now help me out of this dress. I have to tell you what I found out today. The Sisterhood is going to have to move. Fast."

Wei removed the hair sticks while I shimmied out of the dress and into my regular clothes.

"Joan is in danger. You heard that Alert about the GC looking for girls who got away from the fake FeLS training? Well, I overheard a couple of women in the group of homeless that Joan hangs with. One of them wants to turn Joan in for the reward."

"Skivs!" Wei scooted the pile of dresses aside, and we sat on her bed. "I guess I shouldn't ask what you were doing that put you in a position to hear these women."

"I've been taking them food. Joan's cold and hungry all the time. Svette, who lords all over them, took the scarf I gave her. I don't like Svette."

Wei gnawed on her lip. "Okay, let's call everyone. We need to take matters into our own hands."

In a few minutes all the girls were projected on Wei's wall. I caught them up on what I'd heard.

"The first thing is to get Joan away from those women," Brie said. "Do we have any safe houses in town where she can go for a night or two? My uncle can usually help, but if we involve him, the guys will take over the whole scheme."

"That won't do," I said. "She's terrified of men. She barely allows women to help. The only man I know she tolerates near her is the doctor who's been helping her. If a strange guy came up to her, it might push her over the edge. She's come too far for that to happen."

"I overheard my dad talking to one of his friends after that Alert," Dorrie said. "He said maybe it's best for some of them to be treated. At least they won't remember the horrors that happened to them."

"That's not true," I said. "Joan's had some help from that doctor—he gives her meds and basic care on the sly. She's so much better than when I first saw her. It's not right to wipe away all of a person's past, even if some of it is bad. The GC's doing this only so that no FeLS girl will be able to identify her abusers."

"I'm not afraid of a fight." Brie rubbed her chin. "It's just that, well, we've never done anything like this before."

"I say we figure something out," Paulette said. "We can do it."

Paulette supporting me? I kept my expression as bland as possible, to hide my shock.

"It wouldn't be much of a sisterhood if we didn't stick together." Mag nodded. "I'm in."

"All right," Brie said. "It's going to take a day or so to find somewhere to put her until we figure out how to get her out of town."

"Why out of town?" I asked.

"She won't be safe here," Wei said. "Not with that group of homeless knowing about her, and not with so many B.O.S.S. agents around. Out of the country would be even better. I wonder . . . Let me ask my mother about our relatives in Japan."

"She'll tell your father. We'll be stopped," I said.

"Trust me. She won't tell Dad."

"How would we ever get her to Japan?" Mag asked.

"Someone will have to go with her," I said. "She's not capable of making it on her own. Even though she's getting better under this doctor's care, she's still really fragile."

Everyone looked at Wei. "I guess it will have to be me," she said. "Oh well, I haven't seen those relatives . . . yeah, ever. I'm sure they won't mind me popping in for a surprise visit." She pursed her lips. "You know, it will be good research for Sociology. I'll set it up as a school project. Dad can't object to that."

"I think I know how we can do it, too," Brie said. "Uncle

Alfonse has a veljet he's been tinkering with for a couple of years. It's robo-controlled, and if Mag can map out a flight plan, Dorrie can program the controls. Right?"

"Uh-huh," Dorrie said. "As long as I have the coordinates."

I was already envisioning Joan on her way to freedom. "Can your uncle fly them there?"

"He's on the Dark Side for the next month," Brie said.

"A month! We can't wait that long. It could be too late."

"Besides, the veljet holds only two people," she said.

"It won't need a pilot," Dorrie said. "The preprogrammed coordinates and robo-pilot will take care of that. The only thing we'll need is to get Joan to it, or it to Joan. I'm guessing it will be easier to get her to the hangar. It's at Sal's aunt Rita's place."

"I knew we could do this." I was pumped.

"Won't work." Wei was shaking her head. "There's too much security. We'll be spotted the minute we set foot on Rita's property."

"Well, then . . ." Dorrie said. "We need to bring the veljet to her."

"Right." Mag stared pointedly at Dorrie. "Where are you gonna park a veljet in Chicago without the authorities being all over it in light speed?"

"Much as I'd love to know the answer to that," Paulette said, "call me when you have it figured out. I've got to go help my mother with this party." She clicked off.

"I've got to go, too," Brie said. "Don't worry, Nina. We'll figure it out. Your friend deserves to be safe." She clicked off.

"Sorry, Nina. But I know we'll think of something." Mag's image disappeared.

Dorrie just said, "Bye."

Wei and I stared at the blank wall for several seconds. Then she said, "I'm going to talk to Mom about Japan. And don't worry. She won't tell Dad. She doesn't agree with him about keeping girls out of the fray. Your mother and mine were taking on the government as far back as when they were passing notes written in invisible ink in grade school. She understands."

Half an hour later, Mag sent a message to the rest of us: "Brie, Dorrie, and I were talking. We came up with an idea."

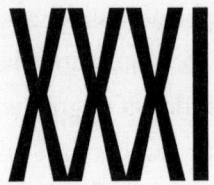

XXXI

I was busy cataloging a shipment of early twenty-second-century performance-art chips when Martin joined me. "Are you all ready for New Year's Eve? Have you found a dress? Percy has been pestering me mercilessly, don't you know? He's so excited about your being there."

"Uh-huh." I didn't want to tell him how uncomfortable I felt about spending the evening in the same space as Paulette. And I also didn't want to disappoint Percy and him. Besides, there was all the trouble that Mrs. Jenkins was going to to make me presentable.

"I know it can be a little overwhelming, your first top-tier event, but with you working at the Institute, I promise it won't be your last."

I smiled, a whole lot more enthusiastically than I felt.

"Don't stay too late. Sleep in tomorrow morning and nap in the afternoon. Well rested is the best makeup. Oh, by the way, we're sending a stretch trannie for you. I promised Mrs. Gold I'd come early to bless the decorations. And"—he leaned forward, conspiratorially—"to rearrange them if need be. She is, after all, from New York, where people still labor under the illusion that they live in the center of all things fashionable." He rolled his eyes and sniff-snorted before straightening up. "I sound like such a snobbitch. I'm not, really. And I do like Mrs. Gold, she's—" He was interrupted by an insistent beep from his chronos. "Oh, dear. If I don't hurry, I'll be late. Remember, home early, lots of sleep." He patted my cheek. "I know you'll be the belle of the ball."

As soon as he was gone, I took my receiver out of my bag and uploaded a message from Dorrie. Transferring the digi to a piece of paper, I had in front of me a map of all the hidden passages in the Art Institute. Turning on my PAV's GPS recorder, I stepped through one of the doors and into the corridors behind the exhibit halls.

Having no idea who, besides Martin and myself, used the passageways, I left my LED off and navigated by the dimly lit wall sconces that flanked the doors to each exhibit space. In between those I was on my own.

I was recording the route, making excellent time, when one of the doors in front of me swung open. Plastering myself against the wall, I sucked in my breath, possible excuses for my presence racing through my brain.

"Can't you read?" a man's voice asked. "Employees only."

"Sorry, I was looking for the men's room," another voice said.

"I'll have to run a scan on you first. Security procedure when a door is breached. If you'll just stand over—" Something banged up against the wall, and I heard a shout. "Stop that man!

That was the last thing I heard before the door slammed shut. My heart was still racing and my knees trembled, but I eventually got myself together and pressed on. With no further scares, it took me maybe an additional two minutes to get to the roof. I knew the door code from the list Martin had given me. All the codes needed to be memorized in case of fire or other disaster. I held my breath as I keyed it in. Success. I walked out onto the roof. A few yards in front of me was a helipad, more than big enough to land a tiny veljet.

Back inside, I locked the door and retraced my steps via the recorded route. It took three minutes and fifteen seconds to get from the roof to the storeroom. I stepped into the office foyer and quickly sent the route information to Dorrie, then erased it from my receiver. The last thing I needed was to be stopped on the way out and have my PAV checked. Security occasionally ran random searches on employees, and after that incident with the guy earlier, I wasn't taking any chances.

***

When I got home, the house smelled like cookies. Following my nose into the kitchen, Dee and Chris were busy whipping up a batch of something delicious.

"Macaroons," Dee said. "You want one?"

"Sure!" I reached for the baking sheet.

"Be careful," Dee said. "I just now took them out of the cook center."

"The ones on the back row are cooled," Chris said.

I selected one that was exactly the right side of warm. "Yum!"

"Chris knows everything about cooking." Dee gazed up at him.

"I know just enough." He tousled her hair. "You're a good student. Listen, I'd better get upstairs. I promised Mom I'd cook dinner tonight." From the doorway, he turned and said, "Don't forget, Dee. We've got a date tomorrow night. Dinner and vids—your choice. See ya."

"Date? I thought you were going to Maddie's?" I snuck another macaroon.

"I was, but she's sick. Her mom thought it would be better if I didn't come over. I might catch what she's got. Anyway, Chris is staying home and wondered if I wanted to watch movies with him. It's okay, isn't it?"

"Of course." Staying home with Dee would've been a perfect excuse for me to get out of going to the party. Gah. I was still thinking of backing out. I had to stop that. The wheels were in motion, and I couldn't get off the express if I wanted to.

Tomorrow night. I wrapped my arms around myself. The only thing keeping me from being absolutely abysmal was knowing that Mrs. Jenkins would make me look good. Small consolation. I trudged down the hall into my room, where I took out my art supplies and spent the next hour sketching what I planned on being the start of my next vid interruption.

XXXII

Between Wei, her mother, and Dee, I didn't have much of a say in how I spent New Year's Eve day. Their excitement was contagious, and I didn't even have to fake a smile when Wei took the digis of me.

"Ultragorgeruso," Dee exclaimed. "You look like a vid star. Can I have your autograph, Miss Oberon?" She held out an imaginary rapido and paper.

I was afraid I would stab myself with the Kanzashi sticks in my hair, or that I'd topple over in the heels I was wearing. I did have to admit, as I surveyed the final product of Mrs. Jenkins's ministrations—I looked hot. Not like myself, but ultrahot. Or maybe it was a part of me I was afraid to explore. That part that wanted to be attractive and sexy. There was no time to think about that further, because the stretch arrived.

"Have fun!" Dee carefully hugged me.

"Happy New Year!" Wei gave me air kisses on either cheek.

"Be careful," Mrs. Jenkins said.

Even behind the dark windows of the trannie, I felt exposed. Which I most surely would be when I walked into Paulette's. The dress, the hairstyle, the shoes—none of it mattered if my brain kept calling me an impostor.

"Are you ready, miss?" the driver asked.

I tore my eyes away from the steady stream of top-tiers being admitted to the building. "Uh . . . I, um . . . give me a nanosec. Please?" Was I being a snob, asking him to wait? I opened my borrowed clutch and took out a mirror, pretending to adjust my hair—which I dared not touch for fear of messing it up.

My PAV beeped. "Are you here, Nina? Percy's going to pull a neck muscle looking for you."

"I'm downstairs, Martin. I'll be right up." At least I knew he and Percy wanted me to be there. What Paulette's reaction would be was anyone's guess. "I'm ready," I told the driver.

In a flash, he had the door opened, his hand extended to help me out. "Have a wonderful evening, miss."

"Thank you." I wondered if I should tip him, with my nonexistent tip cards, but he was back in the stretch and gone before that thought was fully formed. I was left with no choice but to go inside. The man at the door inspected me. Apparently, I passed his approval. "Name, please?"

"Nina Oberon."

"First elport on the left, penthouse suite."

"Thank you." At least my voice was steady, even if I wasn't.

Tucked into a corner of the elport with a mass of partygoers, I closed my eyes, wishing the night was already over.

Nothing could've prepared me for the spectacle on the other side of the elport doors. Sure, Wei was top tier, but her house was comfortable, real, a place where I felt easy. Granted, Paulette's penthouse was decorated for a gala New Year's Eve party, but even without the decorations, I would've felt like I'd stepped into a vid. Everything was sleek, shiny, and oozed ultrachic—just like Paulette.

Like sale shoppers at Mega World, the people in the elport pushed past me, melting into the other revelers. Before the doors closed, I stepped into the swarm. As I inched my way through the crowd searching for Martin and Percy, a familiar voice said, "You're the last person I expected to see tonight."

"Paulette." I wasn't sure what to expect. She'd been almost friendly the last couple of times I'd seen her. Tonight, however, she was anything but. Her icy scrutiny left me feeling for all the universe like a protozoa under a microscope.

"What are you doing here?" she asked.

All the apprehension I'd felt about coming, and all the concerns about what a bunch of top-tiers would think of me, was pushed aside by her attitude. "I'm with Martin Long and Percy Bunton. And if you don't mind, I'm looking for them right now." I tried to push past her, but she snatched my arm.

"I saw your name as their guest, but I didn't think you'd actually show. Nina, you should've told me you were coming," she said. "Be careful. You are so out of your league."

I wrenched out of her grasp. "That's your opinion." I stalked off, sure that my face was as red as the baubles Mrs. Jenkins had woven into my hair.

I'd turned down three drinks and a plate of hors d'oeuvres before I finally heard a welcome voice.

"Nina, over here." I spotted Percy, waving frantically.

Somehow I managed to weave through the other partiers. "I

didn't think I'd ever find you. I am so relieved to see a friendly face. Where's Martin?"

"Marty's there—somewhere." He swept his arm out across the expanse of people. "Oh, see?" He pointed with his drink. "Those are the Golds. Like an Adonis, isn't he?"

I raised my eyebrow.

"Oh, all right, she is, too. And look at my Marty, working them for all the credits they're worth. All for the Institute. Ever the fund-raiser." He gazed admiringly at his partner, before setting his cocktail down and placing his hands on my shoulders. "Let's have a look at you." Twirling me around, he nodded appreciatively. "So retro-ultra-Asian. Jade did the hair, didn't she?" He slapped his hand to his chest and looked skyward. "She *is* the hair goddess. And you, my dear, you are *the* god-dess."

My neck warmed. "Can we not talk about me?"

"Oh, my sweet Nina. Everyone is already talking about you." He leaned close. "Look at the way they're sneaking peeks at you over their drinks or over their companions' shoulders. You're putting these ultrachic snobbitches to shame." With a gesture, he summoned a waiter. "I'm sure you haven't eaten a thing, have you?"

"I'm not hungry." And I certainly wasn't enjoying the thought of being the topic of everyone's conversation. Percy was right: people were looking at me, and commenting—and creeping me out. "Maybe we should join Martin?"

"First, I want to introduce you to someone who's been dying to meet you." Percy secured my elbow and guided me through the masses.

I saw Paulette watching us. She's probably thinking I'll ruin her party. Percy threaded us through the crowd, and we ended up in front of a massive crystalline fireplace, where, surprisingly, there was lots of uninhabited space and two men, deep in conversation. I recognized one immediately: Kasimir Lessig.

Percy cleared his throat. "Kasimir? May I introduce Miss Nina Oberon?" he said.

"Miss Oberon." Lessig took my hand. His was warm and his demeanor so charming it took me completely off guard. I'd expected the same fake persona that came through in Media broadcasts and Alerts. He gestured to the man he was talking with. "This is my assistant, Angelo Fassbinder."

"Ah. The daughter of the late Alan Oberon. What a delight to make your acquaintance." Fassbinder shook my hand, and I immediately wanted to pull it away.

Percy gave my arm a reassuring squeeze. "When Mr. Lessig found out you were coming, he asked particularly if I'd introduce you."

"Really?"

"Yes, my dear. Your father and I knew each other," Lessig said. "He was such a skillful, talented speaker. But I'm sure you know that."

"I've never heard any of his speeches," I lied carefully. "They're contraband." I certainly wasn't going to tell the head of Media, possibly the most powerful man in the country, that I'd listened to illegal speeches.

"Oh, yes. That's true, isn't it?" He shook his head. "The Governing Council worries about the most ridiculous things. It doesn't matter to me or Media. I'll arrange for you to hear his most famous speech. Angelo?" He whispered in Fassbinder's ear.

"Of course, sir. Miss Oberon." Fassbinder noted whatever it was Lessig had said to him, then turned to leave. I can't say that I was sorry to see him go. Something about him rubbed me the wrong way.

Lessig said, "My secretary will be in contact with you soon, my dear." His eyes softened. "I was very sorry to learn of your mother's recent demise. I had the pleasure of meeting her only once. At her wedding."

"You were at my parents' wedding?" His smooth way of talking bothered me—it was like watching a snake smiling at me, full of danger and slick charm. I had never imagined my parents were acquainted with him. Ginnie couldn't stand to watch him on the PAV, but she'd never let on that she knew him.

"Oh, yes. Your father and I were old school friends. Well . . ." He shook his head and smiled. "To tell the truth, we were rivals. As good as I was in public speaking, I was no match for Alan Oberon. I suppose if he had lived, he'd have my job and I'd be doing local broadcasts in the middle of nowhere. He was, by far, the superior orator."

I couldn't do more than nod in amazement. His words were so friendly, could I possibly have been wrong about him? No, Ginnie and the Jenkinses didn't trust him. I knew I shouldn't either.

"I must say, Nina . . . May I call you Nina?" Lessig continued, assuming I'd consented, which . . . well, why would I refuse? "You are stunning. Not at all like most sixteens I've met, decked out in their ultra-chic. And, oh . . . a new tattoo?" He touched my wrist. "Well, you're a Creative. I should've guessed."

"Yes." I didn't like the feel of his hand on my tattoo—no wonder, since it proclaimed the truth.

"I shouldn't be surprised, what with your father's gifts, surely they'd be passed down to his only child." He turned my hand over, studying both the wrist and front design. "Emphasis on truth, I see." His finger drew a circle above the three cursive words surrounding the XVI. "As Pilate said, 'What is truth?'"

"Who's Pilate?"

"Pilate was a man who did what was necessary, while staying above the fray." He met my eyes, then inspected my wrist again, before letting go. "You designed this yourself?"

"Yes. My grandfather says that we should always look for the truth, and that it can't stay hidden."

"How interesting." He flashed what passed for a nice, fatherly type smile. "Your grandfather is a wise man. You are living with your grandparents now?"

"Not exactly." I wasn't sure how much to tell him. But then I realized, he could probably find out whatever he wanted. "I'm staying with friends. My grandmother's in the hospital."

His secretary, who was standing off to the side, was obviously trying to get Mr. Lessig's attention.

"Excuse me a moment, Nina." After a hushed conversation, he returned. "Angelo informs me that your grandfather was recently arrested. How awful. Is he still in custody?"

"He is." I dropped my gaze.

"Oh, dear. It's not your fault. Let's take this into a quieter place, where you and I might discuss the further particulars of your grandfather's case. I do have a bit of sway with the powers that be. Perhaps I can be of some assistance in procuring his release." My heart stopped—could he actually help Pops? Or was this some kind of trick? He glanced around the room. Catching a serving girl's eye, he beckoned her over to us. "A quiet place where Miss Oberon and I can have a discussion?"

"This way, please."

I wasn't sure it was a good idea to go anywhere alone with him. But if he could somehow help Pops . . . As I turned and took a step forward, I caught a glimpse of Paulette out of the corner of my eye. But it was too late. She stumbled right in front of me. I tried to grab her, but she lurched forward, splashing her drink all over Mr. Lessig.

His bodyguards, which I hadn't noticed until that very moment, were on top of us in a nanosec. Lessig waved them off. "An accident. A simple accident."

"I am so sorry." Paulette dabbed at the rapidly spreading stain with a napkin. "Cory! Over here. Right away!"

The same serving girl hurried over with more napkins and took over cleaning up.

"You clumsy cow," Paulette hissed quietly at me.

It was not my fault; Paulette had cut in front of me. But what would be the sense in accusing her? No one would believe me. I remained silent.

"Cory, take Mr. Lessig to Daddy's room."

"Certainly, miss."

"My father's valet will see to your clothes," Paulette said to Lessig, who looked as if he would've rather stayed behind. But Paulette, pure solicitousness and condescension, was not to be denied the role of saving his suit and his dignity.

As soon as they were gone, I spun her around. "What were you doing? He was going to help Pops! You ran into me. I did not—"

She shook me off. "Get out of here, before they get back."

Paulette summoned one of the waiters. "Gene, take Miss Oberon downstairs. Have Reggie drive her home. Immediately."

"Excuse me. I'm not going anywhere. I'm here with my boss and his partner. I have to find them—"

Paulette grabbed my arm. "What you have to do is leave. Right now." Her jaw was set, and there was fire in her eyes.

"You do not get to boss me around, Paulette! For your information, Mr. Lessig and I were discussing my grandfather. He offered to help me get him out of detainment."

She threw her hands up. "Nina, are you really that naive? Go. Now. Before I call security to remove you."

I didn't protest. I turned and went, of my own accord. I'd message Martin and Percy later and make my apologies. Huddled in the backseat of the trannie, I consoled myself as best I could. So much for parties. So much for trying to be someone I wasn't.

XXXIII

When I got home, it was fifteen minutes to midnight. Reggie dropped me off without so much as a Happy New Year. The minute I got in the front door, I stepped out of the heels. "Aaahhh." At least part of me could feel good.

I padded into what I expected to be an empty room. Instead, Chris was on the floor, leaning back against the couch, where Dee was sound asleep. He leaped up, his finger to his lips. I followed him into the kitchen.

"She zonked out half an hour ago. You know, I haven't watched Arianna Lightfoot since Wei was Dee's age. It was kind of . . . wait a sec." He checked out the cook center timer. "What are you doing back so soon? It's not even midnight. Was the party that bad?"

Without any warning, I burst into tears. Chris moved closer, intending to comfort me, but I held up my hand. As soon as I gained control of my emotions, I told him about my whole evening, concluding with, "Kasimir Lessig was going to help Pops, but Paulette spilled wine all over him. She claimed it was my fault and threw me out." I sounded like a sulky Pre. I looked away, catching my breath. "I should never have gone. I don't belong with people like that. They wouldn't stop looking at me. It was awful."

"Wow." He ran his hands through his hair. "It sounds awful. You want me to make you some tea or something?"

"Tea's fine." I sat down at the table while he bustled about the kitchen. In ten minutes, the steaming liquid was evaporating the edges of my disgrace.

"You know, I'll bet people were looking at you because you look beautiful."

I managed a half smile. "I'm not used to that kind of attention."

"Well, you'd better *get* used to it." He reached over, lifting the hair out of my eyes. "You're a very pretty girl."

"In someone else's clothes," I said, swirling the tea in my cup. "It's exactly like playing dress-up."

"It doesn't have anything to do with the clothes, or the hair, or makeup, or anything external. You know, you can't judge a vid by its promo."

My mom's admonition to take a compliment with a simple "thank you" popped into my head, and the words came out of my mouth. "Thanks. But what do I do about the fact that Mr. Lessig was going to help me with Pops? Paulette ruined everything. It's almost like she did it on purpose because he was talking to me, not her."

Chris scratched his head. "Doesn't make sense for her to do something like that. And, Nina, you shouldn't put too much stock in what Lessig says. Remember the Alerts? He twists the truth around all the time."

"But even if there's a chance to help Pops, I have to take it. Otherwise, what's going to happen to him?"

"Well, you said that Lessig told you his secretary would be in touch."

"He doesn't know where I live."

"Think about it, Nina. If anyone can find you, Lessig can."

"True."

"Look." He pointed to the clock. "It's midnight."

We clinked our teacups together.

"Happy New Year." He leaned across the table and kissed me. Without thinking, I kissed back.

Shocked at what I'd done, I mumbled, "Happy New Year," into my teacup, letting the steam moisten my burning cheeks.

Another moment's thought made me realize it was just a traditional New Year's kiss. It must've been. Chris's warm smile was sweet, and he was so easy to talk to, but I was in love with Sal. Damn. This night was not at all how I'd wanted to spend New Year's Eve.

I wanted to be with Sal, or at the very least talk to him. But I wasn't going to message him again. He still hadn't called or messaged back. And I'd reached out three days ago. Maybe I'd ruined things for good. Maybe I'd never hear from him again. I needed to turn off my brain.

Chris's voice brought me back to the planet. "Making resolutions?"

"Nuh-uh. I'm exhausted."

"I should go. You want me to carry Dee to her room?"

"No. Let her sleep. I'll get a blanket for her. And thanks for spending the evening with her."

"Are you kidding? She kept me from feeling sorry for myself. No date for New Year's Eve. What a loser I am."

I smiled. "You might be a lot of things, but you are definitely not a loser."

"Neither are you." He put his arm around me and kissed my cheek. "Happy New Year, Nina. You deserve it."

***

One glance in the mirror brought back the whole night's events. I carefully removed the Kanzashi sticks from my hair and shook it out. There. That was more like me. My fingertips brushed the embroidered crane as I slipped off the dress. It was so beautiful. And I'd felt beautiful in it—even if for just a few hours. I wished Sal had seen me. Without warning, Chris's compliment rang in my ears, and I remembered his lips on mine. My cheeks burned again. Crazy.

I needed sleep.

That was the cure for crazy.

XXXIV

Sleep turned out to be a cure for nothing. My shame at Paulette's throwing me out and my confusion at Chris's kiss were as strong as they'd been the night before.

While I waited for Dee to get ready for our visit with Gran, I called Sal. My hands trembled. One beep . . . two . . . three . . . voice pickup. I really, really needed to talk to him, to hear his voice, to be sure that we could work things out. Why'd I let myself get so mad at him?

Because he doesn't think you're capable, the voice in my head replied.

The whole conversation with Sal played through my brain, again. Followed by the same resultant anger and frustration. I sighed. The Sisterhood would have to show him, and all the NonCons, that girls are able to hold their own and to contribute to the Resistance beyond gathering intelligence and providing technical know-how.

***

"Dr. Silverman says February first." Gran huffed. "I told him I was fine, but he won't budge. Says he needs time to assess my recovery. 'Assess what?' I asked. I'm an old woman. I'm still breathing. And I feel better than I did when I was seventy. He only wants more time to show off his handiwork. He's had his colleagues tromping in and out, practically nonstop, since I got here. I'm starting to feel like a sideshow freak. Oh, well . . ." She sighed. "Any more news about your grandfather? They won't tell me anything here. Mustn't upset the patient, you know."

I told her about meeting Kasimir Lessig at Paulette's party. I wasn't sure whether or not to mention his offer of help. If it turned out not to be true, I didn't want to cause Gran more stress. But I saw the desperate look in her eyes, and thought of Pops.

"Lessig might be able to help us get Pops out. He said he'd get in touch with me about it."

"Dear Lord!" Gran paled, clutching her chest.

"Gran!" Skivs! Had I caused her to have another attack? "Dee, get the nurse. Right away!"

"No, no." Gran stopped her. "I'm fine. Just . . . the shock . . . Lessig. Oh my."

"He said he'd known my father. I was surprised at how friendly he was to me." I was more than surprised. Considering all I'd heard of him beforehand, I wasn't sure whether or not to trust him. But we needed some hope, didn't we?

"They knew each other all right, and there was no love lost between those two. Alan never trusted him. He could twist the truth from here to Holiday and have you believing up was down and east was west. Nina, if Lessig does get in touch with you, be careful."

"But," Dee chimed in, "if he can help get Pops home, wouldn't that be good?"

"Of course, dear." Gran patted Dee's hand. "Of course it would." Her eyes betrayed the anxiety she wasn't admitting to. The anxiety I shared.

***

Outside, Dee and I waited for the trans to show. "Why didn't you tell me you met Kasimir Lessig?" Dee's eyes were accusing. "That's huge news."

"I did tell you, silly. At the same time I told Gran."

"You know what I mean."

Dee and I boarded the number 55 trans.

"I didn't want to get your hopes up," I said. "I'm not sure I should've told Gran either. He might not contact me again. Not after the whole drink thing."

"What drink thing?"

After I told her about the incident, she said, "It was not your fault. I don't like Paulette Gold."

"You don't know her."

"Well, do you like her?"

"I'm not sure." She'd done so many contrary things lately. Driving the getaway car, championing helping Joan—and then treating me as if I were lower than tier one. I really didn't know *what* to think of Paulette.

***

Dee was at Maddie's for the night, and I was pacing a hole in the carpet waiting for Wei. We were going to Soma to hear Derek play.

When she got there, I said, "How about we go down by my old apartment building first. If you're going to take Joan to Japan, she

Julia Karr

needs to meet you. She's not very trusting, and if she's at least met you, she'll probably feel a little more comfortable. I don't want her to freak out."

"Makes sense. Let's go."

I handed Wei one of two bags at my feet. "Food. It's a kind of a peace offering." We headed out to catch the trans.

By the time we got off, it was already dark.

"Do you think they're here?" Wei asked.

"If we walk down by the river, they usually come out of the alleys between the buildings."

"Where do they sleep?" Wei asked. "I'm surprised they survive when it gets this cold. This is awful."

"I don't know." I thought about that for a moment. "They have to deal with it. Especially since there are no shelters."

"There used to be," Wei said. "Dad's grandfather ran one. It was open for anyone who needed refuge. But then the GC took over running all the shelters and made rules about what people had to do in order to stay in them. A lot of homeless refused."

"What kind of rules?"

"They had to work at whatever jobs they were given. No drugs. No drinking. No smoking."

"That doesn't sound terrible. It sounds like what welfare people have to do now. Like Mike's dad doing all that medical testing."

"On the surface, it sounds fine. I mean, we're all going to be doing some kind of work in order to get credits to live on. But I think it was the kinds of jobs."

"Like what?"

"Lots of medical experiments. Not only like Mr. Trueblood

234

does, but they'd implant devices in them, just to see what would happen. They'd give people homes, but the price might be amputation and experimental regrowing therapies. Dad said the amputations weren't always voluntary. They injected them with diseases, giving some of them medicine and others only placebos. Then they started doing genetic engineering."

"Skivs! That was outlawed a century ago."

"Yeah. Most of the homeless revolted and refused to go to the shelters. Dad said that the GC closed them all in retaliation. Then Media started broadcasting messages about how homeless carried diseases and were subhuman because they lived in alleys and scurried around like rats. I guess eventually it became okay to abuse and even kill them without getting into trouble."

"That is sickening." I clutched the handles of my bag, my cheeks flaming, as I acknowledged to myself that at one time I'd believed Media's lies.

We walked down to the oases along the riverfront, then back up to the street, hoping we didn't look like loiterers. We couldn't risk getting picked up by the police. I'd almost given up when I caught a glimpse of movement between two buildings. It was Joan and Svette.

Svette scowled at me, but she was quick to snatch up the bag of food I offered. She thrust it at Joan. "Take this to the others."

"No," I said. "I need to talk to Joan."

"What do you want with her?" The woman's eyes turned to slits, reminding me of the snakes in the reptile house at the zoo.

I drew myself up to full height. "I've got news about her family. It's personal."

"Nothing's personal here." She planted her feet.

Joan, who had been silent, said, "I'll take it over in a minute." She cast her eyes to the ground, flinching, as if expecting a blow.

"You'll—"

"You'll need more help." Wei held out her bag. "She doesn't look like she can handle both of these."

I heard a gasp from the shadows and a strained "Two bags?"

"All right." The leader motioned behind her, and a girl, not much older than Joan, appeared. "Grab that. Do your part."

The girl obediently took the bag, and she and Svette disappeared into the darkness.

"What's happened to my family? Is Mom okay? Mike? Yelena?" She grasped my arm.

"They're fine. I said that only to get rid of the others." I touched her icy hand. "You need these more than me." I pulled my gloves off. "Don't let Svette take them."

"She won't. She's already got some." Joan shoved her hands into the gloves. "Oh. They're warm. Thank you."

"This is my friend Wei. I wanted you two to meet. Wei's someone you can trust—with your life. Come with us a sec." I led her across the street to the DZ oasis. "Listen, we're going to get you out of here."

Joan shrank back. "I . . . I can't go. I belong . . . here." She pointed to the alley.

"No, you don't. You belong where people won't hurt you."

"But how? I don't have credits. What will I have to do?" Her eyes were haunted, as if I was going to ask her to do some unspeakable horror.

"Nothing. You're going to Japan with Wei. She has family there. It's safe, and they'll take care of you. But you can't say anything to anyone," I said. "Especially not Svette. I'm not sure you can trust her, or any of them."

"But they've taken care of me. Svette's good . . . Well"—she glanced around, then said—"she's usually good to me. She needs to keep strong. You know, the scarf for warmth, extra food, things like that. If something happens to her, we'll all be caught."

My blood was boiling—Svette stole Joan's scarf, and here she was defending her. But it wasn't time for me to lose it. "Promise me you won't say anything to anyone. Please."

"I promise." She glanced across the street. "I've got to go. Now."

"I'll come back soon," I said. "Maybe even tomorrow. Keep safe, and warm."

Joan evaporated into the shadows.

***

There was an Alert while we were on the transit.

It was Lessig. It was FeLS. It was Ed.

All of that wasn't surprising to me. What I wasn't prepared for was the picture of my mother that appeared next to Lessig as he said, "This woman, Virginia Dale Oberon, was murdered in Cementville last October. She is the alleged mistress of Chamus, with whom she is purported to have had one child. Oberon was the widow of the late Alan Oberon, mastermind behind the terrorist NonCon organization. Bureau agents are investigating an anonymous tip linking Oberon's involvement with the phony FeLS training station scandal. It is also noteworthy that Alan

Oberon's father, Herbert Oberon, is currently being held by the Bureau on charges of treason, possession of contraband, and resisting arrest.

"Virginia Oberon also had a daughter by Alan Oberon." A picture of me, from Paulette's party, flashed on-screen. I sat watching my PAV, stunned as Lessig continued to rip into my family. "One can only imagine the horrors those children, girls, both of them"—Dee's school picture joined mine—"must have endured at the hands of Chamus and . . ."

I stared at the projection, oblivious to everything going on around me. I knew what was coming next, but like an express bearing down on me, foot caught in the tracks, I was helpless to stop it, or save myself.

". . . their own mother." He held up a chip to the camera. "Bureau agents have given their sworn statements that when they searched Oberon's home the night she was killed, they found pornographic vids in a locked case. Since these were not a part of their investigation of Oberon's death, they were not confiscated." His voice oozed sympathy. "Oh, if only they had been. Then we might have a clue as to *what* those poor girls were exposed to."

Hot tears threatened to spill out of my eyes, but I blinked hard, forcing them back.

"Are you all right?" Wei asked, her hand on my arm. "Nina, I know none of that is true. You know that none of it is true," she said.

"Part of it was." I looked straight ahead. "Those were Ed's vids they found. I turned on the FAV once, and he'd left one of the porn chips in it." Even after all the time that had passed, I felt myself redden. "It was awful. It was so violent . . . It was . . . I never told Ginnie. I was afraid to tell her I saw it."

Wei threw her arms around me. "It wasn't your fault he was disgusting."

"But . . ." I pushed away from her. "I think they watched them together. I think he made her watch with him." A tear trickled down my cheek. "What if she—"

"Nina, don't! Look at all that your mother did to get information to stop what was going on in FeLS. If she watched that kind of stuff, it's because Ed forced her to. Not because she wanted to. She did everything she could to stop girls from being abused. She sacrificed everything to get that information from him." Wei grabbed my shoulders, turning me to face her. "Don't ever think that again!"

My heart ached. Wei was right—I couldn't let lies change the way I thought about my mother. How I wanted my mother back, for one minute. Thirty seconds. Just long enough to say I was sorry I thought those things. Ever.

"Wei, what do I say to Dee? School starts on Monday. Even though kids aren't supposed to see the Alerts, you know all her classmates will know about it. I can't let on, not even to Dee, what Ginnie was really doing. And I can't go to school with her to protect her."

"We'll think of something," Wei said.

The transit pulled up to our stop, and we got off. When we got to Soma, I said, "Go on in, I'll be there in a nano." After she left, I tried Sal's PAV. Of course there was no answer. I thought about leaving a message, but what would I say? I clicked off and was about to go in when I paused. They'd shown my picture in the Alert. My mother. The last thing I wanted to do was go into Soma and be recognized.

A hand touched my shoulder. "You okay?"

"Chris." I made some unnecessary adjustment to my coat. "I'm fine. What are you doing here?"

"I heard the Alert. Thought you might not want to hang with Wei and everyone else right now."

"You know, I think I would rather leave. I don't feel much like fun tonight." I sent a message to Wei's PAV letting her know I was going with Chris.

XXXV

"How about a cup of coffee?" Chris pulled his trannie away from the curb.

"I guess."

"Relax," he said. "We'll go to a little place I know up in Evanston. There won't be anyone there who knows you."

I settled back in the seat. The scenery whizzed by as we drove north on Lake Shore Drive, past the rehab center on Sheridan, where Gran would be transferred to. Eventually, Chris stopped in front of a place with an antique neon sign that shimmered JAZZ AND JAVA.

The smell of fresh-roasted coffee was like a friendly pat on the cheek as we eased into the dim interior. Soft jazz oozed from the walls. Chris took us to a booth in the corner. Seconds later, a waitress appeared.

"I'll have a cuppa regular. Black."

"And you?"

"I'll just have water."

"Don't like coffee? We've got a variety of teas, and our To-Die-For Cocoa is phenomenal. I highly recommend it."

"Okay, I'll take that." I looked around. Posters of musicians playing a variety of new and antique instruments dotted the walls. "You like jazz, huh?"

"Guilty as charged." Chris stretched out in the booth. "It's intricate. Each song is kind of like an unfolding puzzle. A mystery unraveling."

"I've never listened to it," I confessed.

"Well, we are in the right place for your initiation."

The waitress reappeared with our drinks.

Chris lifted his cup. "To a better tomorrow." We clinked them together, like on New Year's. The dim lights hid my blush.

As I leaned back, the cocoa-scented steam filled my head. I closed my eyes, allowing the music to twine itself around my brain, down my spine, and into my belly. I couldn't put words to how I felt—somewhere between nestled in loving arms and being urged to spread my wings and soar. When the song ended, I opened my eyes.

Chris, his cup cradled in his hands, a pensive smile on his face, said, "Nice, isn't it?"

"How could I not have heard this before?"

"It's on the watch list. Media doesn't like it because it's improvisational, so it doesn't get much airplay. Feeling better now?"

"A little."

"So you want to talk? I'm a good listener. And you know your secrets are safe with me."

His face was so open, so sincere. I wanted to tell him everything. But here was not the place.

"Not here."

"Let's take a drive," he said.

I was glad his trannie was surveillance-free.

As we wound north, through areas of Chicago I'd never seen, all the emotions I'd been holding inside since my mom's death came tumbling out. My guilt. My shame. My anger. My fears. Everything. Well, everything except the Sisterhood's plan to save Joan. That wasn't my personal secret to tell. Although I more than touched on how Sal didn't think that I (or any other girl) was capable of NonCon work. "You probably think the same thing."

Chris reached over, covering my hand with his. "Nina, I have no doubt you can, and will, do whatever you need to do. From what I hear, you're a lot like your mother. Something of which to be megaproud."

My chest tingled at the compliment.

"And you have that glint in your eyes, same as your dad. He'll stop at nothing to help set the world right again. I see that in you."

"You know, they both sacrificed everything. Any kind of normal life . . . their love for each other . . . I don't know if I can do that." I turned my face away, willing the unbidden image of Sal to dissipate.

"Until the Governing Council is altered or disbanded, and the Media is reined in, there's no decent normal for anyone. The best we can all hope for in this fight is friendship, dedication to truth, willingness to change, and love where we find it. You can do whatever you set your mind to, Nina. Of that I am certain."

I almost believed him.

"Look at how you saved Wei," he went on. "Without any special training and in the face of a terror I've never had to imagine. And Ed wasn't just threating murder—even though I have a mother and sisters, I can't know what the threat of rape means to a woman. But anyone who can live through that is a power to be reckoned with. A mighty power."

Like a flash, I suddenly got it. Some people are capable of doing things to a woman that would reduce them to a hollowed shell. I thought of Joan. And those men who never would even dream of doing such horrific deeds would do anything to keep women safe from that terror. NonCons don't want their sisters, wives, and daughters to get too close to that kind of danger. Still, they have no idea what kind of strength women are capable of, despite that danger.

I understood a little better why Sal and Mr. Jenkins were dead set against the Sisterhood's involvement in anything that would expose the girls to that kind of sexual threat. But just because they felt helpless in preventing those kinds of attacks, that kind of torture, it didn't change my mind about what girls could do.

Chris drove down a lane that stopped at the lakefront. The light of a full moon shimmered over the water, reflecting inside the vehicle. Chris brushed my bangs aside. "I'd give a card full of credits to know what you're thinking."

Our eyes met, and what I saw in his was not what I expected. I felt an irresistible urge to kiss him. He put his arm over the back of my seat and leaned close. My head tilted up, following my instincts—or was it my heart? His lips almost touched mine when he pulled back.

"Damn. It's Wei." He listened, then said, "Yeah, she's still with me. We took a drive." He shook his head. "Stop worrying. See you in a few." After he clicked off, he said, "Guess we'd better go home."

That break had shaken me. Chris was my best friend's brother, my boyfriend's friend, and my little sister's crush. What was I doing? I was dating Sal—whom I loved. Right? I stared at Chris, steeling my heart. "What almost happened . . . it's wrong," I said.

He traced the moonlight down my cheek. "Nina. I'm not so sure," he said.

"No, Chris. I can't do this. I can't do this to . . ." I trailed off. To Sal, I wanted to say, but I couldn't bring myself to say his name.

"It's okay, I understand. I'm sorry, Nina. I thought—I thought you felt the same." Chris started up the trannie, and we headed back. I leaned back against the seat and stared out the window at the moon, trying to figure out what it was I did feel.

XXXVI

"Nina, wake up." Dee was at the side of my bed, shaking me. "Miss Maldovar called."

"Huh? What time is it? When did you get home?" I sat up, groggy. My brain was still half asleep.

"It's nine-thirty, and Maddie's mom dropped me off half an hour ago. I wasn't going to bother you, but then Miss Maldovar called. She told me about the Alert."

"Why—" Miss Maldovar was the last person I thought would tell Dee anything about this. I sat up, rubbing the sleep from my eyes, trying to buy myself some time. Taking a deep breath, I decided Pops was right: the truth couldn't be hidden forever.

"Miss Maldovar told me the Alert said Ginnie was Ed's assistant in that phony FeLS camp, but she wasn't!"

"No, Dee, she wasn't. That's just what Kasmir Lessig said."

"Miss Maldovar agreed with me, that Mom would never do anything like that. For a nanosec I thought she wouldn't want me to be her assistant anymore, but she said it didn't matter to her."

"Dee, listen to me. Ginnie had nothing to do with Ed's filthy scheme. But Media is saying she did. It's all over the news. I think the government is trying to discredit Ginnie because of her connection to my father—the GC would do anything to ruin his reputation among the people who are part of the Resistance."

"Can't Mr. Jenkins set them straight? He's a big Media guy, isn't he? I'm going to go ask him right—"

"Stop. You can't go bothering him about this. He's already working on it."

"You told him?" Dee came back and sat on the edge of my bed.

"I didn't have to. He knows that Mom didn't have anything to do with Ed, other than, well . . . you know."

"I hate that he was my father." She fiddled with the ridges of my comforter.

It was so hard not to tell her the truth. But it was for her own safety. I pulled up the corner, inviting her to snuggle in with me. "Things will work out. You'll see."

"Everyone at school will know about it, won't they?"

"Probably." I hugged her.

She shrugged free. "Miss Maldovar said that she'd tell them not to believe everything they heard, and that I'm to tell her if someone picks on me. I can stand up for myself, though. I'll tell them the truth, that Mom never did anything like that." Fire flashed in her eyes. "If they don't believe me, then—"

"Deeds. No fighting."

She clenched her jaw.

"I mean it."

"Oh . . . all right." She snorted. "But I'll want to."

"I know you will. But there are things worth fighting for, and things not worth fighting about. This is not worth fighting about."

"But she's our mom."

"And she wouldn't want you scrapping in the playground like

a puppy. You know the truth, that's good enough. And the truth will come out. I promise you. It will."

***

Later on, Dee settled down to watch some vids. I hoped they would take her mind off of the Alert mess. I headed to the cook center to put together more food to take to the homeless.

I wanted to take soup to the women, but there was no good way to pack it. They'd have to settle for nut butter-and-jelly sandwiches. It was better than nothing.

"What's that?" Dee looked up from a vid she was watching.

"Stuff," I said. "I'm taking this to some friends."

Fortunately, she was too engrossed in the FAV to ask any other questions. "What are you watching?" I asked.

"Some history show about the Greater United Isles. It sounds like the coolest place. Hardly anyone lives there anymore. Except in London and Edinburgh. Wouldn't it be weird to be somewhere where there are no other people? No verts. No nothing."

"Sounds like heaven," I said. I couldn't imagine what that would be like.

My PAV beeped—it was Brie.

"You doing okay? I wanted to let you know that no one believes that stupid Alert about your mother," she said.

"Thanks. I'm fine." I didn't let on that I'd been worrying about how the Sisterhood felt about me.

"Cool. Anyway, I have good news. The game is on for Tuesday. My uncle asked me to make a delivery. Dorrie'll get everything programmed. Wei needs to target the exact time when we can move the goods."

"You sound like Notishca Lamb." I giggled, amazed that I could find humor in any part of my life.

"Oh, I love, love *Spy from the Dark Side*," she said. "I wish I'd lived back in those days!"

"So I guess that means you're getting the veljet, and everything else is a go?"

"Yep. We are all set! We'll talk later."

No matter what happened at school on Monday, at least I had a few friends who cared and knew the truth. And who wanted to help.

***

On the way to the riverfront, I thought about the Greater United Isles. No verts. No GC. I didn't know much more about them, other than that Scotland was where Cliste Galad had been invented.

They didn't bother to teach us much about any of that in school, probably because the GC didn't want us to know how different it could be. But I'd learned a lot more hanging out with Wei and Sal.

Sal. I still had no message from him. No call. And now I felt guilty because I'd nearly betrayed him with Chris. It was funny, the fact that we'd argued about whether or not girls were capable of fighting for themselves. Especially since the End-of-Wars Treaty never would have come about without the Fems. They'd taken power from the Corporations government in the Americas, years ago.

They never said as much in History, but even though it hadn't been a bloodless coup, the Fems were more than fair to the conquered. They didn't shuttle anyone off to a prison space station, or doom them to Mars and infection. They took the Corporation moguls out of power but otherwise left them alone. And that was their big mistake, since the moguls got together and revived Media.

Everyone knew Media wasn't anything new. I mean, verts have been around for ages, in one form or another. They even taught us how most corporations worked through Media to spread their version of the truth—I guess never figuring we'd make the connection to the way the GC used Media.

But no, the GC was so much more evolved than that. Ha, yeah right. I glanced out the trans window—I was almost there. Which was a good thing, considering how my anger was rising just thinking about how we were taught that the printed ads and commercials of the twentieth century turned into verts in the twenty-first century, but no one ever questioned whether or not verts were good now.

And so when the Corporation moguls started using Media to undermine women, to sow the seeds of overthrowing the Fems, it worked. It worked so well, women ended up losing all the ground for which they'd fought for centuries.

And here I was. An all but powerless, sex-teen, standing by the riverfront trying to make a difference. But no. I wasn't powerless. What had I been trying to tell Sal all this time? That girls were just as strong as everyone else.

I was pretty sure the remnants of true feminism were out there, somewhere. And I desperately wanted to find them.

I headed over to the buildings, where I figured I was most likely to find the group of homeless. They were huddled in an alley, trying to avoid the bitter wind.

It was hard for me to believe, but a couple of the homeless women complained that I'd brought only sandwiches. Drawing Joan aside, I told her, in guarded words, to be ready on Tuesday. I could feel her anxiety and tried to reassure her that when she was in Japan with Wei's relatives, they'd help her get back to normal.

"I'll bring more food in a couple of days," I told Joan. "Hang in there."

She and the rest of the homeless women disappeared, leaving the empty bags behind. I stuffed them in the trash and walked out of the alleyway. Two guys—they looked about twenty—were coming up from one of the river oases. As they passed me, I caught a whiff of alcohol. It reminded me of Ed, which was enough to make me hurry on by.

"You. Girl."

I speeded up. Their footsteps grew closer, louder. They were following me.

"What's your hurry, babe?" The voice was right behind me.

Nearly wrenching my arm from its socket, one of them spun me around, slurring, "I said . . . what's your hurry?" Shoving up my sleeve, he uncovered the XVI. "She's legal, Punch. Score one for the home team." A smile spread across his face.

His friend sidled up next to me. The liquor smell so strong I nearly vomited.

"Let go." I struggled to free my arm, but he wasn't about to release me.

"You said 'Let's go'? I'm with you, babe." He homed in on an opening between two buildings. "A little alley-cat love for us and our little sex-teen."

Pressing his mouth onto mine, he rammed his tongue between my lips and his boozy slobber drenched my chin. As soon as he came up for air, his friend, Punch, yanked my head around and tried the same. He was so intoxicated, he missed my mouth completely, allowing me just enough time to scream.

"Nuh-uh, babe." The first guy slapped his hand across my mouth. "Don't want a whole crowd. Punch and me's more than enough."

I tried biting him, but his grip was too firm. Out of the corner of my eye, I saw a hire transport. Struggling to get free, I kicked Punch, connecting with his shin.

"Ouch!" He had a puzzled look on his face. "Why'd you do that? We're gonna give you what you want. Right, Gordo?"

"Of course, idiot. Let's get back there before anyone else comes by."

Between the two of them, they practically lifted me off the ground and ducked between the buildings. I kicked and writhed, but I couldn't manage to connect with either of them again.

"Over here." Gordo, his hand still firmly across my mouth, dragged me into a recessed area not visible from the street. He took his hand off my mouth long enough to jam his glove into it. Holding my arms behind me, he said, "Get her pants down."

I kicked at Punch's groin, missing. This could not be happening. I had to get away.

"She's too wild." Punch backed off, shaking his head.

"I gotta do it all?" Gordo flung me to the ground. "You hold her arms."

Punch eyed me suspiciously but did as he was told.

I tried spitting out the woolen mass, but it was too far in. It was all I could do not to throw up. Choking on my own vomit was not the way I wanted to die.

Gordo straddled me, fumbling with the button on my jeans. "You just calm down, babe. We're nice guys. This is gonna be fun. It's what all you girls want." He couldn't get my all-weathers undone. "Dammit!" He pulled a switchblade out of his pocket.

My heart stopped. My eyes widened in terror.

"What? This?" Gordo flicked the knife open, eyeing it lovingly. "Easy access, sweetheart. Easy access." He slit the waistband of my pants. The blade scratched my skin, and warm blood trickled across my belly. "Oops." He grabbed a handful of snow and rubbed it on the wound. "Sorry."

"Skivs! You cut her!" Punch loosened his grip on my arms. "We'll get in trouble, sure enough." I jerked my arm free at last, snatched the wad out of my mouth, and screamed again. Punch quickly clapped both his hands over my mouth. I bit down. Hard.

What happened next was so fast, I couldn't tell exactly what was coming from where.

A war whoop erupted behind Gordo, and two women jumped him. I made out Joan's face as she leaped across me, slamming into Punch.

She bashed his head against the wall, yelling, "Stop! Stop! Stop!" over and over.

Somehow, Punch managed to push her off. Struggling to his feet, he dashed out of the alley, leaving his friend behind. Gordo was thrashing about under the weight of Svette and another woman. I scurried back into the snow away from them. About the time he swiped the air with his switchblade, I yelled, "He's got a knife!"

Svette cracked his arm on her leg, and the knife skidded down the alley. She yanked him to his feet, kicked him between the legs, twirled him around, and delivered a final boot to his ass.

He stumbled toward the street, supporting himself on the building. "Punch! Punch! Wait up! That bitch broke my arm."

"You okay?" Svette pulled me to my feet and inspected the bloody cut on my abdomen.

"I'm . . . fine." I was struggling to catch my breath. "They . . . this . . ." I held out my wrist. "I couldn't get away." I slumped against the wall. That's when I noticed Joan, sitting on the ground, her fists clenched. I slid down next to her. "Thank you."

She jerked her head around. Her eyes burning. "I wanted to kill him. Kill. Him."

I knew just how she felt.

"You can't stay here," Svette said. "Cops. They'll show up. Can you walk?"

Even with knees like jelly, and a tremendous need to throw up, I managed to push my way back up the wall. "Yeah, I can walk."

Svette and the others disappeared around the back of the building. Stumbling to the sidewalk, I looked around to make sure Gordo and Punch were really gone. My all-weathers kept slipping down. Hands shaking, I wove my scarf through the belt loops, tying a bulky knot at the waist, and took off at a run toward the transit stop. I think I could've run all the way home.

XXXVII

Thankfully, when I got home, Dee was in the kitchen and didn't see me come in. The cut on my stomach had stopped bleeding by then. I spread goldenseal ointment on the knife wound. It wasn't so deep that I'd need stitches, but I figured it would leave a scar. Either way, it was something I'd never forget.

By the time I'd cleaned up and changed my clothes, Dee was in the living room watching a show.

I sat down next to her. "What's on?" I asked, struggling to keep my voice light.

"More about the Isles." She glanced over at me. "You hungry?"

I shook my head. "Not really." My stomach was still doing flip-flops.

"Did something happen to you?" Dee curled her leg under her and swiveled around. "You look . . . I dunno, different?"

"Why would you think anything happened?" I gave her a quick sideways glance and then turned my attention to the FAV, which she immediately switched off.

"Nina, in eight days I'll be twelve. Pres are almost teens. You can tell me anything."

Dee was only four years away from potentially experiencing

what had just happened to me. I didn't want to tell her anything about this. How was I ever going to keep her safe? I thought back to what my mother had always told me: safety comes from knowing what you're up against. From being prepared.

"Come on," she prodded. "Something's bothering you. I know it."

"Two guys, well . . . they came up to me. They thought I was . . . you know . . . a sex-teen. I . . . I escaped, but just barely."

"No! Are you okay? Did you call the cops?" She tossed the remote down and scooted next to me. "What can I do?"

"No, I did not call the cops," I said. It's not like they would do anything if I did. "And I'm fine."

"Fine? How can you say that?"

"I *am* fine, they didn't rape me. Some people saw them and helped me. I got away." I wasn't about to show her the cut from the switchblade or tell her any more details.

"The police—"

"Would do absolutely nothing," I said. "They'd take one look at my XVI and say I wanted it."

"But you don't dress sex-teen. You don't act it. You're not like, like Sandy." She grabbed my hand. "I'm sorry. I mean, not that Sandy was bad, but—"

"I know." I swept her hair back from her forehead. "Media is always telling girls how to look and act so guys will notice them. The verts say it, and people believe that it's what girls want. And if girls dress and act that way, why would anyone think they didn't want to attract guys and have sex? That's how it's all supposed to work. And some guys—predators—take advantage of that and do whatever they want to whoever they want. But some girls, and some guys, know how wrong it is. Sex should be a mutual decision, not one that's forced on anyone. Mom knew. That's why she didn't let us dress and act like everyone else."

"These clothes that Miss Maldovar gave me . . ." Dee smoothed her top, which was, in my opinion, a little too tight. "Are they wrong? Do they make me look like I'm trying to be sexy? I don't want that. I'm not trying to be sexy. Honest. I only want to look nice, to fit in. When Maddie and I watch *XVI Ways* vids, it's just for fun, to feel grown up. That's not wrong, is it?"

"No. Of course not." Dee expected me to know all the answers. I was lucky to know half an answer. "But, Dee, you can't expect to dress like a sex-teen and not have certain guys think that you're like Media says girls are. The thing is, there's nothing wrong with being sexy or with sex . . . but . . ." Oh, man. I was in way over my head. I was still trying to sort out all of this stuff in my own head, and here I was trying to help Dee.

"But what? Have you had sex? Have you and Sal done it?" She waited.

Me and Sal, at his house. It had certainly gone through my mind. "I'm still a virgin."

"Those guys expected you to want to have sex with them." She wrapped her arms tight around her. "What if no one had come to help you?"

"No, I don't think they expected me to want it, no matter what they said. I think they were predators. But, Dee, not all guys are like those two. Most guys only want to have sex with a girl who wants to have sex with them." At least the guys I knew were like that. Derek, Mike, Chris, Sal . . . they'd never force a girl. Ever.

"But I don't understand. Why don't the police arrest guys who try to force themselves on girls?"

"That, Deeds, I don't have an answer to." I really didn't. I thought it tied back into when the Fems were around, that all of this was about power, not about sex. But I didn't know how to explain that to myself, let alone to Dee.

We were interrupted by a tap at the door. Wei stuck her head in. "What are you guys up to? Mom wants you to come up for dinner if— What's going on? Did I come at a bad time?"

"Two guys tried to force Nina to have sex," Dee said.

"Wait, what?" Wei asked.

"Dee, why don't you go tell Mrs. Jenkins we'll come up for dinner. I'll fill Wei in."

"No, I should stay with you," Dee said.

"No, you shouldn't." I crossed my arms over my chest. "They didn't do anything. I. Am. Fine." I stared her down. "Go."

As soon as the door closed behind Dee, Wei said, "Are you really all right?"

"Oh, Wei, I thought they were going to kill me. One guy had a switchblade." I proceeded to tell her the whole story. How Gordo had kissed me and stuck his hand under my sweater. How disgusting it was. And how scared I'd been. I started shaking just recounting the details to her.

She threw her arms around me and held me close. We sat that way for several minutes, until the trembling stopped.

"I can't let Dee see how much this got to me," I said. "I've got to be strong."

"Let's go upstairs," Wei said. "Maybe getting your mind off of it for a while will help. I'm so glad they didn't hurt you. Well, not any worse than that cut and some bruises."

We were halfway upstairs when there was a knock on the door. It took both of us by surprise: not many unexpected visitors came by the Jenkinses'. Wei shot me a look and went back down to answer it.

"May I help you?"

"Yes. I'm Angelo Fassbinder. I'm looking for Nina Oberon."

Skivs! Mr. Lessig's assistant. "I'm right here." I walked slowly down the stairs. Despite Lessig's friendly manner at Paulette's party, I knew I couldn't trust him, not with the way he'd linked Ginnie to the FeLS scandal. I glanced at Wei. "Would you let Dee know I'll be right up."

Wei didn't look any too happy about leaving me with Angelo, but what was he going to do here in the Jenkinses' house? I ushered him into our apartment.

He scanned the furnishings. "Nice." His upper lip curled. "Retirement and survivor benefits must pay better than I thought."

"These belong to the Jenkinses." I crammed my attitude down, waiting to hear what he wanted. At least focusing on this meant I wasn't thinking about those two creeps.

"Ah, yes. Jonathan Jenkins does quite well as senior investigative correspondent. How fortunate for you that his family has taken pity on you."

Because of Gran's warning, I didn't say the first thing on my mind—about how the Jenkinses were old family friends, and that's what friends do. Besides, Fassbinder probably already knew everything about me. It's not like Lessig couldn't find out anything he wanted. "Would you like to sit down?"

"No. This will be brief." He pulled out what looked like a tiny LED flashlight and zapped it around the room. "Interesting." He replaced it. "Now, Mr. Lessig has a proposition for you regarding your grandfather."

I took a step toward him. Maybe, just maybe, Lessig was still going to help me. Maybe Gran had been wrong. Maybe the odd feeling I had about him was wrong . . .

Fassbinder curled his fingers into his palm and shined the nails with his thumb. He fanned out his hand, admiring his manicure, or whatever.

I was losing patience. "Yes?" I prompted.

"Mr. Lessig is a very powerful man." He continued preening. "He can make or break people depending on how he tells a story. Just look at the sad truth about your mother."

"That was a lie," I said. "My mother didn't have anything to do with FeLS."

"Really? That's not what the B.O.S.S. agents said. Are you sure there were no porn vids found after your mother's death?"

I glared at him. He knew there were, and he knew they weren't Ginnie's.

"See? The truth always comes out. In any way that Mr. Lessig tells it." A slow smile spread across his face. He was enjoying himself. "So, Miss Oberon. You would like your grandfather free?"

"Of course," I said.

"Well, Mr. Lessig would be glad to deliver him—for a price."

"A price?" My heartbeat quickened. "I don't have many credits, but I have a job."

He snorted. "Credits? As if Mr. Lessig needs more credits. He's one of the richest men on Earth."

"Then what does he want?" I was getting tired of playing games.

"Information, Miss Oberon. Information can buy anything."

"What kind of information could I possibly have that Mr. Lessig would want? I'm sixteen. I go to school. I work part-time as a tier-two clerk."

"Oh, you so underestimate yourself. You're the daughter of the founder of the Resistance; you live in the home of a very wealthy Media employee. And your mother was a NonCon."

I sucked in my breath. Prickles raced up my spine. Careful, I thought. "I don't know what you're talking about." No matter what he knew, I couldn't let on that I knew anything. "My father died the day I was born. Surely you're aware of that. And my mother was a tier-two cashier in a cafeteria. She was not a NonCon. The only thing you got right is that I'm living with the Jenkinses, and Mr. Jenkins works for Media."

Fassbinder sighed. "I told Kasimir you'd be difficult." He drew near to me. "You want your grandfather. Mr. Lessig wants information about Jonathan Jenkins. There have been suggestions made that Mr. Jenkins is a Resistance sympathizer. Especially after he took in the daughter of their founder." He gave me the once-over. "Lessig gets the information, your grandfather lives. You refuse, your grandfather dies. Simple enough even for a low-tier sex-teen like you to understand, isn't it?"

I jammed my fists in my pockets to keep from using them on Angelo Fassbinder's face.

"I won't spy on my friends," I said.

"Really?" He took out his PAV, punched in some numbers, and threw a projection on the wall. "Bring him out," he said to the projection.

I stared at the screen. At first it was just an empty room. A man entered pushing an older man in a transchair. The man in the chair had tubes running into his arms; his head was lolled over.

"Show me his face," Fassbinder said.

The man pushing the chair grabbed the older man's head by his hair and pulled him up so I could see his face.

"Pops! No!" I clapped my hand over my mouth, stifling a scream.

"Please"—Fassbinder rubbed his ear—"it's not like he can hear you." He turned off the projection. "Your grandfather is in reassimilation stage one-oh-one. Mr. Lessig has the power to stop the process. But you seem to think the cost too dear. Too bad for your 'pops.'"

"I didn't say that," I said. The tears welled up inside me. I couldn't make this choice. "I need time to think."

"Maybe you should learn to think on your feet. But as I told Kasimir, in all fairness—and you can thank me for this later—you should have twenty-four hours to give him an answer. It's classic film noir, isn't it? Always give the poor sap time to squirm." He tucked his PAV back in his pocket. "I'll be in touch. Twenty. Four. Hours. Six p.m. tomorrow." Straightening his jacket, he said, "Oh, I nearly forgot. If anything out of the ordinary happens—if the Jenkinses should happen suddenly to disappear, or if anything else suspicious happens—your grandfather's a dead man. I'll show myself out."

I crumpled to the floor. What was I going to do? The Jenkinses had taken in Dee and me without hesitation. They'd treated us like family—they were family, practically all I had. Burying my face in my hands, all I could see was Pops's limp form.

I couldn't betray them—could I?

I don't know how long I sat there, staring at the carpet. A rap on the door brought me back to reality.

Chris peeked in. "Your company gone?"

Before I could get a word out, a tear trickled down my face. Then another.

Chris came in and sat on the floor next to me. "This doesn't look good. You want me to get Wei or Mom?"

I shook my head.

"Who was that guy?"

"Kasimir Lessig's assistant." I could barely get the words out.

"About your grandfather?"

That did it. I burst into tears. Chris took me in his arms, rocking me until I was cried out. I stayed there, my head against his chest, listening to the rise and fall of his breath, the beating of his heart.

"How can I help?" he asked softly, his arms holding me tight.

I turned my face to him, and the next thing I knew, my arms were around his neck and I was kissing him. And he was kissing me. Warmth seeped into me, and I felt myself floating somewhere outside of my head, in an ether that both surrounded and filled me with a sense of infinity and awe. Losing all sense of where I was, the unknown teemed with goodness and truth. I wanted to stay wherever I was forever. But reality intruded.

"Hey! You guys down there?" Wei called.

"Yeah." Chris stood and helped me up. "We'll be right there."

At the door, he leaned down and whispered, "I'll do anything to help you, Nina. Anything. Look, I know that you and Sal . . . Dammit, Nina. Do I have a chance with you?" I started to speak, but he put his finger on my lips. "Don't answer yet. Let me think I do for at least a little while longer."

***

After dinner, I got Wei alone in her room. Ignoring the major guilt I felt about kissing her brother while I was supposed to be in love with one of her best friends—who hadn't contacted me in days—I figured life and death were more important than love. If I looked too closely, that seemed to be the story of my family's life.

I took a deep breath, praying I wasn't signing Pops's death warrant. Several minutes later, I finished with, "That's it. There is no way in hell I will betray you and your family."

"Damn." Wei stared at me for a good minute, before saying, "Did you tell Chris?"

"No, I wanted to tell you first. And, Wei, Brie called me earlier. She and Dorrie and Mag got the whole rescue plotted out for Joan. It's set for Tuesday. But what are we going to do?" It was hard enough not to tell the Jenkinses about the rescue, and now this so-called deal from Lessig was making everything so much worse. "Pops—I can't let him die. And I can't give Lessig information about your dad. What do I do?"

"Correction. What do *we* do? It's time for a meeting. A family meeting."

"What about Dee? I can't put her in danger."

"Okay." Wei pondered for a moment. "Not Dee. Let me get

Mom up here. We need to tell her everything—even about Joan. Dad will go along with whatever she says."

"And Chris?" I was already worked up, so any blushing went unnoticed.

"He'll make his own decision. I'll go get Mom."

I hoped she was right. I'd already lost so much of my family. I couldn't afford to lose them all, too.

***

"Nina, I respect your decision," Mrs. Jenkins said. "A hard one to make, but I believe it is the right one."

"Thank you."

"I'll get ahold of the Sisterhood about the change in plans for tomorrow," Wei said. "Don't worry, it will work out."

I tracked down Dee in the kitchen, helping Chris clean up. I glanced at the cook center clock. It was nine. There was something about nine o'clock on Sunday. Skivs! The interruption with my drawings! With everything that had happened, I'd almost forgotten.

"Do you ever watch *Vacation Destinations of the Ultra-Riche*?" I asked.

"I've been known to." Chris smiled. "You planning on becoming ultra-rich? 'Cause you just had your Holiday vacation."

"May I turn it on?" I asked.

"Sure. Something special going on?"

"Actually—yes."

Wei came downstairs. "Mom's having that conversation," she said when everyone's attention was on the FAV.

The wheels were in motion, and I was powerless to stop them. Might as well enjoy my artistic triumph. It could be the only one I'd ever have.

"You guys all watch this with me," I said.

Dee, Chris, Wei, and I sat around the kitchen table watching as top-tier families traveled to the week's themed resorts. This Sunday was tropical fantasy islands. Right in the middle of a mid-twentieth-century Hawaiian luau, the picture flickered. The next image was the first of my homeless series, with music I'd never heard before backing it.

"Nina!" Dee grabbed my arm. "Those are your pictures!"

"I know."

Chris leaned over and whispered quietly in my ear. "You keep amazing me," he said. "Like no one else."

As we watched my sketches broadcast on the FAV, with the haunting music Dorrie'd chosen behind them, I wondered how amazed he'd be if he knew what I was planning.

XXXVIII

First day back to school after Holiday, and Mr. Haldewick gave us a pop quiz. I glanced over at Wei, who was doodling with her rapido, already done with the test. Up the aisle, Mr. H scrutinized the class, most of whom were bent over their desks, writing furiously. Like Wei, I was finished, and . . . my life as I knew it was about to be finished. The meeting the night before hadn't gone like I thought it would. There were things I had to do that I wasn't sure I could do. But Lessig had given me no choice. And lives were at stake.

Then there was the whole Chris thing. How could I have kissed him like that? I'd gotten so lost in his kisses that I hadn't wanted to find my way out. The thought of his lips on mine made my cheeks burn and my insides tingle.

Sal wasn't in school at all today. And I hadn't heard from him in days. I fingered the half heart dangling from my necklace. We were in love. Weren't we? I mean, I loved him. Didn't I? Whether or not he loved me, I wasn't sure anymore. I didn't love that he thought I needed protecting. I did love how it felt when he held me. I didn't love that he was gone all the time. I had no idea what we were anymore.

I wondered if that's how Ginnie had felt when my dad "disappeared." She'd had to go through years of having the world believe he was dead. Seeing him only at clandestine meetings in the park, when he could get away from whatever Resistance work he was doing. Then, when she got pregnant with Dee, she'd had to . . . Ugh, Ed. That was the beginning of Ed. And then my dad was out of her life forever.

Was that what I wanted? A boyfriend who came and went like a specter—someone who was never there when I needed him but who made me feel like he was everything when we were together?

I remembered, when I was little, crawling into bed with Mom because of some scary dream. As I was drifting back to sleep, I felt her sobbing.

"Mommy, what's wrong?"

"Nothing, sweetie pie." She stroked my hair. *"Go back to sleep. I'm here. Everything is all right."*

Except everything had not been all right. My dad should have been there with her. To comfort her. To help. Could he have been? *Should* he have been? I'd never know. Maybe sometime I could ask him, but even he wouldn't have the answers for what had gone on in Mom's head and, more importantly, in her heart.

Matters of the heart were a whole lot harder to know.

An insistent tapping disturbed my concentration. Cutting my eyes down to the left, I saw Mr. Haldewick's pointer *rat-a-tat-tatting* on the floor beside me. Then following it upward, I ended at his face, which was contorted into a frown.

"Are you going to submit your test answers or sit there wool-gathering for the remainder of the period, Miss Oberon?"

"Submitting now." I pressed the holographic Send button hovering in the lower-right-hand corner of my desk.

"Thank you." He pursed his lips and moved on to his next victim.

***

"You okay, Neens?" Mike shoveled a handful of fries in his mouth. "You seem kinda spacey."

"Yeah, I guess." Even though Mike was one of my closest friends, I couldn't tell him what I was really thinking. "It's just, you know. Everyone's avoiding me, or staring at me. They probably all believe that broadcast." Unrelenting melancholy hung over me like those rain clouds in cartoons.

"Well, we don't," he said. "And we're the only people who count. Right, Der?"

"Yep," Derek said. "I think you need some F-U-N. Riley and I are playing Saturday. Wei's coming." He glanced over at her. "Right?"

She smiled up at him, her fabulous, warm smile. "I wouldn't miss it."

I was afraid she would.

"Hey," Derek said. "Did you catch that great vid interruption? I nearly missed it, but Riley called and said that these ultra drawings were being accompanied by some amazing ancient spirituals. It was über-ultra! I've never seen anything like it."

I grabbed a fry and allowed myself a brief moment of pride. It would pass soon enough.

***

After school I headed straight to the Institute. Even though I knew he had an event later on, I had my fingers crossed that Martin would still be in his office. As luck would have it, he was.

After our conversation, I asked, "Will I need anything special to get my friend in?"

Martin handed me a token. "Give this to the guard. It's a building pass. You won't have any problem getting her in. As far as the rest, I've got it covered, don't you know?" His hand lingered on mine. "Nina, you're sure this is the right thing?"

"It's the only thing," I said. "I'm sure."

"I hate to leave you," he said. "But there's an estate acquisition I have to oversee."

"I understand." I rose up onto my tiptoes and kissed his cheek. "I'll miss you."

He drew his lips into a strained smile. His eyes misted over. "It's been my pleasure, my dear. Unequivocally."

I spent half an hour cataloging the loan of several late-fifteenth-, early-sixteenth-century paintings by Hieronymus Bosch. His triptych of *The Garden of Earthly Delights*—the Hell side— seemed particularly suited to my situation. Like those poor, tortured souls, I had no way out.

I left work at four-thirty. The trans ride took forever, and I was terrified that I'd get home and Fassbinder would've come and gone and Pops would be killed. But I got off the trans with a good hour to spare.

Chris was still at work, Mr. Jenkins, too. Mrs. Jenkins, Wei, and Dee had left me a note that they'd gone to visit Gran. Gran. What would she think of me? I might never know.

I knelt on the sofa, looking out the window, waiting for Angelo

Fassbinder to drive up. He was prompt. Three minutes to six. Just enough time to gloat before I gave him my answer.

I was at the door before he could knock. "Come in," I said.

"All alone, are we?" He nodded up the stairs.

"Yes."

"Good. No reason to get comfortable, Miss Oberon. A simple yes or no will suffice." He held his wrist out, taking stock of his chronos. "Mr. Lessig is waiting for my call. And your answer is?"

I took a deep breath. The entire conversation with Mrs. Jenkins flashed through my brain. "Yes," I said. "I'll do it."

"Hmmm." He sized me up. "Mr. Lessig demands proof of loyalty. Tomorrow afternoon. Receipts from Mr. Jenkins's trip to the Southern Protectorates shouldn't be difficult to find. I hear he's quite anal about keeping things. Oh, and Mr. Lessig will want you to confirm what you know about the blocking devices that are in use in this building. A schematic would be good. After school. I'll be waiting."

As soon as he was out the door, I snuck into Mr. Jenkins's office. The receipts were easy to find. The schematic for the house? No way.

I called Dorrie. "Can you have me something by three?"

"I'll send it to your PAV."

Twenty-four more hours.

XXXIX

" What are you doing?"

I lifted my head to see Dee standing in the doorway. "Looking for some clothes to give to a friend. She, uh . . ." I couldn't tell Dee the truth. Not now. She couldn't know about Joan, about any of what I was planning. "There was a fire. She doesn't have anything. She's about Ginnie's size."

"Oh, that's nice of you. Are you going to see her tonight?"

"No." I selected a pair of Ginnie's jeans and a sweater that wasn't too expired. Dee and I had already pulled out anything that was important for us. I felt bad lying to Dee about Joan. But I felt worse being so enveloped in the smell of my mom. And knowing that after tonight, I'd never smell it again. Ever. I was using one of her scarves, but it smelled more like me now. Don't think about that; focus on the task at hand, I told myself. "How's Gran?" Another never again. "Did you tell her I love her?"

"Of course. She missed seeing you. She's doing really well. Dr. Silverman was there, and he said she'll be out by February first." She frowned. "She asked about Pops, but I didn't know what to tell her. You think Pops might be out by then?"

Pops. This was all for him. "I hope so, Dee. I really hope so."

She picked out one of Ginnie's dresses, a fancy one she never wore but used to let Dee play dress-up in. "Remember how I'd dance around the room like I was at a ball?" She held it up to herself and gazed in the mirror. "I bet Mom looked beautiful in this."

At that moment, Dee looked a lot like Ginnie. I couldn't help tearing up.

"What?" Dee dropped the dress on the bed. "Did I say something wrong?"

"No. I have something in my eye." I ducked my head down quickly so she couldn't see my face.

My PAV rang—Wei. "Can you come up? We need a quick run-through with everyone."

"Be right there." I clicked off. "I'm going upstairs for a few" I left Dee with the box of memories.

***

Up in Wei's room, the Sisterhood was present via PAV projection.

"Paulette, you and Mag will provide distraction in the main lobby, if needed," Wei said.

They both nodded.

"Brie and I will land at three minutes to four. That gives Nina and Joan exactly enough time to get to the helipad. Nina, be sure to unlock the door, so if anything happens, we can get inside and leave some other way. The veljet is untraceable. It's expensive, but better it should get impounded than any of us get caught."

"Everything will go perfectly," I said. "And you and Joan will end up in Japan. And Brie leaves with me as my visitor."

"That is the plan." She smiled at me. "See everyone tomorrow."

"You didn't tell them what's really happening?" I said after she shut down the projection.

"Dorrie's the only one besides you who knows. She'll tell Brie right before they leave to go to the Institute."

"This is going to work, right?" I tried to keep my voice steady, but it shook slightly.

"Mom says Dad has everything in place at B.O.S.S. to get your grandfather out. We'll all be watching the sun rise from the mouth of the Hoke no Domon on Hokkaidō. Mom says Aunt Hiroko will be able to help Pops and Joan, too. She's a healer."

"I can't believe your family is doing this for me."

"You're part of our family, too." She put her arm around my shoulder. "I wish we could take Dee and Gran, too. But Mom says they'll be safe, and we'll get them out eventually."

I was trying not to think about leaving Dee behind—even for a little while. How would she cope without me? I thought back to Dee twirling around holding Ginnie's dress to her. How strong she was—even now, at eleven, she was stronger than I'd ever felt. More aptly, how would I deal without her?

"Maybe the GC will get taken down," I said, knowing as the words came out of my mouth that it was just an idealistic hope. "The truth about FeLS and the lies that Lessig is spreading have to be exposed at some point."

"I sure hope so." Wei ran her hand across her bedspread. "Then we could come home. You know, this is the only home I've ever known."

I couldn't help the twinge of jealousy I felt. I'd lived in four different places in sixteen years. And none of them was home anymore. Even the people who made them home weren't there.

"Have you heard from Sal?" she asked. "I know you can't tell him what's happening, but I had hoped he'd call you."

"Nope. Nothing." I shrugged. Sal. That was the worst of all. I hadn't heard from him in days. And the way I'd left things . . . "Maybe we were just fooling ourselves about how we felt."

"Not Sal," she said. "He might be mad at you, but he would never stop loving you."

But what about me? I thought. Would I stop loving him? Had I already? Sal still meant so much to me. Surely I couldn't feel so connected to Chris if I was still in love with Sal. And how could I have let anything happen with Chris if I'd loved Sal the way I thought I did? Or maybe Sal was just the first guy to make me feel that way—to make me realize that I could fall in love. That I even wanted to fall in love. "What about Chris?" I asked. "Has he decided what he's doing?"

"He didn't tell Mom," Wei said. "And he hasn't talked to me at all. Most likely we won't know where he's landed until it's all said and done."

It suddenly hit me how monumental were the sacrifices the Jenkinses were making to save me. Sure, Mrs. Jenkins had pointed out that if Lessig was suspicious of Mr. Jenkins's loyalty to Media, then it was only a matter of time before they'd need to disappear. But to see them uproot themselves entirely, leaving this ultra home and everything they had, everything they'd worked for. Possibly never seeing their daughter, Angie, again. And possibly not even Chris.

Chris. My breath caught. I knew there was a chance I'd never see Sal again. But I hadn't realized Chris, too. How would *I* deal with that possibility of never seeing either of them again?

***

During dinner, Dee had to reassure me at least twice that no one had harassed her in school over the Alert about Ginnie. "No one under sixteen even thinks about Alerts," she said. "How about you?"

"Some kids looked at me funny," I said. "Mostly, they couldn't care less. I'm just a tier-two nobody."

"You're not a nobody." Dee pursed her lips. "Miss Maldovar says we should cultivate our sense of self-worth."

"I'll get right on that."

"You know what I mean," Dee said. "By the way, Chris is picking me up after school. We're going to a place that sells all kinds of culinary supplies."

"Culinary? You are serious about this, aren't you?" I was so proud of her.

"Yes, I am. Chris and I were talking, and I'm going to get my Creative in Culinary Arts."

"I'm sure you will." I smiled to cover the rush of sadness that I would probably not be around to see that. "And you'll probably end up a chef in a top-tier restaurant, making a fortune in credits. Will you take care of me?"

"Of course, silly. We're family."

My heart nearly broke to hear that, and I had to excuse myself from the table before I burst into tears in front of her.

***

Later that night, I started laying out what I'd need. I had already decided what I'd take with me. The animated digi Dee'd given me for Holiday; Pops's ginger tin; and a digi of Ginnie, Dee, and me. I placed them in my bag, along with my rapidos, my sketch pad, the originals of my bought-out FeLS contract and my Creative designation, and a copy of the court decision about Dee. I laid out my clothes for the morning. The clothes Miss Maldovar had given me were of better quality than anything else I had, so I'd chosen them. Closing my eyes, I smoothed the sweater's ultra softness against my cheek. Maybe someday I'd have more nice things. But for now, these would have to do.

I went out to the kitchen to sneak a few energy bars and some food pills—just in case. I stopped by Dee's room to say good night. She was in bed, reading a real book.

"Whatcha got there?"

She handed it to me. *Keena, the First Fem.*

"A history of the founder of the Fems? Since when are you so interested in history? First the Greater United Isles on FAV, and now this?"

"Mom used to tell me stories about Keena when I was little. After that show, I was wondering about Fems. I asked Mrs. Jenkins, and she said I might want to read this."

"I don't remember Mom ever talking about the Fems."

"When you were in school, Mom and I would play 'what if.' Like what if Keena was still alive? Wouldn't it be great to be strong and powerful? Keena is the one who started the Cliste Galad martial arts. That's what Wei does, isn't it?"

"Yeah." I thumbed through the book until I found the chapter Dee was talking about and read aloud: "'Keena created Cliste

Galad—a combination of Scottish warrior traditions and ancient Far Eastern mysticism and martial arts—as a defense against the opposing forces in the Oil Wars.'"

"It worked," Dee said. "Fems defeated enough of their enemies to bring about the End-of-Wars Treaty and take over power." She flounced back on her pillow. "Then they lost it. All because of stupid guys."

"Guys aren't stupid." I thought about Sal and Chris, and every other Sisterhood girl's male friends and relatives who thought they should be protected. That wasn't stupid. Misdirected concern—yes. But it wasn't stupid to worry about the people you loved.

"You could be right," Dee said. "Maybe it's women who are stupid. We believed what the media said about how it was more important to be safe and have a man than anything else."

"Women aren't stupid either. Maybe people aren't so sure about right and wrong. Although, what's going on right now is definitely wrong." I tucked the covers around her shoulders. "We aren't going to figure it out tonight, though. Lights out."

I padded on to the kitchen, thinking how I might never be the person to help Dee figure out life. She'd have to learn it like me— the hard way. I didn't like that. Not at all. But maybe, just maybe, she would be a top-tier chef and her life would be easier. I had to find some bright side to look at, or I'd be lost in the dark forever.

XL

erek, Mike, and I were in our usual booth at Mickey's having lunch. Just like a normal day. Normal. That was how it had to look. Perfectly normal.

"So Nina, you coming to Soma with Wei this Friday?" Derek asked.

"Yeah, it'll be fun. You're coming, too, Mike?"

He nodded, his mouth full of fries.

"Hey, have you heard from Sal? Our homeroom teacher said she thought he'd transferred schools. Do you know anything about that?"

I nearly choked on my Sparkle. "I hadn't heard that. I thought he was just, you know . . . away."

"Yeah, me, too. But she said that Mrs. Marchant told her he was gone. Did you . . ."

I knew he wanted to ask if I had known. And I hadn't. He'd left. The last thing I wanted was to leave Derek and Mike this way, but I couldn't sit there anymore not knowing what had happened to Sal. I snarfed down the remainder of my lunch.

"I've got to check on something," I said. I hurried back to school to find Mrs. Marchant.

***

I hadn't seen Mrs. Marchant since the writ hearing. She looked up when the secretary let me into her office. "Miss Oberon. To what do I owe this pleasure? Most students come here only because of infractions."

"Mrs. Marchant, it's about Sal Davis," I said. "Is it true that he transferred?"

She scrutinized me before saying, "He's your boyfriend, correct?"

"Yes, ma'am."

"And he's told you nothing?"

"No, ma'am."

"Then I'm afraid I can't either. School policy aside, Miss Oberon, if Sal wanted you to know what he was doing, I'm sure he would have told you before he left."

That was not the reply I'd expected, not from Mrs. Marchant. "I guess . . . I mean, I know you're right. I'm sorry. I shouldn't have bothered you."

"No problem. I'm always happy to have students visit."

"Thank you."

I had the doorknob in hand and was struggling to keep my tears at bay when she said, "Often people don't divulge their plans in order to keep others safe. Don't you agree?"

My heart leaped. "Yes, ma'am."

"Carry on, Miss Oberon."

Closing the door behind me, I let out a sigh of relief. At least he was still alive. I hadn't even realized how scared I was for him until just now. I'd barely admitted to myself the possibility that he could be hurt or killed on one of his missions.

***

The closer it got to my last class, the more worried I became about Fassbinder. He'd said he would meet me after school. Did that mean he'd be outside waiting? Was he going to call? Would he show up at the house? I fretted the entire fifty minutes of Language and Lit.

Miss Gray motioned to me as the bell rang. I was torn between being the good obedient student and getting outside. I bolted, leaving her standing there, shocked at my behavior. At least I wouldn't have to explain tomorrow.

When I got outside, Wei was waiting. And so was Fassbinder.

She gave me a thumbs-up and slipped around the side of the building, off to set her end of the plan in motion. I took a breath and then marched down the steps to Fassbinder and his waiting trannie.

The driver opened the door, and I slid onto the backseat. Fassbinder sat next to me, practically hidden in the shadows.

"Well?" he asked.

"It's all here." I held out an envelope. "What about my grandfather?"

He opened the envelope and perused the contents. "Assuming this is what Mr. Lessig wants, you'll be hearing from him," he said. "You're going to work at the Art Institute now?"

"Yes, and I'll be late if I don't hurry. May I go?"

"Mr. Lessig insisted that I be cordial to you. A task I hardly relish. However, since I'm meeting Mr. Lessig at the Palmer, I am going in your direction. Would you care for a ride?"

"No." I let myself out of the trannie and took off to the transit stop. I couldn't be late to pick up Joan.

***

Two transfers later, I was in front of my old apartment building. Rushing down to the riverfront, I saw Joan waiting, alone. We huddled in an alley, and she changed into Ginnie's clothes. "How'd you get rid of your friends?" I asked.

"I told them I was turning myself in. Svette wanted to take me down there herself and get the money. But one of the others knocked her out and told me to run. Said she wouldn't be a part of taking money for my life." She turned her sad eyes to me. "Tell me it's going to be all right, Nina. I'm so scared."

I squeezed her hands tightly. "You will be fine. No one will hurt you ever again. Now"—I helped her up—"let's go do this."

When we got to the Institute, I ran my handsert through the employee entry gate while Joan exchanged the token for a visitor's pass. That hurdle crossed, we made our way to the elports. Tuesday was Free Day, and the lobby was jammed with people. I hoped that would work in our favor. Spotting Paulette and Mag, I gave a quick jerk of my head to them. Mag winked in acknowledgment, then pulled Paulette back into the crowd.

Joan and I got into the elport and took it to the floor where I worked with Martin. It was twenty to four.

I led Joan to the storeroom. "You stay right here. I'll be back in six minutes."

I hurried through the tunnels to the roof. Three minutes there. Unlock the door. Three minutes back.

When I stepped into the storeroom again, I could see that leaving Joan alone in an enclosed room had not been a good idea. She was pacing, rubbing the back of her neck with her hands.

"They're going to hurt me." Her eyes darted around the room. "They're coming for me again, aren't they? Why don't you do something?"

"Joan, it's all right," I said. "No one is here but you and me. No one is ever going to hurt you again." I kept speaking softly to her, trying to reassure her of what we were doing. It took me way too long to pull her back to reality.

Finally, I opened the doorway to the tunnels, and in walked Brie and Dorrie.

"What's wrong?" Brie attitude was all business. She took in the situation. "Joan?"

Joan hung her head. "I'm sorry. I'm sorry."

"Joan, it's okay. It's all right." I reassured her again.

"I know. I know." She turned to Brie. "I freaked out." She gazed up at us. "I'm sorry."

"It's okay. We've got plenty of time, if we leave now."

"Nina—" The tone of Dorrie's voice scared me. "There's been a change in plans," Dorrie said. "Japan isn't--"

A knock on the storeroom door stopped us in our tracks.

"Go. I'll get rid of whoever it is," I whispered, motioning Brie and Dorrie to hide behind a pile of packing boxes. Joan was officially logged in as my visitor, so it'd be odd if she disappeared as well, but I couldn't risk anyone finding her. I pushed her to follow Brie and Dorrie behind the boxes. I went to the door and looked through the viewer. It was a security guard. I cracked the door open. "I'm sorry, Martin's not here today, can I—"

"You've got a visitor." The guard stepped aside to reveal Kasimir Lessig standing there.

"Miss Oberon," he said. "Not looking nearly as appealing as when we last met. Worrying adds years and wrinkles, you know." He patted my cheek and sauntered past me into the room.

"Was there a problem with the information I gave you?" I glared at Lessig.

"Manners, Miss Oberon. Manners."

"The information," I said to Lessig, "was it not what you expected?"

"Oh, I haven't even seen it yet. Angelo, stellar assistant that he is, offered you a ride to work so you wouldn't be late. You declined. He thought that odd. So did I. Since I was just across the street, I thought I'd see if something was wrong. Is there something wrong?"

"No. I'd rather be late than accept a ride from Mr. Fassbinder. I don't like him." Or you, I added in my head.

"Honesty. How refreshing. He doesn't care for you either. Oh, but I suppose I should be careful what I say—me, of all people! After all, wouldn't want it on *News at Eleven*." He laughed and waved his hand around to reference the surveillance. "Lucky for me, I control *News at Eleven*."

It dawned on me that Lessig didn't know that this room had a surveillance block. One that I could control. If I could get Lessig to admit to his lies and his blackmail . . . could Dorrie record it, maybe even broadcast it through Rogue Radio? It might be too late to help me, but she could give it to the NonCons after I was gone. But how could I tip her off?

"No worries here," I countered, trying hard to keep my voice airy and light. "This room is surveillance-free to protect the art. Talk all you want. No one's recording this." I hoped that would be enough.

"Oh, little girl, no place is free of surveillance, except perhaps my penthouse and your current place of residence." He raised his eyebrows. "Besides, you think you can fool me?" Lessig snorted.

"Fine, if you don't believe me, try to contact Angelo on your PAV," I said. "It won't work."

He took out his receiver, frowned, then put it back. "Well, then. Shall we have a frank heart-to-heart?"

"Why not?" Dorrie's PAV wouldn't work with the surveillance shields up either. I'd have to turn them off. Acting nonchalant, I perched on the corner of my desk, keeping the lever hidden from Lessig's view. Leaning on my arm, I pushed it down. What I hadn't anticipated was a single beep, probably indicating satellite connection.

Lessig jerked his head around. "What was that?"

"What was what?" I shrugged.

"That electronic beep." His eyes narrowed. "Nina, Nina. Are you trying to pull a fast one on me?"

"You mean the temperature control? The thermostat is automatic—it beeps when the temperature changes. You know, to safeguard the art. I don't even notice it anymore." I got off the desk and approached him. "Listen," I said, "I held up my end of the bargain. I spied on Jonathan Jenkins—"

"I have yet to see if that information is valuable. I've been waiting for years to set up Jenkins. Never liked him. Never liked anyone who was friends with your father."

"You said you'd get my grandfather out of custody, if I did what you wanted. I did it. Now, I want my grandfather back." My voice sounded steely, but I was shaking inside.

"Your grandfather." Lessig wet his lips. "Alan Oberon's father." He cocked his head. "I think you must have misheard me. I can't imagine helping anyone who's related to Alan Oberon. Ever."

His pointed stare was infuriating. "You promised me—you said, if I spied on the Jenkinses, you'd save my grandfather!" My heart thumped in my chest, and anger raged through me. I knew something like this would be coming, but I didn't realize the sheer fury I would feel at hearing him say it out loud. "I should've known not to trust you, not after you spread those lies about my mother and the fake FeLS station."

"Lies?" His eyes bored into me. "And just what do you know about FeLS that I don't?" He grabbed my arm.

I jerked it away. "Since we're being honest, *Mister Lessig*"—I practically spat the words out—"I know all about FeLS. My mom's the one who found out the truth about the government's liaison program—that it was a sex-slavery ring. And I know you lied about her involvement in it."

"Ah, yes. The perks of being the most trusted newscaster in the Americas. The face of Media. I can show whatever I want, say whatever I want, and people believe me. Fake space station"—he snapped his fingers—"no problem. Sex-slavery ring? Pin the scandal on Ed Chamus and your mother. Piece. Of. Cake. The basic details on FeLS were true—nice of Jenkins to give me that information—but I couldn't let the world know that we were trafficking girls through FeLS, let alone who the girls went to. Can you imagine what would happen if I let the idiots in our society know that their most trusted leaders had a taste for virginal sex-teens? So I created the rest of the story—the fake space station, Chamus being the ringleader. All of it."

"You made those Alerts up? You are sick."

"Sick? Little girl. What I am is the most powerful man in the world. I can make or break anyone." A smile twisted across his face. "I could even bring down the GC president if I wanted to. That old pervert loves the FeLS girls. What he doesn't know is that I've got the vids to prove it."

Suddenly, there was a furious pounding on the door. Fassbinder's voice came through, screaming, "Kasimir! Stop! Shut up!"

Lessig spun around, and I raced back to the wall. He flung open the door, and Fassbinder stumbled into the room, flailing to keep his balance.

"Kasimir—she's broadcasting this. It's all over the airwaves. Everything. FAVs. PAVs. Alerts. Everything!"

"What? There's no reception in--" The realization dawned on him. I looked around for an escape, but he was too quick. With murder in his eyes, he yanked me to him. Searing pain stabbed through my shoulder, but I bit back a scream. "Turn it off!" he yelled. "Now!"

"I'm not recording anything! Look, I'm not doing anything!" I held out my PAV, and he brushed it aside.

"You lying bitch! No worries, Miss Oberon? We'll see about that. Angelo, get the old man on the view." He twisted me closer, wrenching my shoulder more. "See this?"

I looked at the screen of his PAV. It was Pops in a transchair, those same tubes pumping liquid into his arms.

"No." My voice was shaking. I couldn't take my eyes off Pops. He looked so weak, sick.

Lessig spoke into the viewer. "Charlie. Do it."

The same goon who'd yanked Pops by his hair now pulled the tubes out. Pops shook violently. He slipped out of the chair, writhing on the floor. Convulsions racked his body, and although I couldn't hear it, he was screaming in agony.

"Stop it!" I punched Lessig in the gut with my good arm. "Pops! No!"

Fassbinder moved to grab my free arm when suddenly Brie and Joan came flying out from behind the boxes, a flurry of arms and legs. Joan clawed at Lessig, and I pulled away from his grasp. Brie was quick and efficient in her attack—in a heartbeat, Angelo was on the floor unconscious, and Lessig was crumpled in a heap on top of him.

I lunged for the viewer. "Pops! Pops!" He lay still on the floor. The guy who'd killed him toed him with his boot and then walked away. "Pops." I couldn't stop looking at his lifeless body lying there.

"Nina. Nina." Brie helped me up. "Nina, I'm sorry, but we can't stop. There's no time. You and Joan have got to get out of here. Lock the door and turn the shields back on."

I pushed the lever up, and the viewer screen went black. I hurled it across the room. "The door locks automatically," I said, touching my shoulder gingerly. "I think he broke my arm."

Brie's hands moved quickly over my shoulder. "No, it's just dislocated. Lie down. Joan, Dorrie, hold her for traction." Joan looked dazed but did as she was told. A few seconds of searing pain, and Brie had worked my arm into place. At least now I could move it, though carefully. Brie took Ginnie's scarf and fashioned a sling out of it. "Come on," she said. "We've gotta move."

"What about them?" I asked. Fassbinder and Lessig were still out cold.

"I think we did enough damage. B.O.S.S. will clean up that garbage. Dorrie, let's move—we don't have much time. Joan? You okay?"

Joan was white as a sheet. She stood up. "I'll be fine. I just want out of here."

"Let's go, then."

We ran through the tunnels as fast as we could. I tried to keep the image of Pops's body out of my head, just concentrating on moving one foot in front of the other. Finally, we reached the veljet, and Brie shoved us inside.

"First aid kit and energy bars are overhead." Brie pointed to two sliding doors above us. "If you've got to go, unlock the seat like so." She pressed a button. "It swivels around to the rear. You'll have to wiggle out of your all-weathers and scoot onto this." She showed me the toilet. "Flush like so." Another button, another problem solved. "If you're thirsty, there's a full water reservoir. Straws on the door side of your seat." I nodded, still unable to speak.

"And, Nina, you're ultra. That was awesome, what you did back there." She looked across me. "Joan, stick by this girl. She's definitely got your back."

Dorrie reached in and put a chip in the dash. "This is a self-destructing chip. It's programmed to take you to Castle Combe in the Greater United Isles. That's where your dad is. He's expecting you."

"My dad? Why aren't we going to Japan? What about the Jenkinses?"

"We tried to tell you earlier, but we were . . . interrupted. Mrs. Jenkins's relatives were arrested by the Nippon Council for harboring subversives. I don't know where Wei and her family will end up. They had to leave—Mrs. Jenkins is already gone. I don't know where Wei and the rest will go."

A wave of panic washed over me. Dee. "Chris was supposed to take Dee to Martin's. Did he?"

"I don't know. We'll find her—we'll make sure she's okay. Brie and I, or someone, will get word to you. Nina, you *have* to go *now*. We've got to get downstairs and out of the building before we're discovered. Don't worry about piloting or landing. The jet takes care of itself. As soon as I'm clear, press the green button. And, oh . . . I figured you'd want to know—I found out who Miss Maldovar is. Adana Maldovar is Ed Chamus's twin sister. Nina, I'm sorry, we're out of time!" On that note, she clamped the door shut and ran over to Brie. I looked at them through the window, dumbfounded. Miss Maldovar was Ed's sister. The Jenkinses were on the run. Dee was . . . I didn't know where Dee was.

"Nina?" Joan touched my arm. "We've got to go."

I looked down and pressed the green button; the veljet sprang to life and spun upward. Within moments, it leveled out and shot forward. We were off.

XLI

When the adrenaline had finally worn off, and the veljet was far away from Chicago, my shoulder started throbbing, and my eyes got heavy. Soon the drone of engines had put both Joan and me to sleep. The insistent beeping of my PAV woke me. It was Chris.

"Chris—thank goodness! What's happening?" I asked. "Where are you? Is Dee all right? Your family? Tell me."

"Nina, it's okay, but I have to be quick. Everyone's safe for now—Dee is safe. B.O.S.S. will be attempting to track you. Remove your earpiece and flush it and your receiver out of the craft. And, Nina . . . I love you." He clicked off.

I removed my earpiece. The pain in my shoulder was insistent, but I somehow managed to fish my receiver out of my bag. Swiveling around, I tugged the seat up and dropped my only links to the people I loved into the void.

At least Dee was safe. At least there was that.

And Chris loved me—I didn't even know where to begin thinking about that.

Joan was still asleep next to me. I stared out the window for what seemed like an eternity. Miss Maldovar was Ed's sister. She had to be treating Dee so well because she thinks Dee's her niece. What will happen if she finds out the truth? I dared not dwell on that.

And Gran— With the Jenkinses gone, where would Gran go when she could no longer stay in the rehab facility? Who would tell her about Pops? Pops. Oh, Pops. Tears streamed down my face. I felt Joan's fingers wrap around mine.

"I'm sorry, Nina. So sorry."

We sat silently, staring into the dark of the night, speeding toward a destination neither of us had chosen.

***

A robotic voice woke me. "Landing preparations have begun. Please secure cargo. Fasten seat belts." It repeated the directions twice, then the thrusters kicked in and the landing gear dropped. Lights on the bottom of the veljet illuminated the ground. The craft made a sharp turn. If we hadn't been restrained, I would've been sitting in Joan's lap. It veered right and left as if looking for a place to set down. Then, without warning, it dropped to the ground. A perfect landing. The nav chip ejected from the dash, a tiny poof of smoke confirming its destruction.

"I guess we're here," I said.

Before we could even unbuckle our seat belts, I saw a group of women carrying torchlights come through the trees. Two of them had a stretcher. They unlatched the doors to the veljet and helped us out.

"Here, put these on. It's cold." A woman held out coats. When she saw my arm in the makeshift sling, she said, "You must be Nina. I'm Layla. We heard you'd been hurt." She gently laid the coat over my shoulders. Dorrie and Brie must have gotten word out. "We didn't know how bad. Do you need the stretcher?"

"Walking's no problem." I glanced at Joan. She shook her head. "We're both fine."

"Let's get you back to town. You must be tired and hungry," Layla said. "The doctor should look at that shoulder, too. Your father's been in the north country. He would've been here, but we didn't find out about your arrival until a few hours ago. He'll be back later today."

Shortly after we slipped into the darkness of the trees, I remembered my bag. "I left something in the veljet. I have to go back."

"Betts is bringing everything," Layla said. "Don't worry. You're safe. There is nothing to harm you here."

We emerged from the trees at the edge of what was the most beautiful place I'd ever seen. Snow was softly falling as we crossed a stone bridge. Ancient houses lined the street; smoke curled from the chimneys of some. I recognized certain things from pictures I'd seen at the Art Institute. That thought vanquished the beauty of the moment. My family. My friends. What would be their fate?

"We'll stop at the infirmary first," Layla said. "Then I'll take you to your father's house."

"We can speak freely here?" I asked. "There's no surveillance?"

"You can say whatever you want, whenever you want," she said.

"But I don't understand. Isn't there a council?"

"There is a GUI Council headquartered in London, but they are council in name only. The Greater United Isles have nothing of value to offer the various world councils. After the outbreak of glandular fever in 2035 killed off over half the population of the United Kingdom and left any survivors sterile, most of the remaining citizens relocated to the European mainland. Despite a cleanup, most areas of the GUI have never been reinhabited."

"The Media never told us any of that."

"Of course not, they're Media," Layla said. "It was more convenient for the council to have the Isles uninhabited. Fewer people to keep track of and no surveillance to install and man. Every so often they revive the story and broadcast a supposed update about sterile men and women and infected lands. No one wants to take that chance, so they stay away. Which is just fine by us. We have twenty children in our school; all were conceived and born here by people who have lived here for years. And, we're all healthy. So much for the truth of anything Media reports." She stopped in front of a neat, two-story house. "This is Dr. Churchill's. She's expecting us."

Dr. Mauri Churchill had steel-gray eyes and a warm smile. After examining me, she said, "You'll need to stay in this sling for at least three weeks. Fortunately, you're right-handed." She gave me a dissolve for pain. "One under the tongue every eight hours. But be careful, they will probably make you drowsy."

"And you, Joan. I want to see you again tomorrow. I think some nutritional therapy will do you a world of good."

Drowsy had been an understatement. I barely noticed what my father's house looked like. The minute my head hit the pillow, I was asleep.

I woke up in a panic, having no idea where I was. I rolled over and cried out when pain cut through my shoulder. Moments later, there was a tap at the door, and a man's voice said, "Are you all right? May I come in?"

"Sure." I managed to push myself up to sitting with my good arm. As I adjusted the sling, memories of what had happened played through my head. I looked up as the man entered.

"Nina." He started toward the bed but hesitated when our eyes met.

"Dad?" This wasn't at all what I thought it would be like. We were supposed to rush into each other's arms, crying and laughing and immediately loving each other. But at this moment, I wasn't sure what I felt.

He moved a step closer, like I was a wild animal he was afraid to spook. In the end, he sat in a nearby chair. "Layla told me you were hurt. What did Doc Churchill say?"

"That I'll be fine in a few weeks." I watched him looking at me. Wondering if he saw traces of Ginnie in my face. I wondered if he was even thinking of her. Maybe Layla was his girlfriend, or his wife. I had no idea what his life was all about. "Where's Joan?"

"The girl you came with? She's in the next room, still asleep, I believe."

"I should be there. She might freak out when she wakes up."

"Betts is with her. She was a nurse before she joined the Resistance. She's dealt with reclaimed FeLS girls before. Your friend's in good hands."

Speaking of hands, I looked down at mine; without looking up, I said, "Pops is dead. Kasimir Lessig killed him."

My father didn't say a word. Eventually, I raised my eyes. Dad was staring out the window, his eyes misty—and a deep need to comfort him rose in my chest.

"He was so proud of you," I said softly. Spying my bag in the corner, I maneuvered myself out of bed. The bag wasn't easy to open with only one hand, but I managed. "This was his." I held out Pops's ginger tin.

My father took it. He ran his fingers gently across the dented lid. "They discovered our man inside." His shoulders heaved. "There was nothing I could do."

I threw my good arm around my dad, and we cried.

EPILOGUE

I've been in the GUI for almost a month.

Joan's getting better every day. Betts is so patient with her, and Doc Churchill has her on a special diet. She's starting to look and sound like the old Joan. Mike and his mom would be so happy to see her this way.

The day after the Sisterhood exposed Lessig, we heard about the major shake-up it caused. Kasimir Lessig and Angelo Fassbinder are enjoying the hospitality of B.O.S.S. at a special facility in New York. I'm guessing B.O.S.S. wants information before those two will be reassimilated. I sincerely hope Lessig suffers, a lot. Oh, and the GC relieved Xander Critchfield of his presidential duties. Apparently, they haven't dismissed the FeLS program yet. Its fate, and that of the girls in it, still hangs in the balance.

I've received one message from Wei. Her mom fled the country, mostly having to do with the arrest of her relatives in Japan. But her dad risked everything and stayed—remaining a Media employee. After Dorrie's broadcast, when everyone saw Lessig admit to setting up Mr. Jenkins, Media offered him Lessig's job in an attempt to save face. Although he hasn't said yes for sure,

Wei thinks he'll probably take it. That can only be good for the Resistance.

Wei is still at her home with her father. Gran will be joining them when she gets out of rehab, and Dee will move back with them then. Though Wei said Dee really loves living with Martin and Percy. She told me they threw Dee a huge birthday party in one of the rooms of the Art Institute. Wei sent a digi. Dee's radiant. I cry every time I look at it. Not just because I missed her special day, but she thinks I'm dead.

I understand why they told her that. The reasoning behind it makes sense. Miss Maldovar is Ed's sister, and she's obviously going to keep inserting herself in Dee's life. The risk of Dee's letting it slip that I'm alive to Miss Maldovar, to this woman she may trust, is too great. Wei said she's dealing with it pretty well— or as well as can be expected.

Dee and Gran both know about Pops's death. But neither knows the truth of how it happened. Thankfully, Dorrie had cut off the transmission before it was broadcast to the world. It's better that way, I think. They miss him enough as it is; they don't need to know the details of how he suffered.

Dad and I put a stone marker in the church's graveyard. I go there pretty much every day to talk with Pops. Sometimes my dad's there, too.

I was right. Layla's his girlfriend, wife, whatever. I want to hate her, for Ginnie's sake. But I can't. She's nice. She loves my father. And he seems to love her. Although I overheard him one day, when he was talking to Pops, say that he wondered if he'd made the right decision all those years ago. That Ginnie was his one true love. I couldn't help but feel sad—for both of them. But the past can't be changed. We've got only the present and the will to work for a better future.

Wei said Paulette told her that she'd located Sal. He's out west, on NonCon reconnaissance. She didn't know how long he'd be gone. When he returns, she'll tell him where I am. If he even wants to know, I thought.

And Chris. She said Chris left after taking Dee to Martin's. He told Wei that he had something he needed to work out and he'd come back when he knew what to do about it. She doesn't know that he means me.

Sal or Chris. Not a decision I'm prepared to make yet.

I found myself at the graveyard once again.

"Pops, it's your Little Bit." Tears stung my eyes. "You told me to always seek truth. It's easier to find when it's about people's rights and how they should be treated. But the truth about one's heart . . ." I threw my arms around the cold stone, wishing it was my grandfather. "Pops, that truth is so hard to find."

I'm not sure how long I'd been prostrate on that marker, but a growing warmth on my back caused me to glance up. The sun was shining through a break in the clouds. I imagined I heard Pops saying, "Truth never remains hidden, Little Bit. Sometimes you just have to look a little harder for it."

For the first time since I'd arrived at Castle Combe, I felt strong and hopeful. Pops always did tell the truth.

Turn the page to see where Nina's journey started . . . in

I

"Nina, look." Sandy jabbed me in the ribs.

I glanced up at the AV screen expecting to see the latest vert of back-to-school fashion for sixteens.

"No, there." Sandy jerked my arm, bringing my attention to the doorway.

Four guys approached us, lurching and swaying through the moving express. They sat across the aisle, immediately crowding together in a knot. A low buzz of unintelligible words, accompanied by the occasional rowdy snort, rose from their cluster.

"They're eighteen," she whispered. "I bet it's that one in the middle's birthday. He's cute!" She wriggled in her seat.

By the way he kept admiring the tattoo on his wrist and fingering the Band-Aid behind his ear, where his GPS had been, I knew she was right. I involuntarily touched my own tracker. The tiny grain-sized pellet embedded beneath the skin barely registered on my fingertips. What would it be like to be able to go someplace where you were untraceable?

Before my thoughts went any further down that path, Sandy said, "They're going into the city to celebrate. I wish—"

"No, you don't." My stomach turned at the thought of

eighteenth celebrations. We'd heard all about them, particularly the Angel affair. I quickly blocked the images from my mind.

Sandy "humphed" back into the seat, crossing her arms over her chest. "Those stories can't be true. Guys wouldn't do stuff like that. I mean, look at them . . ." She leaned toward me conspiratorially, but I saw her peeking at the boys from under her bangs. "Someone that cute could never do those kinds of things. Listen . . ." She fished around in her bag and handed me a rapido. "You're the one who took all those art lessons. Draw the tattoo. Okay?" She stuck her wrist in front of me.

"Sandy!" I pushed her hand away. "We could get arrested!"

One of the guys, not the birthday boy, must've heard us and looked over. He ogled Sandy the way I'd seen her stepdad do when he thought no one was watching. I grabbed her wrist and thrust it toward him, showing the absence of the obligatory XVI tattoo. He shrugged and turned back to his friends.

"Hey!" She pulled her arm away from me. "He was going to talk to me."

"It's not talk he wants, Sandy. Those stories aren't all made up. Ginnie said that ever since they started the tattooing twenty years ago, girls aren't safe. She thinks that—"

"She's your mom. What do you expect?"

"I dunno." I shrugged, letting it drop. Sandy was so caught up in all things sixteen that there was no reasoning with her. Her mother and mine were galaxies apart in just about every way possible. Mrs. Eskew not only allowed, but encouraged Sandy's sex-teen ways. She was even prepping her for FeLS. My mother, Ginnie, on the other hand, was doing everything she could to keep me from applying for the program, even though it was about the only way out of our tier-two status. When I tried talking about it with her, she'd say not to worry. I wouldn't be a low-tier forever. But she never told me how I'd move up. It wasn't like I wanted to join FeLS, but outside of marrying some upper-tier guy, I didn't have many options.

Sandy snatched a retractable zine chip from the rack on the back of the seat in front of her. She let go and it snapped back in place. She grabbed another, doing the same thing. I sighed. If she'd reached for a third, I would've stopped her. Sometimes I felt more like Sandy's mother than her best friend.

Her mood suddenly changed, thank goodness. "Scoot over," she said. "We're almost to that big farm and I want to see the cows. Can you believe people used to eat meat? Makes me want to puke just thinking about it."

Sandy's almost as crazy about cows as she is about boys. Truthfully, we're both animal lovers. That's one of the reasons we got to be such good friends. When Ginnie moved me and Dee out of the city and into Cementville, I didn't think I'd ever find a friend. But the first day of school, I met Sandy. We were both wearing the same shirt, with a horse on the front; and after school she got off the transit at the same stop as me. It turned out that we lived right next door to each other. We've been best friends ever since. Even if she does get on my last nerve sometimes.

The dull monotony of suburbia and Cementville finally gave way to an oasis of rolling hills and clumps of trees. As the express approached Mill Run Farm, Sandy and I both pressed our noses to the window like little kids. A herd of black-and-white cows was grazing in the distance. Two horses appeared, racing along the white board fence.

"They're so beautiful," I whispered.

Sandy gave my hand a squeeze. "Nina, I know you don't want me to do anything stupid," she said softly. The farm faded into the distance, and we settled back in our seats. "Hey, did you get all your homework done?"

"Yep," I said. "Regional Government and Twentieth-Century Literature. Love the Lit. Hate the Gov."

We both laughed.

"I'm dying in Lit," Sandy said. "You have to help me out. Promise?"

"Of course." She always depended on me to explain books to her, and I didn't mind. It wasn't like she couldn't or didn't read, she just didn't get the deeper meanings. I don't always either, but Ginnie talks with me a lot about what I read and helps me work through it.

"So. Are you going to take the FeLS prep?"

"Sandy, you promised." I half glared at her.

"Sorry, I forgot Ginnie won't let you." She tickled me. "Come on, don't be mad."

I couldn't help laughing, and I didn't want to stay angry with her—so I didn't.

"Are we going to your gran's first, before we meet up with Mike?" she asked.

I nodded.

"You know your grandfather freaks me out." She dug into her pocket, retrieving a small bag. "Want one?"

I stuck the frosted lemon drop into my mouth, rolling it around on my tongue until the rough sugar smoothed into puckery sourness. I sucked on the candy. "Yeah, Pops is a little strange. But I'd think you'd be used to him by now."

Sandy put several drops in her mouth and the bag back in her pocket. "No way," she mumbled, arranging the pieces with her tongue so she could talk. "I don't get a lot of what he says, and it creeps me out when he takes his leg off."

"I'll try to keep him under control," I promised, chuckling to myself. As if anyone could control Pops. "Maybe we should go to the zoo. It's probably the only way we'll get Mike away from all the new verts downtown."

"We are going to Gran's before we meet up with him, right?"

I laughed. We both knew that if Mike came with us, he'd talk Pops into taking his leg off. Mike was fascinated by the prosthesis. "Sandy, it's just an old GI leg."

"GI-wha?"

"For the billionth time, microbrain . . ." I tapped her head. "Government issue. Remember back in the 2000s the soldiers were called GIs because everything they had was issued to them by the government? That's where Pops got his leg after the accident, from the government. He says that's why it doesn't work right. It's cheap. Like something from Megaworld or Sale-o-rama."

"Hey, come on! These jeans are from Sale."

"I meant that when rich people get body parts, they get the good stuff, bionic, acts like the real thing." We both shopped the discount stores, like everyone else who was lower tier. "And," I added, "I love those jeans."

Sandy smiled and ran her hands around her waist. "Thanks," she said. "They fit good, don't they?"

Her clothes fit her a lot better than mine fit me. As Gran would say, "She's built like an MK lunar pod." Which I'm sure is why her stepdad looks at her the way he does.

The men I knew were either crazy, like Pops; half creepy and weird, like Sandy's stepdad; or mean cheaters, like Ed. He's Ginnie's married boyfriend, who also happens to be my little sister Dee's dad. I had no idea what it was like to have a father, real or otherwise, since mine died the day I was born. All I had was an old photo chip and the stories Gran used to tell me about him. Sandy pulled a mirror out of her purse and fluffed her hair, pouting at her reflection.

"Do I need more lipstick? Mascara?"

"Come on, Sandy, we're just meeting Mike and Derek—you know, friends." That's how I preferred guys, as friends. Any other way freaked me out. Sometimes I wondered if I was some kind of freak myself. Most every girl my age was getting primed for turning sex-teen. I had my reasons for never wanting to have sex. I just didn't have anyone to talk about my reasons with. Especially not Sandy or Ginnie.

Sandy sighed and put her mirror back. "You never know who might be looking at you." She gazed longingly across the aisle.

The guy who'd noticed her earlier glanced at me, quickly taking in all the important details. He cocked one eyebrow and licked his lips. I held my breath, scared he was going to speak, but the other guys drew his attention back into their huddle. I exhaled. At least for a few more months I was fifteen—and safe.